'ADVENTURES OF THE CHEMO KID'

The Black Eye and The Black Heart

By Mike Love

edited by:

Jeff Powers- creative edits

Paul Smith- line edits

graphic design:

Jason M. Harmon

Jeff Powers

Erich Adie

Print by: RJ Communication.

Printed in the United States of America

ISBN: 978-0-9859154-0-7

'ADVENTURES OF THE CHEMO KID'

BY MIKE LOVE

BOOK ONE:

THE BLACK EYE AND the BLACK HEART

For Trey

Introduction

'Fast Cars and Long Faces'

1

"We have to take Duke to The Children's Hospital!" Maggie Dillan screams through the phone as her husband, Jesse puts the receiver to his ear; the phone barely reaching his horseshoe earring before he pulls it away again with a wince.

"Hello?" he shouts as he raises the phone back to his ear again, ready to let her have it for screaming like that. He can't make anything out amidst the noise all around him. "Hold on!" he yells, annoyed, as he kicks at the couple of shovels tangled at his feet. He stumbles through the jobsite, which is littered with tools and materials, toward his truck. He gets a sideways look from his co-worker, Billy, to which he replies with a rolling of his own eyes. The paver walkway they have been working on for the last couple of days is merely a hole in the ground at this point, and filled with all types of precarious obstacles. Billy watches for a moment with a chuckle as Jesse makes his Godzilla-like rampage through the seemingly booby-trapped trench finally leaping past the edge of the section of pavers they had just laid, being sure not to knock anything loose on the edge.

"Now, what's the matter?" he shouts into the worn cell phone.

Jesse makes it over to his truck, having to catch his breath after his fifty-foot dash. He grabs the t-shirt he had discarded earlier from where it lay slung over the toolbox and wipes his face and hair before using it to wipe off his phone too. He can still barely hear her crying and screaming on the other end. He's not even paying attention to the phone as he tries to gather himself. He opens the driver side door and slides into the seat. Inside it's about a thousand degrees and he nearly drops the phone as he quickly tries to get the window rolled down. Maggie's already in the middle of a frantic screaming fit when he finally gets the phone back to his ear.

"Wait, wait... Mag, Mag, Mag! I can't... Can you slow down, please?" he shouts with the phone out in front of his face. "I don't even know what you're talking about! I can't understand you! Hello?"

By now, he's got the truck started and the air-conditioning running. "Maggie?" he asks. Her screaming is replaced by silence at first, leading him to believe that he'd been disconnected somehow as he calls her name again, but then he can hear her crying... very hard. He can hear his son Duke, crying too in the background. Immediately he remembers the pediatrician's appointment she had reminded him of the day before... the black eye. He hadn't actually forgotten. He'd simply stored it in a part of his mind where he didn't have to look at it. He had been sure that it was nothing when it happened without even a yelp from their 21-month old two weeks prior. He had been able to concoct a reasonable explanation almost every day for the last two weeks as the bluish-green ring held steady around his son's right eye. He was still sure last night when he scalded his wife for worrying that it could be something serious. He was so sure of all these things that he hadn't

6

even worried about the appointment at all.

She's sobbing uncontrollably. "Maggie… What is it?" he says, still with an impatient tone. She can't speak. It sounds to him like she can barely breathe. He gathers himself realizing that whatever has her this upset must be a big deal, and impatience certainly won't help. He's always assuming she's exaggerating everything, and let's face it, he's received screaming phone calls before that turned out to be nothing at all. But it's her inability to even speak that tells him that this is something different. Maggie can yell and scream with the best, but silence is not part of her DNA. "Babe? What's going on?" he gently asks, and waits for the answer.

2

She cries hard for another minute before speaking, and only after clearing her throat three or four times with a series of hacking coughs, does she manage control her emotions. She takes a breath, "Whfhoooooooo," the same kind she'd taken when she delivered Duke into this world; deep, long and controlled.

"She said that she feels something in his… abdomen, like a mass…" Maggie says as she fights through the urge to break down again. "First she said she'd send us for like labs and stuff, and then she left to get the prescription, but when she came back in… she said that she wants us to go to Children's Hospital instead... Oh Jess…" She can't stop the tears now.

"Well what does that mean?" he asks. No answer. He thinks of the way his little sister used to cry so hard that she'd actually stop breathing until the wail would come back around again like a police siren. It's just like that. "What does any of this have to do with his eye? Mag!" he

7

begins to get impatient again. She still can't answer until abruptly she clears her throat and says, "She's coming back in... I gotta go."

CLICK.

Silence.

3

Jesse doesn't want to panic, but he's starting to. "Mag... Maggie," he calls, but it's too late. As he pulls the phone away from his ear he gives the steering wheel a swift, hard punch, causing the horn to honk. He grabs hold of the wheel and holds on so tight that his knuckles turn white as he tries to process what he just heard. "God, please... just... Please!" he shouts as he sends another punch into the steering wheel. "Please God!"

Stepping one foot out of the truck and poking his head above the door, he hollers across the ruckus, "Dude!" and waves his hands at Billy. The saw-blade quickly grinds to a halt. Jesse turns back into the truck and doesn't wait for a response from the cloud of dust that hangs over the cutting area. He stares straight ahead, with both hands on the steering wheel, trying to suppress bad thoughts, and struggles to come up with a theory on how this can't be as bad as his wife is making it out to be.

Billy runs over to the passenger side door of the dust-covered beige work-truck and hops in. The radio is on inside the truck. Jesse's vacantly mouthing the words of the song, but his head is too full of worry to process the ironic nature of the lyrics,

"Don't worry... 'bout a thing, 'cause every little thing is gonna be alright..."

"What's going on?" Billy asks as he turns the volume down, snapping Jesse out of his trance.

"It's Duke… Maggie called… the black eye… Something about his spleen… It's something bad…" he mumbles. He's making no sense to Billy, but his friend knows the story behind the matter and catches on quickly.

"They're sending us to Children's Hospital!" Jesse abruptly shouts and gives his steering wheel another hard punch.

Billy knows what that means, and it's not good. They don't send kids to the city for black-eyes. All he can think to say is, "Well, Children's is the best hospital in the country, trust me, I spent a lot of time there when I was a kid." Jesse doesn't flinch though. He knows Billy's story, and that Children's is the best. He also knows that you don't go to the best hospital unless you have the worst problem. He's already compartmentalized that thought. He's gotten a head start on dismissing a lot of the thoughts that have popped into his head in the last few minutes.

4

He peels out of the parking lot, with Billy in the passenger seat, never even considering whether the tailgate is up or if all the toolboxes are closed. He's driving eighty in a twenty-five zone, but he wouldn't stop even if a cop rolled up behind him. Besides, he just has to make it to the end of the street. He slams on the brakes fifteen feet short of the light. "I'll call you," he says to Billy and jumps out in the middle of the street, causing an oncoming car to slam on his brakes and squeal his tires. The driver lays on the horn, but Jesse doesn't even look back to see his good friend exchanging hand signals with the road-raged driver as he does the old Chinese fire-drill, and circles the truck to jump into the driver's seat. All Jesse can think about is his son, Duke. He's saying silent prayers as he hustles to see him, begging God to make it all OK.

He sprints over the little hill and into the parking lot. He hasn't run at an all out clip like this since his days playing flag football in the micro-brewery league, but his adrenaline is pumping so hard that even in his work boots he's able to continue all the way to the elevator before stopping. He climbs inside the first car, and as the door closes, slumps against the wall. He touches the button marked three and tries once more to push aside the anxiety that is etching itself into his mind and his stubbly, bearded face. He hums the tune that's playing in his mind and mumbles the words. "Three little birds, on my doorstep." When the elevator stops on the third floor the door slides open. Stepping out into the office he'd been to ten times before, he doesn't recognize it. Sure, he knows where to go and he knows to use the door to the right if you don't want to walk through the sick-kid waiting room, but it just looks different; it feels different. He steps to the desk and smiles at the young woman seated there.

"Duke Dillan?" he asks, but the words don't feel right coming out of his mouth. He puts a hand to his mouth, his eyes suddenly vacant.

"Room 3," she says rather abruptly. The polite smile returns to his face, but hers is no longer a true smile. He could feel her worry mingling with his. He could see it in her eyes. Maybe the paranoia is setting in already. Maybe she doesn't even know anything.

She's pointing to the hall to her right. "Thank You," he says as he turns and walks away, giving the desk a happy little thumpity-thump with his knuckles to try to complete the illusion of his own composure.

He steps his mud-encrusted boots down the hall of this sterilized place as he sees the hand-drawn pictures made by patients in frames on the walls and in the brightly lit rooms with the examination tables. He feels like a big germ walking through this clean office. He buries his hands a little deeper in his pockets, wishing he could stop for a quick shower rather than soil the carpet with one more crumb of dirt. At this point he'd settle for some moist towelettes and a stick of gum. He wonders again as he passes two pretty young nurses whether they too maybe had a hidden sorrow behind their polite smiles, as if they know who he is and why he's here.

The trail of dirt nuggets sticks out like a sore thumb as he looks back; straight from the elevator to the room where his wife and son sit, like bread crumbs into the middle of the forest. The image brings another smile to his lips, until he remembers the rest of the fairy-tale. "God…" he says as he looks up to the ceiling tiles. He just shakes his head as the words won't come. He wants to say something poetic about the big, bad wolf, but he just sort of smiles figuring that God probably already got the idea. He looks back down to the door handle and grabs it. "Please don't take him away," he mutters as he presses on the handle.

5

When he opens the door he sees his wife crumpled over in a heap staring out the window with mascara stained tears in her eyes. Blake and Sydney, the two kids for

11

whom she nannies, are with her, as they always are when she needs to take Duke to the doctor. They are standing off to the side playing with coloring books and Duke is slung over his mommy's shoulder like a baby. It is the first time he has seen anyone hold his son like that in a long time. She looks up and immediately catches his eyes as he comes in. She can't hold back her tears and crumples back against the wall once more. He goes to her, pulls her up and gives them both a great big family bear hug and says, "Everything's gonna' be alright."

"Nothing's alright!" she screams into his dusty t-shirt which is now stained with the mixture of dirt, sweat, and tears. "They're sending us to the Children's Hospital! Do you know what that means?" Her emotions are pouring out now. Duke begins to cry again and the other kids are standing looking down at their shoes, surely wondering what's going on around here. As he hugs her, she pulls herself together like any good mother does, even in the face of the fiercest adversity. With her well manicured hand she wipes away the tears along with her mascara and pink eye makeup, and then gently raises her son to her husband. Duke wraps his arms around his dad and hugs him back.

"Hey buddy… how are you?" he asks his son. For the last six months he has worked so much that he hardly ever even gets to see his curly haired boy. Now, in the light of this new uncertainty, he's feeling like the almighty dollar is about as worthless as a sack of dirt when compared to the time he missed spending with Duke.

"A-good," he replies in that hoarse way of his when he's been crying. His dad knows that he's wise beyond his years, and he's always been amazed at how much this little boy loves him, even though he's always working. Duke gives his dad a big smile and then another bear-hug around his neck to break the tension. His dad is relieved to see that Duke is still able to crack a smile, but then he sees his wife staring out the window once again trying to stop the tears raining down her freckled cheeks.

"Just wait…" he abruptly begins without a hint of compassion. Then he stops himself and re-starts his thought with a much calmer and gentler tone in his voice. "Just wait until we hear what they have to say. It could be anything. What did they say about the black-eye?"

"Don't you see? She feels something in his abdomen! I knew it was something serious! You didn't want to listen! You said you were sure it was nothing!"

As she's shouting, the doctor returns and Maggie stops. She's embarrassed that the doctor saw her losing her cool, but the feeling quickly fades because her worry for her son far outweighs any care for keeping up appearances. If Maggie only knew what it is that has the doctor nervous enough to send them immediately to their parent hospital, she'd realize that a family feud is the furthest thing from the doctor's mind.

Jesse shakes her hand, as they have met several times before. She's trying her best to keep her composure, but he can see in her eyes that she is really worried. Jesse doesn't let it get to him but Maggie is staring daggers at him as if to say, "See, I told you this is bad…"

As she ushers them out of the room, she explains that she's not sure what she feels, but she definitely feels something that's not supposed to be there and his belly is distended. These are all the reasons she needs to send them to The Children's Hospital. She escorts them back through the office and past the kids with the stuffy noses and the baby-acne. All the parents are staring as the family huddles close together, mother full of tears, with their pediatrician right behind. The office is silent as they cut through. The faces of the people are filled with sorrow. They all know that this can't be good. They all watch as the family exits the office and their doctor hugs them before they pile into the elevator. Blake and Sydney are glued to Maggie's leg. It must have been like something out of their worst nightmares. Here they are, without their parents, and the only person they know is sobbing uncontrollably. Everyone keeps saying that there is something wrong with their new friend, and now they might have to go to the hospital. Blake is holding his sister's hand and sleep-walking. Sydney has the remnants of frightened tears in her eyes. She saw those people's faces. And she's smart enough to know what could make them so sad.

In the elevator they stand motionless and silent until Blake utters a faint, "Maggie… I want to go home."

7

When the elevator dings open, Blake's wish comes true, and his eyes open like saucers when he sees his dad waiting on the other side. "Daddy!" both kids scream as they run and re-attach themselves, this time to his leg, almost pulling him down in the process.

"Hey, I'm Justin," he says to Jesse as he reaches out his hand the best he can under the weight of the children who have now advanced upward and hang from his neck and waist. They all get a chuckle out of that one as Jesse grabs the belt loop on Blake's pants and raises him up, before shaking Justin's newly freed hand. "It's great to finally meet you."

"It's a shame we couldn't be meeting under better circumstances," Jesse adds, which sobers the mood quickly once again. The sad truth is not lost on Justin as he nods in agreement. He looks at Duke and begins to well up with tears of his own. Nothing is worse than seeing a grown man cry. Maggie gives him a big hug and apologizes for making him leave work to come pick up the kids. He looks at her and says with a huff, "Please... don't apologize to me. Besides, you know I work from home! You guys just call us and let us know what's going on." He gives Maggie another hug and disappears around the car as he loads the toddlers into the SUV. Maggie opens the door on the other side and says, "Thank you Justin. Bye kids, I'll see you soon..." as she leans in for one last hug from Sydney.

Screams of "Dukey! My little baby!" suddenly come from the other side of the parking lot. GG, Maggie's mom, is running across from her car. She's got tears streaming from her eyes and Jesse immediately hands Duke off to her. "I love you, I love you, I love you!" she says as she showers him with kisses. Duke usually wouldn't approve, but under the circumstances he lets her get away with it. GG is one of the most important people in Duke's life, and she's around just as much as anyone. He gives her a big hug. Jesse opens the door and guides GG over to it to load Duke in his seat. GG runs to the other side and climbs in.

As Justin and the kids pull away, Maggie hops in the car and tears out of her parking spot. She doesn't even look before she makes a right-on-red onto Lancaster Avenue with car horns sounding from every direction. She just slams on the gas and tears down the busy street. Maggie explains all that happened, arguing and screaming, as she flies down back roads towards the highway. They all say silent prayers.

She keeps the pedal to the floor the whole way, and anyone who has ever driven The Suburban Expressway knows that it's no place even on your best day to be driving with tears in your eyes. Their car however, is on auto-pilot. The overhead must look like a video game, with the Red SUV careening through and changing lanes, braking and accelerating at all the right times. It would have gotten the high score for sure. How they don't get pulled over or wreck is a miracle. Maggie Dillan will never even remember driving there, but it was probably the best driving she's ever done. They make it there in about a half an hour, and anyone who's ever tried to get into the city in any kind of hurry knows that it's never that easy. When they exit, the hospital is just a few blocks away, through the most beautiful part of the city, a part of the city that is home to the brightest young minds getting an Ivy League education. Maggie swings through the Emergency parking lot, jumps out the driver side door and runs inside with GG and Duke. Jesse hops in the driver's seat and pulls up to the security guard station. The guard instructs him to go down the ramp and into the garage below. He spirals down the ramp and disappears.

Chapter 1

'Emergency Room Blues'

1

Jesse finds his spot and jumps out of the car without locking any of the doors, sprints across to the elevators and climbs into the first car that comes down. When he gets to the first floor, another security guard points him to the E.R, and still another guard stops him before he can go toward the main desk where a line has formed. At first he goes toward the end, but he doesn't see his family anywhere. He looks back toward the guard as if to say, "Here?"

The security guard says, "You can just go right up."

That's the first sign that things may be even worse than he's willing to admit to himself. He speaks Duke's name, and the receptionist looks to a young woman who comes around the desk and escorts him to a small triage room where Duke and the girls are. He looks back and realizes that they had been ushered past the other 25 or so families that had most likely been waiting for hours. He has had deep cuts on his hands, mild concussions, and even once took a softball off of his right eye, but he's never been escorted to the front of the E.R. line before.

When Jesse gets to Duke, he is crying hysterically. GG hands Duke off to his dad. He's a mess, and totally inconsolable. He's been shuffled around like a deck of cards and his head is spinning. His mind is filled with thoughts of uncertainty and fear. He may be wise beyond his years, but nothing could have prepared even a Harvard scholar for this. The nurse somehow manages to get his vitals through the screaming and writhing. The tension in the room is as thick as peanut butter. No one can even look at each other. Maggie and GG are totally freaked and Jesse is acting like they are making too big of a deal, although he knows it's worse than any of them could even imagine. The nurse comes back in and tells them to gather their things. She is going to show them to a private room. They march through the hall a little way, passing doctors and nurses who all seem to have that same look of concern for the family. Duke looks past his own tears and sees all of the people working on computers and with all sorts of machinery that beep and flash. He calms for a minute, intrigued and a little frightened by it all. Once they are inside, they shut the door and pull back the curtains.

2

Duke is dropped on the bed. Everyone is in a frenzy. The room is in motion. Duke's been thrown around and passed back and forth between parents, nurses and doctors. He's not currently crying out loud, but he still wipes his eyes as he tries to look around at the various monitors and equipment around the room. There is an uncomfortable silence as they try to get him situated in this scrubbed, white room with a multi-colored light of fractured glass on the ceiling. He tries to focus on the light for a moment, which makes him rub his eyes some more. GG climbs in behind him and he rests back on her.

"Here we go," Jesse says as he swings the white arm holding the TV. GG ducks Duke's head as the metal arm almost smacks him right in his already bruised eye.

"Jesse! You almost hit him right in the head!" Maggie snips as she runs over to join her mom in an affectionate shower of kisses and hugs. Jesse pays it no mind as he positions the screen right in front of Duke's face and scrolls the digital tuner for age appropriate programming.

"Does he like any movies?" the nurse asks.

"Gary the Green Dragon," they all reply in unison. They bust up laughing and share glances and eye rolls at their uncanny timing. The brunette nurse vows with a certainty that glistens in the tear forming in the corner of her eye to find some Gary videos and bring them back for him to watch. Then she kindly smiles and leaves them alone.

The laughter has stopped and an awkward silence starts again. Duke is starting to sense a theme. Just in the nick of time the door slides open again, allowing the hustle of the halls to come alive. Duke is captivated by the sounds of the bustling E.R. that seem to sing together like an orchestra.

A handsome young man walks into the room, closing the door behind him. This draws a smile to the lips of both GG and Maggie as they catch eyes. Jesse notices but doesn't comment. He just shakes his head and continues searching the dial.

"Hi, I'm Steve. I'm going to be with you guys today. Is this Duke Dillan?" he announces exchanging nods and smiles with each of the adults. "Wow! What a cool name!" he comments with a smile, never stepping more than a couple of steps into the room. Duke's attention is still on the hall, trying to look past the new guy and see what's going on out there.

"That's him," Jesse says. "My name is Jesse Dillan, this is my wife Maggie and this is GG, Duke's grandmother." They each take their turn shaking the hand of the young male nurse. As his back turns to the women, they look at each other and make a 'he's cute' face.

"Can I take a look at you, Duke?" he asks.

"Aaaawkk!" Duke screeches. His best pterodactyl impersonation is enough to have the adults reaching for their ears. The reaction makes him crack a smile and he does it again.

"Aaaaaawk!"

"Wow! That was loud!" Steve shouts and smiles. Duke can't help but laugh a bit at what he had done and he even lets out another smaller screech as they laugh. Jesse tells Duke "That's enough," and after one more, and another stern look from dad, he quits it.

"Well, can I take a look at you now?" Steve asks. There's a moment of trepidation while Duke looks at his dad again. They all brace for another screech. He fakes it and smiles at the nurse before he slinks back into the bed.

"Well, can I?"

Duke nods, and Steve steps into the room.

2

"So... does Duke have any medical conditions or allergies?" Steve asks as he opens the manila folder containing Duke's chart. He wheels the rolling stool around the side of the bed as he awaits the answer. He's looking for something, but coming up empty on whatever it is.

"He has WPW... Wolfe Parkinson White syndrome. He takes propranolol," Maggie answers with a burst of words. She talks faster when she's nervous, and she is as nervous as could be.

"WPW… OK… when did they find that?" Steve says as he rolls the stool back to the table with the chart on it.

"He went into SVT at birth. His heart rate went up to 280 about two hours after he was born. He was on Digoxin until he was two months and then they saw delta waves on his EKG which told them it was WPW so we had to stay here for a night when they switched him over to Propranolol," Maggie rattles off faster than Steve can write, causing his eyes to open wide, which gets everyone smiling for a moment. After making a quick note of it, he hops up and excuses himself as he squeezes past GG to the other side of the bed, still looking for something.

"Here we go!" he says, as he pulls a tiny cuff out of the rack. He wraps the blood pressure cuff around Duke's skinny arm. "It's ok, just giving your arm a hug… just sit as still as possible," Steve says with another big smile.

Duke feels like some kind of lab rat sitting here on a strange bed in this weird place. There are so many nurses and doctors running around. He can see them past the edge of the curtain, up and down the hallway, carrying clipboards and wearing stethoscopes around their necks. He feels them leering in as they walk by. "And this arm coming out of the wall… I don't know if I should trust it, even if it does have a TV on the end of it!" he silently jokes to himself, causing him to smile a little.

Just then the door flies open so abruptly that the pastel rainbow curtain inside it almost comes of the metal clips. "Awkk, Awwkk!" Duke screams as they all duck and cover. The two in the door look highly annoyed at the pterodactyl impersonation. Duke can see his family

21

as well as nurse Steve looking rather un-nerved as well; nobody is laughing. Duke starts bawling once he realizes that his antics aren't funny anymore.

"Is this Duke Dillan?" the older one in the doorway asks. The young one stands by quietly. Duke's attention is on the white streak in the front of the young one's hair. "Awkk, Awwkk!" he screeches again through his tears.

"Duke, that's enough!" Jesse snips.

The two doctors stand in the doorway, exchanging opinions without much regard for the family who sits inside, stunned. "It looks like his eyes are looking in two different directions…" the younger one states as more of a question and looks around the room for agreement. She finds nothing but a sharp "Awkk-Awkk-Awkk!" from Duke. Jesse doesn't bother to give him any grief this time.

"We may have to sedate this child if we can't get him under control," the older doctor says as the pair abruptly exit back into the hall. Everyone in the room looks at each other with a 'do you believe that?' look on their faces.

Steve winks his eye at Duke and says, "Don't worry about them… I'll stay here with you." Duke smiles a little, but Steve's the only one who notices. Actually, Duke pays no mind to Steve as he does his thing. He's got his eyes focused on the action in the hallway since the door is still open a bit. His focus is on the doctors and nurses as they move around each other like clockwork. A couple more doctors come in and Duke greets them with the prehistoric screech, but it's an auto-response now as he's totally captivated by what he's seeing past the curtain. It's like a dance as they dip, duck and dive.

They twirl through the halls with their clipboards in hand, leaning in close for a signature, or craning their necks amid a huddle for a word of advice. They all work in unison as they run from room to room, some with panic in their eyes and others with a sigh of relief. Each one looking both ways before they cross the hall, careful not to get smacked, until "Whack!" two of them collide, sending papers flying through the air.

'Ooh!' Duke winces as they both go to the floor.

Still mesmerized, he even agrees when Steve asks him if he and another nurse can give him an IV. He doesn't snap out of it until they're just about to do it. He suddenly tries to reconsider, but there are now four adults holding him still. All he can do is let rip several more screeches until they are done. Duke sulks back into GG's lap, feeling like he had been suckered. Steve wraps a big blue splint around his arm, so he can't get at it.

The Brunette nurse hands Duke a bear that has an IV on too. "See, he's got one too!" she says with a smile. Duke likes the bear, but he won't give her or anyone else the satisfaction right now. "Well, what about these?" she asks, holding three Gary DVD's. Duke sits up and grabs them out of her hand.

"Duke… What do you say?" Maggie asks, and he faintly mutters, "Thank you."

3

As they try to load the DVD's into the player, another doctor walks in. This time, it's a young male doctor stepping through the curtain, smiling but with sad eyes. He clearly feels for the distressed family, especially considering what he already assumes of this young boy's health. He clears his throat before he introduces himself.

"Hello, I'm Tim Houston. I'm one of the Oncology Fellows." Tim shakes the hand of the three adults. He then leans in just in time to get an "Awwkk!" from Duke. He pulls back quickly with his index finger in his ear. After his outburst, Duke buries his head in GG's lap. She's become a permanent fixture on his bed, as he won't let her or anyone else out of his sight.

Dr. Houston is not what any of them expected to see. He can't be much older than Jesse, and he's got a baby-face that rivals Duke's! Once he begins to speak though, it's clear that, young or not, this guy knows his stuff.

The DVD finally starts to play. Duke pays no mind to the doctor now that he's got a good Gary movie to occupy his attention. He is excited to immerse himself into the story and snuggle with his stuffed Gary dragon that GG brought to the hospital for him. However, it's not far into the opening credits when he drifts off to sleep.

4

In his mind he is dreaming, just like he often dreams. He's following the meandering path that leads through the twilight, toward the clearing at the end. His bare feet find their way through the undergrowth. A warm breeze blows, but he is, as always, comfortable. Somehow, the winding path always remains free of stumbling blocks, and the narrow trail leads him toward his destination, which is never within sight. His feet always find solid footing on a stepping-stone though he never actually looks down to find the next foothold. His eyes just stay focused on the path ahead.

In his dreams, it's his trust that leads him through the

landscape far more safely than his eyes ever could anyway. Faith guides his body as it moves entranced through the forest and into the backlit clearing. Faith in what, he isn't really sure, but he has always been sure that no matter what comes up, both sleeping and awake, that there is something watching over him; protecting him.

The sun is slowly creeping toward the horizon in all its purple majesty, sending the last orange and yellow-red bursting out beneath it as darkness tries to rid the world of another day's light. His eyes leave the path for a moment, and his head turns to look up to the unpolluted sky. The sun kisses his face one last time before drawing back again. He closes his eyes and tries to recapture it, but the warmth is gone. When he opens them again, dusk has fallen on his forest dream. A chill has replaced the suns kiss, and the wooded trail now seems to darken with every passing moment. The horizon is now a few shades short of its previous splendor, as if he had closed his eyes for too long and missed the sunset altogether. He stumbles forward, almost reaching, but the sun goes down even that much faster with each step. Another look around and he can see that night has fallen, and the forest has come alive with shadows that play with his mind. He hugs himself a bit, suddenly cold against the persistent breeze that feels more like a wind without the sun to warm it's touch. What's that! He spins around to see, but no one is there, only shadows.

5

"Duke has ahhh… a… a-a mass in his abdomen," Dr. Houston says, tripping over his words a bit, like a man who doesn't want to have to say what he is about to say, and definitely doesn't want to say it wrong. "We need to do some more tests to know for sure, but we believe that it is a tumor."

The family is floored. To think something like this could be possible was beyond any of their imaginations.

"Ok, but it could still be benign, right?" the ever-optimistic Jesse chimes in.

"I believe that we will most likely find that not to be the case. We think that this is Neuroblastoma," he replies.

"What's that? I've never even heard of that!" they all reply in a chorus of chatter.

"It's a solid tumor that often stems from the adrenal gland or the spinal column," he replies. "Usually in children about Duke's age. A black eye is a very common symptom of NB, but I don't want to speculate too much about that until we do more tests."

"Why? Is there a chance that it could be from something else?" Maggie asks.

"Sometimes with different types of cancers, proteins can move into the bloodstream, and collect in a place like the eye, and cause a black eye." he replies.

"So it could be that, right?" Jesse asks. "That would be a good thing, right?"

"Yes, but it's highly unlikely. The other reason that a black eye could appear is that there is a metastatic tumor behind the eye. Like I said, I don't want to speculate either way until we have all of the facts. Over the next few days we'll be running a lot of tests to determine the accurate diagnosis."

The family sits there, in complete disbelief. No one can believe that their little Dukey could have cancer. How could such a horrible thing be possible?

Jesse breaks the silence as he sits back with his hands buried in the curly mop on top of his head and says, "Nothing will ever be shocking to me again. There could never be anything anyone could say that would shock me more than this!"

6

Duke is running now, from an invisible stalker. He can feel eyes on him from all around. He is sprinting, hoping to find a place where the darkness doesn't feel so deep. He manages the path as if he'd run it a thousand times before. He can see a place ahead, a clearing, where the moonlight has broken through the trees. He sets his mind to it and silently asks for swift feet to take him there safely. As he approaches, he can see the light. Once he reaches it, he smiles and closes his eyes, letting the moon shine on him. He falls to the ground, feeling safe again. The eyes of the forest still lurk behind him, but he feels as if they cannot get to him here. Still, he scurries to his feet as he spins further away from the edge of the darkness. The forest breathes deeply and blows a cold wind back at him, but it quickly dissipates in the light of the moon.

Turning away, trusting in the safety of the starlight, he sees that he's come upon a great canyon. Had he run any further he would have run right over it. He shuffles his feet toward the edge, knocking some loose gravel down. It clicks against the sheer cliff a couple of times before the sound disappears. He can see nothing below, but darkness that seems to play host to the same hidden horrors as do the woods. Looking out into the night, he can see nothing but infinite, star-filled night, and the great beyond.

The clouds swirl in a certain conjunction with the millions of stars as they seem to be blown by the same wind that chilled him moments before, but now, in the light, has calmed. The crescent moon hangs as if on a string, almost seeming that it could hook the swirling cumulous as it floats by. The sky is not polluted by the light from any town or city, which makes it like nothing his crystal-blue eyes have ever seen before. He has the urge to step off the edge and join the stars, but he somehow knows that he can't leave this path. He closes his eyes and imagines flying across that night sky. Disoriented, he slips a bit and goes down on the rocky ledge, startling himself awake.

7

Duke is thrashing and flailing his limbs as the young doctor and Duke's family try to keep him from throwing himself off the bed. Dr. Houston pulls back from Duke, feeling that he had startled the boy with his attempt to read his pulse while he slept.

"It's a night terror," Maggie tells him looking back as Jesse and GG take turns holding him and trying to calm him. "He's had them all of his life. Sometimes he'll do this for fifteen minutes or more."

This time it only lasts for a minute, and GG lays him over her as he she climbs again into the bed. Duke reclines on GG as he opens his eyes, rubbing the bruised one as he has for the last couple weeks. Stressful looks paint each of there faces as they all sigh collectively, causing a few hysterical chuckles around the room. The whole fit may have only lasted a moment, but to them it felt like an hour, especially with the day they've had.

Duke squints his eyes in the bright lights. They are bloodshot, and he can hardly see through the blur left behind by the tears. As his eyes clear, he sees them all standing around him. He gives a bashful smile as he nuzzles into GG's lap.

"Duke… I'm Dr. Tim… Can you say Tim?" Dr. Houston asks.

"Chim," Duke replies as everyone in the room smiles and cheers.

"May I check you out?" Dr. Tim asks his young patient. Duke nods and sticks out his arm for another squeeze from the blood pressure cuff. Dr. Tim grabs his wrists with a thumb over Duke's vein. He looks back at the clock and seems surprised to find that Duke's heart rate is very normal for a kid who's just had a night terror episode.

"So, he does that often?" he asks the family as he rolls back toward the desk to make a note of the strange occurrence. "Actually he used to do it all the time… but not as much as when he was a baby. Are night terrors normal?" Maggie asks. She's been told by everyone else that they are, but was not going to pass up the opportunity to get the professional opinion of a doctor. "It is *quite* common actually," he says.

He leans back into Duke just in time for another "Squawk!" from the youngster. Duke smiles a bit to tell the doc that he's just playing a little, but he's a bit wary of this new doctor. Dr. Houston grabs Duke's wrists again and begins his exam. It's standard stuff: ears, nose, throat, knees; Duke's done this a hundred times before.

Dr. Houston looks Duke in the eyes for any erratic movement or laziness. He sits back and addresses the family. "Everything looks alright aside from his blood pressure being a bit high. We're probably going to start him on some Amlodipine to bring that down. "As he gathers his things he says "I'll be back in a little while, when we have the rest of the blood work back. You all just stay here and try to be as comfortable as possible."

Reclining on GG, Gary the Green Dragon lulls Duke back to sleep.

8

He finds himself right back where the dream had left him. But clouds now gathering overhead quickly steal away the light of the moon. With just a few steps back toward the forest, the light is gone, as if a curtain has been drawn between him and the sky. He tries to turn back again, but he can't move. Everything has gone black all around him. He begins to fear for his life. The eyes that had hidden in the shadows are on him again. He can feel them leering at him from all around. The forest has come alive. He momentarily lapses into panic as he tries to breathe but he chokes on the air, which is now thick and rank. Instead of filling his lungs, it invades his soul. His baby blue eyes are almost consumed with black as the unbroken darkness causes his pupils to dilate. He begins to struggle in vain, as the brush at his feet now begins to pull him under the shifting earth. The landscape which he always believed to be a fern-covered path beside a babbling brook now appears as no more than a sinking pit of quicksand bound with twisted vines which wrap around his arms and legs, relentlessly trying to pull him down into the dark and never-ending mire. He looks back to the path from whence he came, but the trees have bent over it, and thickets are now packed in all around him, leaving him no hope for escape. The nothingness envelopes him in its suffocating grip, taking every breath as he barely squeezes each one through his constricted windpipe.

He's struggling now with every ounce of energy that he has. He fears that he will succumb to the clawing vines that threaten to drag him under and end up too deep to get out. He can't loosen the grip on his hands and he's now up to his throat in the muddy goop. He closes his eyes and remembers something he's heard in one of his dad's lullabies. "Though I walk through the valley of the shadow of death, I will fear no evil, for you are with me." He repeats it in his head with his eyes clenched shut. The grip around his wrists seems to tighten, although he feels the binding knots on his ankles begin to let go. He opens his eyes to see as he continues to repeat the Psalm, but shuts them immediately when he sees that the blackness has now been replaced by a light so bright that he can't even look at it. The vines on his wrists no longer cut at him, but instead are now gentle as a mothers caress; the hands that now are lifting him up and out of the muck.

9

Duke's eyes open to a darkened room, where he and GG lay together on the bed and Mommy is sending a text. Gary is still dancing on the screen, but with the excitement of his dream, he can't get into it. He can still feel the fear that gripped him as the vines tried to drag him down. He is really wondering though, what it was that pulled him out of it, that amazing bright light. Whatever it was may have saved his life, dream or not.

10

When Dr. Tim Houston left Duke Dillan's room that day, the perplexed look returned to his face immediately. He had managed to compose himself after an initial lapse, but the child had done something that he had never seen before.

Dr. Houston is a new Fellow, which means he's been here only a few years, but in that time he's seen things that have changed him in a way few people would understand. Though not many lines of age have marked his face as of yet, he's seen things in this place that most could only imagine.

This child however had done something that made him think that there is more to him than even just a genius in the making. This child is special.

"John... John!" Dr. Houston shouts as he runs into the weekly conference where Duke's case would be discussed with the rest of the doctor's who specialize in this deadly form of childhood cancer. The rest of his colleagues had not yet settled into their seats, so his shouts weren't totally out of place, although a few of them turned their head to see what the fuss is about.

As he reaches his friend and colleague, he extends a hand and receives a firm shake from the middle-aged man. His hair is fully gray but Dr. Houston knows he's not too much older than him. His status, however, is legendary. When it comes to Neuroblastoma, Dr. John Masters is the man you want to see. What Dr. Houston wants to say to him, however, has little to do with NB.

"What's up, Tim?" Dr. Masters asks. "You look like you've seen a ghost! Is this about the new NB admit from today?"

"How do you know about that already? I haven't even filed any of the paperwork yet," he asks. Now the look on his face is even more confused. He knows that Dr. Masters is pretty high up in this place, but he didn't realize that he's a mind reader!

"Relax, Tim… I just got off the phone with Nick Maloney of Ophthalmology. He must have been by after you left. He said everyone was all shaken up about something." Dr. Masters has that look in his eye, asking the question if his friend knows anything about it.

"That was probably my fault. I was in there breaking the news. But after that, the kid really threw me for a loop. He was sleeping, and I was trying to examine him without waking him. He was having a nightmare, and he was really upset. All at once he was freaking out, and then he woke up. The parents say it's a night terror… he has them all the time." Dr. Houston is visibly shaken by what he's trying to tell his colleague.

"What's the matter Tim, neither of your daughters have ever had a nightmare before?" he muses, although he can see that Tim is not laughing. "Sounds pretty normal to me."

"All I know is that the kid woke up and his heart rate normalized instantly. He just seemed like… I don't know… different. He's got these deep blue eyes…" he trails off for a moment before finishing with, "I'm telling you John, there's more to this kid than meets the eye. He's special." Dr. Houston finishes his last sentence as their meeting is beginning, his colleague laying a hand on his shoulder with a concerned look.

Just as the final few docs get to their seats, John leans over to Tim and says, "You know, it's funny," he whispers, shaking his head and laughing a bit. "Nick said pretty much the same things you're saying. I told him he was crazy too!" He smiles at Dr. Houston. "Just kidding, Tim. Keep your eye on him though. Let me know if it starts to seem like he's like the others."

Chapter Two

'Nightmares in Reality'

1

CRASH! An exploding blob going off just inches from his head sends shards that seem to chinkle and crack, like crystals as they fall to the floor in a spectral array of fragmented light and color. Quickly another one splashes its payload, like a water-balloon filled with radioactive sludge. "Sssssssssssssss," it hisses as it melts down the wall with its electric lava. BOOM! BOOM! Another, and then a bigger BOOM! Then CRACK!... BANG! And BOOM! again, like lightning touching down on a live transformer. He keeps his eyes clamped shut, begging God to be back in his forest dreamscape, and for these to be the sounds of an electrical storm which is ripping trees from their ancient roots and making the earth groan as the bursts of light illuminate the sky. Shaking, he feels himself succumbing to his fears. Silently he mouths the Psalm over and over; "Even though I walk through the valley of the shadow of death, I will fear no evil, for you are with me," until his heart rate slows and he regains his composure, and opens his eyes.

Bzzz... Crack!... Z-Z-Z-ZZZZ.... crackle sparks of light as they fill the room like static in the air he breathes. Sizzling shrapnel is flying all around as the sound snaps through the air. The room is hot with the electricity left behind by these dirty bombs as they do their worst.

Without warning, he's been thrust into some sort of war-zone. He wonders, as he's trying to wipe away the cobwebs from the inside of his mind, how he could have ended up in this new place that is so much different from the dreams he's used to.

His wondering is cut short when, BOOM! another, then BOOM! another loud crash explodes above. His head is pounding now from the noise and the pressure of squinting his eyes. The shockwaves are rattling the teeth inside his mouth and he sends a hand to the side of his face to try and soothe the pain.

The sounds and sights begin to run together like fireworks on the fourth of July, the booming all around him like drums beating an evil rhythm. Battle cries of an unseen enemy call out from the other side of this place, seeming to make a demented song filled with horrible laughter and the cries of children. Closing his eyes once more he can see a dark figure standing before him with his arm outstretched and a long finger pointing in his face.

Laughing, the dark man joins the chorus and begins to shout to the rhythm of Duke's dream. The voices, low and then loud, sing, "Ooh- Ha, Ha... Ooh- Ha, Ha..." The voices all join together and swirl around him in a terrible chant that invades his mind and paralyzes him with fear, unable to move. "Ooh- Ha, Ha!" they shout as the whole world begins to spin. Duke tries to squeeze himself deeper into the corner, but he can't manage to squirm any further. Out of control, his mind is spinning a tapestry of fear that is blanketing him. "Ooh- Ha-Ha!" they chant as the tears fall down his cheeks. "Ooh- Ha, HA! Ooh- Ha, Ha!" He's squeezing his eyes so tight that the vein in his temple is bulging out. "Please God, make it stop!" he cries. "I know you're with me, please God, please!"

2

Instantly there is silence and darkness. All of the chaos that previously surrounded him has been replaced by a faint hum. The sweat on his clothes now chills him as he starts to shiver. He's backed up in a corner. He puts a hand out and presses it against a cold metal wall. He pulls it back fast, because it's so cold that he initially thinks it's hot and that it may have burned him. Steam is coming out of his mouth when he breathes. The silence and darkness are almost as scary as the chaos he'd found himself in a few moments ago. He sends a hand back up to his head, which has stopped hurting a little, but is still throbbing a good bit. Totally dazed and confused, he tries to get to his feet. There is a metal pole beside him that he uses to stand up, still cautious of what might be on the other side of this frigid metal wall.

"Crrr---rushhhh---shhhhhh---Bzzzz---chunk" comes from the wall in front of him. The sudden electrified crash sends him back to the fetal position in the corner, only this time he whacks his head on the metal pole he had used to help himself up before.

"Oww!" he yells as he swings his arm around at the inanimate object on which he had just smacked his head. As he holds his wrist, he looks up to see that above his head there are several monitors and pumps that have all lit up simultaneously when he hit the pole with his hand. From his position, the pole now looks very intimidating. It seems to loom over him and the monitors and pumps make it look all too animated for his comfort. The thing looks like it could read his mind if he'd let it. He scurries back up to his feet and tries to slide past the newly

37

illuminated pole. It looks like it has come alive and is now staring at him. He trips over the pole's base and falls down again. He's tangled up in its star shaped bottom and the thing looks like it's going to come down on top of him.

"Ahhhhh…" he starts to yell as he puts a hand up over his face, fully expecting the tall rack to come toppling down on him.

3

Click. The door opens. Duke mistakes it for the pole falling and wraps himself in a ball on the floor. A man in dark blue hospital scrubs flips on the light and peers inside.

"Man, what are you doin' in here, man? How'd you get over here?" the custodian asks as he puts a hand on the pole that has seemingly followed Duke out of his hiding place. "You need to be careful not to knock over your pole, man!"

Duke looks through the opening between his fingers and sees a middle aged man with a purple and yellow hat on his head and a smile on his face. The man has pushed his cart into the doorway to hold the door while he moved the pole around to the other side of Duke. He reaches his hand out to try to help him back to his feet, but Duke coils himself back up on the floor.

"Aww, it's alright, lil' man…. James not gon' hurt ya'." he says as he reaches his big hand down and grabs Duke under his arm. "Here, hold on like this." he says as he wraps Duke's right hand around the pole. "You just need to hold on now. You ever ride a skateboard before?" James asks with a wry smile. He pulls Duke out into the

open and wheels him awkwardly around the room on the
buzzing and vibrating mobile pole.

4

He's struggling a bit, but James has a good firm grip
around his right hand on the pole. Duke looks at his hand
and then the pole and then up at James again. At first he
feels scared, but James looks like he actually might be
trying to help. "What is this place?" he whispers.

"This the Nursh-ment Room. They got all kinds a' soda
and milk in there. You want one?" As he says all of this
he opens the door of the metal fridge and reaches in,
pulling out a carton of chocolate milk and drinks the
whole thing down in one gulp.

"I love me some chocolate milk, man!" James laughs
as he sprays the leftover milk from his mustache scruff.
Duke has to duck and cover as the milk comes showering
down.

Duke looks over at the place he had been hiding when
he was dreaming. He points his finger and James says,
"That's the ice machine, man!" and with that he pulls
the door up just in time for a fresh batch to dump into
the hopper. Duke scoots back and wraps himself against
James' leg as his mind goes back to that scene, moments
earlier when he was trapped behind there, scared for his
life.

"S'alright man… watch you don't pull your pole down
now.," James says. He spins around trying not to get
tangled up. "S'matta wit you… look like you seen a
ghost. Here, let James get ya' back to ya' room."

39

"You still not doin' it right. Now, stand here and put your hand on the pole like this…" James says as he repositions Duke on the star-shaped base. Duke's still a little jumpy as he's distracted by the little spot behind the ice machine. "C'mon man, pay attention now," James says snapping his fingers in front of Duke's face to try to break the trance. "You gonna need to know how ta do this, so you need to pay attention."

Duke looks at James and says, "Where am I?"

"You in The Children's Hospital, and my name's James. I'm the head of En-vi-ro-mental Services on this Unit; Three South," he says as he grabs the left breast pocket of his shirt and shows Duke where it says, Environmental Services, James.

"What's yo name?" he asks.

"Duke Dillan," Duke replies.

"That black-eye what got 'em all worked up right?" James asks as he peers down his glasses at Duke's face. "Yeah, old James seen a lot of them in my day."

"Yeah… I guess. They were messing with my stomach though." Duke chimes in, wondering what this guy could know about it anyway.

"Yeah, well, it's all the same man… don't make it no diff'rent. You still gotta fight it all the same. Don't matter what they tell ya; only the big guy upstairs can tell ya when it's yo time to go." James pushes his cart away from the door as he's still talking. He pulls Dukes pole faster than he had expected and Duke wobbles a bit and grabs hold with his other hand.

"You gotta hold on tight now… You don't know where this thing gonna' go sometimes! Ha-Ha!" James says as he continues to pull the pole and his cart out into the hall. He's walking backwards and looking over his shoulders as he talks.

"What do you mean? I don't…" Duke starts before James interrupts with, "This pole gon' take you wherever you want to go. You just gotta be careful when you ridin' it though… don't want to fall and break your head!" And with that James busts into a full belly laugh. Duke's not quite sure what the joke was, but he chuckles a little just to be polite. James laughs right up until they pull up to a room with the door closed.

"Well, here's yo room," James says as he clicks the door open. Duke's parents are asleep inside. He wonders how they got here and why they didn't miss him when he was gone, but he's so tired by now that he doesn't think about it too much. James has him in his bed and is walking back out the door before Duke whispers, "Hey… Mister…. Uhh, James… thanks."

James looks back and winks and says, "Anytime kid…. I'm right across the hall." He points to a closet across the hall that says "Soiled Utilities." That's my office. Just knock on the door like this if you ever need me. James knocks a silly rhythm on the door jamb. He smiles and winks again. "Goodnight little man" he says. By the time the door clicks shut, Duke is asleep from exhaustion.

Chapter Three

'A new day'

1

Beep, Beep, Beep….. Beep, Beep……….Beep, Beep, Beep….. Beep, Beep he hears as he wakes up to find his situation and his surroundings to be much different, far less chaotic, but none-the-less strange as ever. A pretty young nurse rushes in, silences the beeping, checks the monitor, looks Duke over, and exits with a wink and a smile.

"Hey, Buddy! How are you? You alright this morning?" he hears as he unsuccessfully tries wiping the sleep from his eyes. One might believe that hearing the sound of his daddy's voice would have been just what the doctor ordered, and it's usually true. But right away he's stricken with paralyzing dread. There's a twisting knot in the pit of his stomach and a bead of sweat appears on his temple as he replays the image of the dark figure he saw when he closed his eyes last night. Like a movie playing reel to 'real' on a screen inside his mind, he can see the huge figure cloaked in rags of pure black, which sag with the weight of their own filth. His rotten smile drips with motor oil drool and, as he croaks a hideous laugh, the stuff sprays all around; what lands on the floor sizzles and steams away. Looming above, staring down with burning red eyes, he strikes a fear so deep that makes Duke shudder as he jerks awake.

"Good Morning!" his dad shouts as he reaches in and

tickles Duke under his leg. Duke twists away with a whine. Above him a blinding light shines down; the lids of his eyes slam shut at the sight of it. He starts to prop himself up on his elbows but is quickly grabbed under the arms by his old man. He tries to wriggle away again, expecting more tickling, which he's not ready for at this early stage of the day.

The pulsing inside his head is still there as his dad picks him up and gives him a hearty squeeze. The oversized bear-hug he gets from his over-stuffed dad is a little more than he was bargaining for. The extra pressure makes his eye throb even more than it already had been.

"Good Morning!" his mommy says as she grabs him from his dad. She hugs him and kisses him before laying him down on the bed again. Standing above him with the bright light at her back, she looks like an angel. It shines through her silken blonde hair, which frames her face, until she brushes it away and tucks it behind her ear. She is smiling down at him. From his vantage point, the blur at the outer reaches of his vision gives her an angelic aura. She mouths the words, "I love you," and the world stands still.

In this still moment, he begins to feel relief. The terrible events of the night before recede to distant memory, like one of his many heavy dreams. Duke's night visions have always been nightmares, which is why, in his waking hours, he daydreams triumphant fantasies. He regularly envisions himself as a super-hero, a boy destined for greatness. In his bathrobe and his dad's bandanas, leaping off cushions and running down hallways, Duke feels like he will change the world someday.

As the world comes back to full-speed Duke realizes that something is going on here that he doesn't understand. His mother's smile is wrought with fear, which can be seen in her beautiful blue eyes, now bloodshot and dim. His heart skips a beat as it slides into position at the bottom of his throat, just in time to stop his own tears from raining down. Duke holds off the storm clouds for his mother's sake, because, for her, when it rains, it pours.

"Mommy… moke." he faintly mutters. He is back to playing dumb again, and some baby lingo for 'milk' does the trick as she wipes her most recent tears from her pink cheeks, which are still smeared with the remnants of yesterday's mascara. She's just so happy to hear that he's finally up for something to drink. She goes on, half crying and half laughing at the sound of his voice. Jesse takes off running out the door, and GG now joins the laughing-crying frenzy. Feeling a bit embarrassed he slips back down under his blanket, and pulls it up over his head.

3

Duke's become pretty good at pretending that he's not as smart as he really is. Although his special qualities have been showing since he was first born, he's been doing his best to squash any signs of his genius. His motor skills had quickly evolved, just as his speech had, but he had decided after one particular instance, that he would keep most of these things under his hat.

One spring morning at the ripe age of 14 months, he had been playing Duke of Dragons in his room. It's a game he invented over the past year on those sleepless, nightmare-filled nights. He has collected enough dragons to build an army of them. He'd line them all up on every free space in his room and bark orders like a medieval king. It's quite the thing to see, but he's always careful to play like a baby when anyone is around. He is also always adamant that his dragon warriors fight fairly. One time he even had his dragons attend their own Geneva-like convention in which they developed treaties and protocols to establish standards of dragon warfare. Duke called these the Dragon Rules.

Mommy was out of the house on this particular day, and Daddy was running in and out of the back door trying to clean up a nasty mess their dog, who Duke aptly named Doggie, had made in the back yard. The back yard had been a puddle of mud for months now, ever since Duke's epic first birthday party. Jesse was totally oblivious to what was happening inside. He has always given Duke a little extra leeway when mommy wasn't around. Besides, he was too wrapped up in his task, annoyed that the dogs had gotten a hold of another pair of his sneakers.

There is this nice older guy that lives down the street. He stops by sometimes, and he'll let himself in if the front door is open and no one comes. This is because Duke's mom and dad once told him that they couldn't hear when he knocked on the door if they were in the back room. Needless to say, this guy took it more like an invitation to walk into their house rather than a polite way to say, "go away". Well, on this day, he chose to stick his nose in the door. The dogs, which were crated and snoozing by the back door, didn't even notice the door opening. Good thing for the old man, because Doggie would have surely pummeled him as he unwittingly stepped through the door. Doggie isn't a mean dog, but this particular unexpected houseguest would have found the energetic boxer on top of him, licking his face like an overturned plate of steak scraps topped with a can of Alpo. Of course the other dog, Baby, the six pound Chihuahua, might have taken off his ankle at the first sign of forced entry!

Daddy was out back and Mr. Neighbor-Dude could hear Duke in his room playing with his dragon army. He says to himself, "Well, I'm already inside the house... better just go make sure the little guy is ok." His intentions were good enough actually. He mistakenly assumed, that since no one answered and he had seen Jesse working in the yard earlier that day, that the kid was indeed in the house... alone. Jesse is definitely one who would leave Duke to his own devices, sometimes even a little longer than his wife was willing to tolerate, but he always knew where the kid was at, and what he was doing.

Now, Mr. Crazy Neighbor is not any threat to Duke, and even Duke's parents don't really mind him stopping by, even if he is a little long-winded on the topics of religion and politics. But you can't go walking into someone's house unless you're fully aware that you very well might get your butt kicked, either by the doggie or the daddy, and in their case, the mommy too! Lucky for him, though, Jesse is outside for a little longer this time, and Mommy still won't be back for a while.

He stepped lightly through the hardwood-floored living room and past the dining room table. He stopped to examine the large scratch in the table top, making a tisk,tisk,tisk sound between his teeth while wagging his index finger. Mr. Nosy Neighbor doesn't have any scratches in his dining room table. Maggie Dillan would be none too thrilled if she knew he was looking at the scratches. She's been begging her husband to re-finish it for months.

Nosy-Neighbor was around the corner. Duke's door was open. He looked inside, seeing his fourteen-month old neighbor doing something he couldn't believe. Duke had climbed up the side of the crib and was seated, perfectly balanced, on the top edge of the rail, like the captain of some pirate ship, aloft, scanning the sails. He was sporting his blue bathrobe, using one of his daddy's bandanas as a headband. Looking down on his host of dragon warriors, Duke shouted instructions and enforced the Dragon Rules. "Protect the colors of this flag!" "Fight with honor and dignity!" "Our Fore-Fathers fought for our freedom!" He even threw out phrases like "This great nation" and "God Bless," every bit as eloquent as Winston Churchill or John F. Kennedy. But this was no Prime Minister, this is just a child!

As the baby stood before him, facing his troops, reciting the final stanza of his great speech to the dragon forces laid out neatly on the floor, Mr. Nosy Neighbor could have simply slipped out the way he came, and no one would have ever been the wiser. But the stirring speech and the amazing comprehension of the English language, which he spoke with all of the confidence of a Rhodes Scholar, had him stone-frozen.

The nosy neighbor just stood there, dumbfounded. It was the first and only time someone snuck up on Dukey Dude while he was doing his thing. Mommy, Daddy and GG walk around here like a herd of elephants. You can hear everything as someone walks across this wood floor. And Duke is quick as a flash when his parents are coming. He can get his outfit off and be, goo-gooing and ga-gaing again in three seconds. But somehow this guy walked in there and caught him red-handed.

Suddenly Duke stopped and looked up, realizing that he

was being watched. He smiled at the man. Mr. Neighbor-Dude, still trying to pick his jaw up off of the floor, stumbled backwards, smacking his head on the side of the hallway door-jam. He turned around to see what hit him and immediately saw Duke's daddy, bounding toward the back door from the outside. This was the first moment that the Nosy Neighbor thought how it didn't look really great, what, with him standing there in his neighbor's house, staring into a child's bedroom. The problem was that he still couldn't get a hold of himself after seeing this kid balanced there, acting like a full-grown man, speaking as clearly as the most silver-tongued orators. It was too late for a quick exit. He would have to stay right there and try to explain why he was where he was. He figured the best bet would be to inform this guy that his kid is some sort of freak of nature.

"Who's there? Who's that?!" Duke's dad hollers as he raced in the house. He stopped one step inside the back door. He wasn't expecting to see anyone standing in his house, but he also wasn't surprised that this guy was the one standing there. As ticked off as he was, he would give him one chance to get out before he threw him out. He was poised to lunge and make sure that from now on he understood that if no one comes to the door, you just turn right around and leave!

The neighbor began to stammer, "You-you-you're boy…. He was t-t-talkin…" but he couldn't fully get the words out. Daddy pointed his finger toward the door. The neighbor didn't hesitate and raced toward the front of the house while Duke's dad went to see if his son was ok. In his hurry, the neighbor tripped over his own feet, hitting the ground hard. Duke's dad looked at him and yelled, "What are you doing?!" The man couldn't even respond. He thought for sure that this guy was going to kick his butt.

"You better start makin' a little sense or I'm going to have no other choice but to physically remove you from my house!" Duke's dad shouts at the man on his living room floor. Finally the neighbor man started to compose himself. "Y-Your kid was in his room. He was talking like a full grown man and I-I…… I swear! I saw him!"

"What are you doing in here in the first place?" Jesse hollers. He towers over the much smaller man.

"I-I-I…. The door was open! I-I-I-I didn't mean to be nosy! I just wanted to see if you folks wanted any tomatoes from my garden!" Saying this, he pointed over at the table by the door where several plump tomatoes sat. Duke's dad looked over, perplexed. The man decided it'd be best if he just skedaddled. He hopped up and took off. Jesse stood there looking through the storm-door window, as the man, who is at least in his fifties, ran for the first time in twenty years. Jesse watched long enough that he would have known if the man had pulled a groin or something, then turned his attention to the tomatoes on the table. He stood there shaking his head. "Well, they are some nice tomatoes… That guy is so weird!"

He walked into his son's room and stared at the little boy. Duke stared back at him with a loving gaze, and said, "Daddy…" in his cutest voice, then quietly continued to play with his dragons. Jesse didn't ask, but wondered what the heck that was all about. He stood there for a good long time before going back to his chores, that is, after he locked the front door.

The neighbor-dude never came back, but every couple weeks in the summer, there would be five or six plump red tomatoes on their front step. Daddy had looked at him a little differently ever since, and Duke had decided that he would have to be a lot more careful if he was going to keep his special talents a secret.

4

Duke's Daddy scurries out of the hospital room, as if he's just been given orders from the President of the United States himself. "I wonder what he's all worked up about?" Duke thinks to himself. He looks back to his mother who is weeping uncontrollably, and he has to look away. He cannot stand to see her cry, not even for a second. If he doesn't divert his eyes, he'll begin blubbering too. That wouldn't be good for anyone.

That's when he notices the pole standing where his daddy just took off running. As he peruses the six-foot tall pole, he sees, much clearer by daylight, the lighted monitors churning and pumping. Some have syringes on top, and others are pumping liquid through tubes with blue motorized pumps. The collection of medical apparatus is arranged in a way that somehow resembles a human face. As the numbers and the words flash through the screens, it's as if the monitors are showing expressions and even trying to make him laugh. The screens are all obscured by clusters of dangling tubes hanging down from bags which are hooked onto the pole's top. Another set of tubes swoop down toward the floor. As he begins to trace them up to his bed he realizes that they are all condensed into a pair, neatly tucked up under his shirt above the waistband of his pants.

What the….? he gasps silently as he begins to lift the shirt. What he sees next shocks him more than any of the events of the night before. The tubes are connected to a central tube, which has been placed under his skin snaking its way up to his neck, then disappears. It's like a bad sci-fi movie, where the alien worm gets under your skin and begins to make a slow trek toward your heart. Only it doesn't look like this worm has very far to go at all!

All of the gasping and horrified expressions send GG and Maggie to Duke's bedside in an instant. He shrugs them off as they try to fix his shirt. He wiggles away as they try to stroke his hair. Ever the vigilant mother and grandmother, the two would go to the ends of the earth to protect and comfort this little boy. Some kids would feel lucky if even one of their parents were around all of the time, now Duke's got three!

When he looks back up in the direction of the pole, his Daddy is standing there again, with a small carton of milk in his hand, and Duke's Mom-Mom Jo under his other arm.

"Look who came to see you," Jesse says as he opens the milk and sticks a straw in it.

Duke hardly even remembers asking for the milk, and he certainly wasn't expecting to get it, and he definitely wasn't expecting Mom-Mom Jo at his early hour. Before today he would have been lucky to get anything without saying "please," let alone in seconds flat! Jesse turns and gives his mom a kiss on the forehead and says, "Everything is going to be alright, Mom. We just have to have faith."

She just buries her head in his chest. She is trying to speak, but the only things he can make out are sobbing cries and," He just has to be ok!"

Once again the kid is confused. Now not only are both

his parents at his bedside, but both of his grandmothers as well; all with poorly hidden worry on their faces and red, tear stained eyes. Mom-Mom is hugging and kissing him on the top of his head as he picks up the carton, puts the straw in his mouth and downs half of the milk before he puts it down. They are all now staring at him as if they had never seen him do such a thing. As a matter of fact, he can't remember the last time he was so thirsty. All he knows is that something has everyone all worked up, and by the looks on their faces, it can't be good.

5

Soon Duke becomes more aware of his surroundings, and when the confusion starts to turn to realization, the anxiety starts to set in. This is one time that he wished his brain hadn't developed so quickly. An ordinary two year old would still be thinking about some toy they wanted, or their favorite Sesame Street character, but he's here making logical deductions about where he is and why he's here. It has to be the black eye. He knows it. This shiner had come out of nowhere. He could remember the day, but he still can't remember what happened.

About two weeks ago he was playing with the kids for whom his mother is the nanny, Blake and Sydney. The boy is a big lug, only about a year old. He's the type you might find actually eating mud pies, not just pretending like the rest of the kids. His arms are like ham-hocks, which explains why having a catch with him is always an adventure. The poor kid couldn't hit the broad side of a barn, catapulting with those great big arms. The girl is about three, maybe even four. Typical girl, you know the type. She'll haul off and whack you, then go running away crying to her mommy that you did the hitting.

Then, while she's getting her make believe boo-boos kissed, she'll give you that look, the one where she sticks out her tongue and crosses her eyes, as if to say, "I'm a girl and you're a boy, so tough luck to you." He was sure that's how everyone assumed he'd gotten the shiner in the first place. Maybe he'd taken a shot to the eye from a girl who ran off tattling about how he tried to kick her or something, or maybe he was in the way of a catapulted baseball from the arm of a one year old. As far as he could remember, it may have even been either way. He just couldn't remember how he'd gotten the bruise either.

Mommy and Daddy have moved to the other side of the room, and are sitting on the couch. Duke doesn't notice them at all. He's deep in thought trying to remember how he got this nasty black eye. He sits up, suddenly recalling having been with Blake and Sydney just yesterday.

He remembers going to the doctor's office. The doctor was feeling his belly, which ticked him off. What would the doctor be checking his belly for when he's got a black eye!

The next thing he knew, they were saying goodbye to Blake, Sydney and their Daddy. GG, of all people, was pulling into the parking lot of the doctor's office. Daddy was yelling. Mommy was crying her eyes out. He doesn't really remember what he was doing, which probably means he was crying too. He always spaces out when he's upset. He vaguely remembers a speedy ride in the car with all three of them, which must have ended up here, although he doesn't remember a thing that happened since then.

He looks over to the couch where Mommy, GG and Mom-Mom Jo are sitting, and notices for the first time that he's in a room with huge windows, which peculiarly, don't look outside. There's only one place he could think of where there are windows that look out to more 'inside,' and that's a hospital.

They must have been headed to the hospital in the car yesterday, while Mommy was crying and Daddy and GG were telling themselves that everything would be ok. And now that he's getting a better look around, he knows he's been here before, a long time ago. The room was a little different then, and he remembers having a roommate. Actually, that's the whole reason he remembers at all. The poor thing didn't stop crying the whole time. She was just a baby, but as far as he remembers, he was too. His mommy and daddy were both there. It was only for a little while, but he remembers the nurse was very nice.

That's right around the time when everything started to become clear in his mind, at the meager age of two months. When he left this place before, he could see things in a whole new way. His senses had changed and he became aware of his surroundings in another way entirely. Since then he's found that he can do things that no child can do. He became super.

6

This time has to be different though. Before nobody else was crying except for that little girl. Now everyone seems to be crying. This has to be something much worse.

He can't remember a thing about the day his mommy pointed out the bruised eye for the first time. He didn't even believe it until he saw his reflection in the side-view mirror of their SUV. Blake and Sydney's parents stood there for a while debating if it was even possible for him to have gotten a black eye without either of them hearing him holler. Mommy even sent off a quick text message to his dad, who was at work, to ask him, "Does it make me a bad parent if I don't know how Duke got a black eye?"

Of course, optimistic Jesse was sure it was nothing and told her, "No, I don't think so. He's a tough kid. He probably got whacked and didn't even feel it." Duke's dad, the positive thinker, always has a way of shrugging these things off as 'no big deal.' He was still telling Mommy that everything would be ok as they were getting ready for bed, the night before his appointment with Dr. Schectman. He didn't want to hear anything about her 'crazy' ideas... which maybe aren't so crazy sometimes.

Now they're in this place, and he wouldn't be surprised if someone told him he'd been here for a week. Chances are good that nothing will ever surprise him again after he and his family see the doctor who is now entering their room.

7

Duke immediately sees the faces of his family brighten as the young doctor pokes his head into the door. He is smiling with a hint of sorrow in his eyes. It is obvious that he is the leader of a flock of doctors that are standing in a group outside of the room.

Duke recognizes him; suddenly remembering a little bit more from the Emergency Room, and as he takes a second look at the doctor's blonde hair, they catch eyes.

"Good Morning, Duke," he says as he breaks away from the others and enters the room. The rest follow, but it's clear that Dr. Houston is taking the lead in this case.

There is an attending doc named Dr. J with him, along with the nurse practitioner, named Miss Colleen, and the resident. As he's stepping into the room and shaking hands with Duke's dad and mom, he again locks eyes with Duke, who grins at him, and then gives an ear-piercing pterodactyl squawk to the others.

"Aaaaaawk!"

It halts them in their tracks. As the rest of the docs hold their ears, Dr. Houston says, "It's alright Duke… they're with me. These are my friends." Duke immediately stops his screeching. The other docs begin to comment to each other on how good Tim is with Duke and pull their fingers out of their ears. Dr. Houston just looks back at Duke, smiles, and says to him, like they are sharing an inside secret only they understand, "He's my buddy…. Aren't you, Duke?"

Unable to resist, Duke starts to crack a smile of his own. He hears his daddy saying "He must really like you, Doctor Houston," and the rest of the family agrees in unison at the sentiment. It seems everyone likes the young Doc. Duke isn't even really sure why he likes Dr. Houston so much. It's almost like he's known him his whole life.

8

Duke can't make out much of what Dr. Houston is telling his family and most of what he can hear gets lost in the never-ending commotion coming through the open door left ajar by the last doctor to enter the room. Two words do stick out in his mind though: tumor and cancer. He knows they are bad words once he sees Mommy run out of the room crying and GG chasing after her.

Now being a kid, even a highly intelligent one, those words don't really compute. It's not that he's not intelligent enough to understand their meaning, but most people can't comprehend those words even when they're fully grown. They are heavy words; the weight of which no child should ever have to carry. Duke is in such a state of shock that even seeing his mother run by in tears doesn't rouse him out of it.

His life has been spent in a very happy home, and the language has always been of the positive variety. So there isn't a lot of talk about these types of things. He has heard these words before, though. Recently he's heard a lot about cancer when he's listening in on Mommy and GG's conversations about his great grandfather, Pop-Pop. He always pretends to be sleeping in the car so that he can eavesdrop on the real conversations.

From this espionage, he knows that his Pop-Pop has cancer, and apparently, he's had it for a couple of years. He heard them saying that they thought they had gotten rid of it, but then just after his six-month birthday, he heard everyone start to talk about how it had come back, and now the doctors don't know if there is anything else they can do to help him.

9

Pop-Pop is a very old man. He and Duke have always had a very special bond. Ever since Duke was born, Pop-Pop would always say, "There's something about that kid. He's special." Pop-Pop had given him his first silver dollar. He kept it taped to the head of his bed, so he couldn't lose it. That coin is one of his prized possessions, probably his most prized possession. Duke has always guessed that their connection was because

Pop-Pop recognized his extraordinary talent.

Recently though, Pop-Pop has seemed like he's getting older every time he sees him. Mommy and GG cry whenever they have to leave his house, and then they talk about how he doesn't look good at all. It's because he has cancer. It's making him really sick, and they all think he might die soon. Of course they never say any of this in front of Duke, and if they knew he could understand them when he's pretending to be sleeping, they would never say any of it at all.

Thinking of this, makes Duke want to cry. Not because he's about to hear that he too, has cancer, but because he'll miss his Pop-Pop very much if he dies.

Now they are coming toward him, Daddy and the doctor. The doctor wants to take a look at this tangle of twisted tubes that is embedded in his chest, just below his right nipple. He refers to the main tube as a central line, a Med-Comp he calls it.

"Hello," he says, as he looks Duke right in his eye. He smiles and although Duke doesn't want to, he smiles back at him.

"Will you sow my friends how you can say Tim?" Of course Duke could say it. Heck, he could even read the chart the guy is holding, but he's not going to. He's still busy thinking about Pop-Pop.

"Well that's alright, maybe later. I'm just going to look at the tubes, OK?"

Dr. Houston takes a look at the tubes and points out a couple of things about them that makes them different than others. Daddy's writing it all down in a notebook, which Duke can see has stickers of his favorite green dragon all over it. His old man has been taking notes in that thing ever since they got here.

Dr. Houston tells Jesse that it looks pretty good, and that they should let him know if there are any changes. The doctor then starts to feel around his belly like the doctor yesterday did. This actually makes Duke a little mad for the first time since Doctor Tim walked in. He pulls on his shirt until the doctor takes his hands off. He wonders why everyone is so concerned with his belly when he's obviously got something wrong with his eye.

"What is Neuroblastoma, Dr. Houston? Is it like leukemia?" Jesse asks as he scribbles a few more words in his book. Duke sees that his dad has the first five or ten pages filled up and he once again wonders exactly how long it is that he's actually been here.

"Neuroblastoma is a cancer that attacks developing nerve cells in the body, while the baby is still in cellular form, shortly after conception. The gene responsible for this simply has an on/off switch which in the rest of us is switched off, but in Duke's case is switched on. The cancerous cells start in the nerve endings, usually in the abdomen, chest, or around the spinal column. The tumor, which in Duke's case stemmed from his left adrenal gland, grows unchecked until certain warning signs appear." Dr. Houston makes it sound so simple, but Jesse is having trouble keeping up as he feverishly scribbles it all down in his book.

"So in Duke's case, it's the black eye which was the first symptom, right?" Jesse asks Dr. Houston.

"Well, yes and no. We are looking at the results of the CT-scan Duke had last night in order to see if the eye symptoms are related to proteins given off by the tumor in his abdomen, or if it is actually a metastatic tumor."

"Which one are we hoping it is?" Jesse asks, although he thinks he knows the answer.

"When there is a tumor inside someone it begins at Stage I. When the tumor spreads or metastasizes to another part of the body, it usually brings it up to a Stage IV," Doctor Houston explains as Mommy and GG are walking back into the room. Maggie only caught the tail-end of the conversation, but she's eager to know what Dr. Houston thinks about the stage that Duke's Cancer is in.

"Wha… what stage is Duke?" she fearfully asks, still wiping away tears from her eyes.

"We really won't know for sure until we do some more testing, but I think we are going to find that it is Stage IV," he concisely yet compassionately replies. Never-the-less, his response sends Maggie and GG running out of the room once again. As they are rushing through the doorway, they almost plow over another young doc, who slides to the left side of the door frame and sucks in his breath to allow them to pass. Duke, Jesse and the Doc all look at the new guy as he looks back at them, having nearly been run over by the women. They are actually able to snicker a bit at the way that he was almost flattened. He comes in and immediately gets the screech of terror from Duke. Aaaaaawk!

His news is no better, as he re-introduces himself as Dr. Nick from Opthomology. "His eyes seem good, and the good news is that it doesn't seem that the tumor is damaging his eye or his vision."

"So it is a tumor?" Jesse asks. "Not just proteins?"

Dr. Nick quickly responds and puts an end to any more speculation. "I just saw the results of the scan. It's definitely a tumor."

10

It's probably best that the girls didn't hear that. It's been nothing but bad news so far, and they are both taking it very hard. Dr. Nick takes a few pictures of Duke's eye for his file. He needs them to document what he calls a 'text book case of NB'. As Dr. Nick snaps a few last shots, he tries to get a smile from his young patient. Duke is having none of it. He's too busy wondering if he'd ever see his Pop-Pop or any of his other friends or family again. Finally Duke rolls over completely in his bed and faces away from the doctors and his dad. He's feeling sick to his stomach in the light of the news, and he's staring blankly as the adults continue talking. That's when he once again notices the tall pole with the monitors and pumps. He looks up and sees bags of saline solution hung on hooks. He scans the tubing as it feeds into the pump, and watches the fluid pump through the tube that connects to him, under his shirt. It's freaky enough that they've got this stuff tucked neatly into his chest, but the feeling that this pole is actually looking back at him is more than he can handle.

The funny thing though, is that he's not really scared of the IV pole. He's more intrigued than anything else at how the churning sounds of it's pumps, and the strangely life-like formation of it's monitors make it seem alive. As he rolls back over, he begins to imagine what it would be like if the pole really did come to life.

"It looks like you and I are going to be pretty close, so I'd better introduce myself. I'm Duke Dillan. That's the

61

name my parents gave me after I was born," he would say.

"Nice to meet you," he thinks its response might be, recited in a monotone robot voice.

"Sometimes my dad calls me Dukey Dude, like a super-hero. You know what a super-hero is?"

"Oh, of course I do," the IV pole would reply.

He's smiling a little at his mental rendition of a robotic dialect, but he's still being careful not to actually say any of this out loud. He doesn't want them to think he's sick and crazy too… or does he? He is rehearsing a conversation he *might* have with a robotic IV pole; so go figure.

"Well, we'll just make this our little secret." he says as he glances at the pole, winking one eye, to see if it got the joke. Even though it looks like the right pump is winking back at him, as the beeps are simulating a laughing sound, Duke goes on assuming it's just his imagination.

He takes a glance back toward the hall, where his dad and the docs are still talking. They're discussing how the Med-Comp will be used to administer all of his meds and his chemo, obviously not having noticed his little pseudo-conversation with his pole.

When he looks back at the pole though, it is beeping and flashing away, with "ERROR-ERROR" flashing on it's screens as if at any moment it may burst into flames sending a shower of sparks over the whole room. He gets to his feet and has his finger over his lips, saying, "Shh! Shh!" The pole is now jumping off of the floor and steam is pouring out of the main monitor like a tea kettle. "Daddy!" Duke cries as he tries to scale the side of his bed and get out of there. Jesse runs in and asks, "What's the matter Duke?" but when he turns and looks again, the pole is standing perfectly still, as if nothing had ever happened. Doctor Houston and the nurse stride hastily into the room together, having heard Duke's cries.

"Are you playing games with me?" the nurse coyly asks Duke seeing that everything is ok. A burst of rosy red fills his cheeks and Duke flips over burying his head in the pillow. "I'm gonna' have to keep an eye on you!" she jokes as she punches some numbers into the pump.

"It looks like you've got an admirer!" Jesse remarks as she's leaving the room, "You're the first nurse who's come in that didn't make him shriek like a pterodactyl!"

"Bye, Duke!" she says in a flirty voice on the way out. His head is still buried in the pillow, though. The crazed beeping IV pole he could excuse, but his own Daddy exposing his emotions like that; that's below the belt!

After all of this, or because of it, the doc and Daddy decide that's enough discussion. Doctor Tim, flashing his most bewildered yet charismatic smile yet, says his goodbyes.

As Dr. Houston heads back into the hall, Duke sees his mommy giving the doctor a big hug as she wipes more tears from her cheeks. Duke can hear Dr. Houston shout, "Dr. Mahoney… Can I have a word with you?" then looks at Maggie and says, "Don't worry, we're going to do everything we can to help him." Maggie turns to her husband and buries her head in his chest as Dr. Houston runs to catch his colleague.

Maggie and Jesse see the two docs down the hall talking and looking back over their shoulders in their direction. They decide to go back into the room so they don't seem to be eavesdropping. As they are entering the room, Jesse looks back to see another doctor joining the conversation. He briefly wonders what they could be discussing, then shrugs his shoulders and walks into the room.

11

"So, you saw what was going on in the ER too, right? I've never seen a kid's heart rate return to normal so fast after a night terror. It's like he has extraordinary control of his involuntaries." Dr. Houston says to Nick Maloney. "Please tell me I'm not crazy, 'cause that kid was in my head, and it sort of freaked me out… I think I probably sent those poor people into a tizzy!"

"Well, you did, but I tried to smooth it over. I think they were most likely in a tizzy already. I did notice that there was something different about him than the other kids, but I couldn't quite put my finger on it."

"John thinks we need a vacation," Dr. Houston jokes to his young friend. "Seriously though, there's something up with that kid."

"I know… He was checking me out when I walked in… I was waiting for him to ask me for my credentials!" The two docs break out into a loud laugh with that, which is only cut short when Dr. Masters walks up on them.

"You two really *do* need a vacation, don't you?" the salt and pepper haired doc remarks. There is a certain level of respect the two younger doctors have for John Masters, but he treats them as equals. Still, they know that this is the guy who has the answers to their questions. He's seen it all. "Let's walk and talk," he says. "I'm late for a meeting."

"We were just in with the kid. He's doing well. Nick saw the scan and confirmed a metastatic tumor above the right eye," Tim says.

"Classic Neuroblastoma," John replies.

"The parents are eager to know the prognosis. We kept it pretty vague, but I did tell them I would be surprised if it was not Stage IV," says Tim. For a young doc, he is pretty sharp.

"Tim, I'd like it if you'd accompany me to the Solid Tumor Conference tomorrow afternoon. Nick, you can come too, and bring those pictures you took of Duke's eye and distended abdomen. There have been a lot of major advances in NB treatment, and this boy may have come to us at just the right time…" Before he could finish his sentence he's exiting the hallway through a doorway for which he has to use a keycard to exit.

"I think he means *he's* made some major breakthroughs in NB treatment." Tim says. "The guy's like the Michael Jordan of Neuroblastoma research!"

12

Duke turns his head slowly back in the direction of the pole. The thing is winking at him again, he swears it. He almost thinks he can hear its laughter inside his head. I'm losing it, he thinks to himself with one eye still glancing back over his shoulder, afraid the thing might try to zap him if he turns his back completely.

When Duke's daddy returns, he is just standing over him, gazing, as if he is a newborn baby. It's like he has never seen him before, or maybe like he would never see him again. Duke is giving his dear-old-dad a death-stare in return for embarrassing him in front of the nurse. But Duke could be shooting him with real poison darts and Jesse would never budge from this moment of taking in *all* of his son. Something's come over Duke's parents, and now it seems like *he* is their only concern.

"G-Gary," Duke says, and once again Daddy is running around like a man named Jeeves, whose one sole purpose is to serve his every whim. Before he can even begin to give his daddy a hard time, his favorite TV dragon is doing the pre-historic Irish jig on the screen. Before Gary can even get through a couple stanzas of his classic "I am Gary, you are you, do the best that you can do" routine he is nodding off again for a mid-morning nap. Actually, Duke has no idea if it's morning, noon, or night, given the fact that this place stays lit up at all times. Before he closes his eyes, he takes one last look at the IV pole that almost blew up earlier. "This keeps getting weirder," he thinks as he watches the pole with a wary eye.

"Stay!" he whispers so his daddy won't hear. Then he closes his eyes and falls into a much needed, dreamless sleep.

Chapter Four

'Automatic Friends'

1

When Duke awakes from his nap, all is quiet in the halls of 3 South, except for some beeping coming from down the hall. He notices that Gary the Green Dragon, his trusted stuffed friend from home, is sprawled out on the floor next to his bed.

"Sorry, pal, but you know the rules," he groggily says.

As he reaches for his sippy cup, he starts to realize that the lack of his bedtime companion is not the only thing that has changed from before he fell asleep. His room is dark. There is no sign of anybody. Once again he starts to re-live the moments of his far too vivid dream of the night before. He can't shake the idea that someone else was there with him in the woods, and fears that it was that same dark figure who haunted him in the nourishment room. It's the first time he's ever felt the presence of a stranger in his recurring dreams, but now that he feels it, he wonders if this invader has been there all along, or if he'll ever go away. He actually has himself all worked up over the notion until he's startled out of his trance by an abrupt series of beeps from his pole, similar to that of an alarm clock.

He snaps out of his paranoid trance, and smacks his head on the prison style bars of his children's hospital bed. "Oww!" he snaps in the direction of the pole, once again acting as if it's more than an inanimate object. Now he's staring at the thing as if he's not sure whether or not the rolling rack could actually be alive. He's staring daggers in that direction and rubbing his right hand on the small lump that's forming on the back of his head.

As he peruses the pole, he becomes increasingly more aware of the noise coming from down the hall. It's a familiar beeping sound, similar to the one that had woke him up this morning. But his beeping was quickly extinguished by his pretty young nurse, who smiled at him and pressed a couple of buttons. This particular beeping, however, is not stopping.

He realizes that he has not seen anyone walking in the hall since he first woke up from his nap. He hasn't been here for that long, but it seems like the halls had been bustling with people before he went to sleep. As he is lying there his eyes close again. As he begins to dream, it's as if it had been a parade that had gone by earlier that day.

Da, Dum, Da-Dum, Da-Da, Da-Da, Da-Dum. Duke hears the marching band leading the procession with a string quartet following behind. He'd been really excited this past New Year's morning when he and his family had watched the Mummer's Parade, a local tradition, filled with men in feathered costumes strutting down Broad St.

James the Janitor leads the Environmental Services Staff at the front, in their blue jump-suits, twirling mops and doing figure eights around each other atop their wheeled buckets. Drops of water splash over the sides then fall into the nearest bucket in unison, as the procession continues. Others make a crazy "Rat-a-tat-tatttley-tat-tat" drumbeat on flipped over trash cans, like those urban percussionists you see playing on street corners in New York City, keeping the beat for the marching pedestrians as they file by, sipping their lattes on their way to their high-rise yoga studios. They mop the floors in time for the next wave to slide by, nearly crashing together, before using their trash bags to parachute to a graceful halt.

Top Doctors in lab-coats come marching by next, never noticing the wet floor signs that are quickly collected just before their shiny leather shoes clap on the barely dry floor, nearly missing a painful spill. They're all skulking along with their massive brain-filled craniums so deeply planted in some manila folder that they would never stop in time if their colleague had bent down to tie his shoe. Good thing for all of them, their massive brains are too full of theories on how to solve these horrible riddles that have stumped the brightest minds since the dawn of time. At first sight, they might seem like they are nothing but giant skulls bobbing down the halls, on a stick, being operated by a hidden puppeteer beneath the hem of their coats. Most are clad with pocket-protectors, glasses taped in the middle and every other stereotypical nerd adage, but it would be they, who would be finding the cures for all that ails the children who grace the rooms along either side of these halls, so it would be most prudent to look past their sometimes scary exteriors, to see their true faces.

Then come the Jolly Good Fellows, who, both men and women, contrary to the name, seem to walk to the beat of their own drummers, stopping along the way to poke their heads in doors and say a cheerful "Hello" as they be-bop along the path. Duke can hear the many different musical grooves coming from this group, and how they all seemed to meld together into one beautiful harmony. This group reminds him most of the hippies from the

'60's, wearing their brightly colored tie-dye t-shirts and headbands, complete with hempen jewelry, mood rings and Birkenstock sandals. This image has Duke laughing especially hard, but not at them. It would surely be their amazing bedside manner which will ease the suffering of the children, while they endure what would usually go as torture in any other setting. These amazing people have hearts that will not fail to rid the world of these horrible diseases.

The Jolly Good Fellows are closely followed by the massive grouping of Residents. They have only just begun their tenure, although you likely wouldn't be able to tell by their cock-sure strut. They walk with their chest puffed out and their head in the clouds. Bright plumes stick out from their lab-coats as they march, proud as peacocks, down the hall. So full of pride in their newfound status that they miss the next turn and begin to fall over each other as they smash one by one into the wall! The ones who have enough sense to see past their own feathers, stop short of the pile up. They have to pull the rest up by picking them up under the arms. Surely these would be the doctors of tomorrow, but for now let's just be thankful that it's still today!

Next, the disjointed conga line includes the Lovely Young Nurses, whose harps can be heard all throughout the hospital, singing their sweet songs of healing and compassion. They are calmly floating along, as if they rode upon a cloud, smiling always, and shining the brightest glow into each and every room they pass. Like angels, they watch over the youngsters as they each battle their own demons. And it would be through them that all these kids, including Duke himself, would find the greatest comfort. They are family and friends to these kids and their parents, as long as they stay.

Lastly, the Never-Ending Stream of Well Wishers bring
up the rear. Some are crying, whether tears of sorrow
or joy. Some are laughing, though they might not know
whether their laughter was bred from humor or sheer
madness! Some from this crowd carry the children
through these halls, either to aid them in the most difficult
moments of their lives, or to exalt them as victors, making
their way back to the real world. Still others travel along
individually, devoid of any outward emotion, trudging
through their own private hell, waiting for the answers,
or the end. Through their dark eyes can be seen the fear
of the unknown, and the greatest of all sorrows.

Duke slowly wakes from his momentary dreaming
with a tear in his eye. He rolls over as he wipes away the
wetness from his cheek, still fully expecting the halls to
be filled with a circus of action; but at least for now, the
halls are eerily silent. The parade has, at least for the time
being, ceased altogether. And the silence is deafening.
Silence that is, except for the persistent beeping coming
from down the hall. Every moment that goes by he's
expecting help to be coming for whoever it is that needs
it, but so far, none has come.

2

The beeping down the hallway is so pronounced now
that it feels like the alarms are going off in his head.
Scanning the room he begins to feel like all eyes are on
him, even though there is nothing but inanimate objects
around.

"What is that?" he says, looking over his shoulder, trying
to break the tension. When he looks in the direction
of his Gary the Green Dragon friend, he imagines the
stuffed animal staring back, posing a silent question. He

responds to the imaginary inquisition.

"What do you want me to do about it? I'm just a kid!"

This time he could swear he sees the glimmer in Gary's eye that he recognizes from his TV shtick, where he twinkles his eyes and BAM! he's a full-grown dragon come to life!

"Don't get any ideas," Duke dryly remarks to his friend. After all, this is the very set of circumstances that lands Gary on his can, on the floor, each and every night. No stuffed animal of his is coming to life in the middle of the night, singing about the alphabet and telling him how much he loves everybody! The thought does amuse him, though. However, he's not sure if it's the idea of his toy coming to life or that he's actually afraid enough to launch him from his crib at night to prevent it!

Regardless, that beeping needs to be addressed. Duke feels a sudden urge to climb aboard his IV pole and ride it down the hall like a star-shaped skateboard with a hat rack mounted to its frame. He can picture himself gliding down the halls in search of the source of all this incessant beeping. Oddly enough, at his mind's mere suggestion, his pole is buzzing and beeping and almost coming off of the floor, as if it were a dog who's just been told that they'd be going for a walk and is eager to go darting off to find his leash. The possessed pole is already as far away as she can be without yanking the tubes out of Duke's bony chest. He crawls over to the side of the bed where it stands. He reaches his hand out from between the bars of the fence. As he extends his fingers, he closes his eyes to concentrate on stretching that last couple of inches so he can touch the plastic casing on the blue pump. He's still short by at least a foot.

When he opens his eyes he can't believe what he sees. The monitors simultaneously light up and the pole does an about face, turning it's information screens toward him. Then it draws closer to him, and closer, and closer, until its plastic handle is in the palm of his hand. Duke jumps back, scared out of his mind, and hits his head again.

"Oww!"

Now he's freaked. Momentary tears have turned to cold sweat. "Mommy… Daddy….." he mumbles as he once again rubs the sore spot on the back of his head, darting his eyes around the room. They are nowhere to be found. It's just him, Gary the Green Dragon and his IV pole, which is apparently set to auto-pilot.

"Please don't hurt me," he mumbles as he closes his eyes.

"I don't want to hurt you," he hears a sweet woman's voice say. This turns Duke around with a jerk to try and see where the voice came from. No one is there. He's totally baffled. Maybe the strangest part of it all is that it feels like the voice came from inside his head.

"D-Did you just say something?" he asks out loud, now actually talking to this coat rack come-to-life. His IV pole just stands there, as if nothing ever happened. He's starting to think he's lost it altogether.

Duke once again crawls back to the side of the bed where his pole is standing on the other side of the safety bars. He stands up on the mattress to look over the top of the rail. There's at least a four-foot drop to the ground from here, but it feels like a few stories to skinny baby boy. He looks back over his shoulder at the door, and finally decides that he's never going to get any answers locked up in this cage. With all the grace of an Olympic gymnast, he swings his legs up and over the rail, pushes off with his hands like he's dismounting the pommel horse, and lets go just in time for a gold medal landing.

Now having completed his trick, Duke turns and bows, like a trapeze artist who has just dazzled the crowd with death-defying stunts, and a pin-point landing. The IV pole immediately starts buzzing and beeping. His athletic antics are certainly not wasted on her... or him?

3

Duke walks closer to the pole. It scoots just far enough away with each step so that it is still just out of his reach.

"I don't want to hurt you. You don't want to hurt me, do you?" he asks. Duke is shaking from expending all of the energy he had stored up in his body, and because he's scared out of his wits that this contraption may truly be alive. This time it does not reply. It just stands there. He once again reaches his hand out, and at the mere suggestion of his mind, it rolls toward him, and the pole lands right in his hand.

"Alright, you're really starting to freak me out! If you don't start talking I'm going to get the nurse and throw a major tantrum!" Duke knows that the threat of a tantrum is all it takes to get what he wants from Mommy, Daddy, GG, and just about anyone else he's ever been left alone with. He's just hoping that this thing responds in the same way.

The answer he is seeking comes in action, not in words. The illuminated pole, whose handle rests in his hand, suddenly shifts closer. Duke is suddenly swept up off of his feet until he's seated on his tiny little butt on the star shaped base of the wheeled rack. He begins to get to his feet but is thrown back as the thing propels itself into a Tony Hawk-style trick expo. Duke has to hold on for dear life!

After a few tense, white-knuckle moments with his eyes closed repeating the twenty-third Psalm, Duke actually begins to enjoy being vaulted around his hospital room. He even gets to his knees, and then his feet, all while the pole is spinning and jumping; it seems like he's a natural at it. They are jumping up onto the heating unit which sticks out a foot from the window-wall, and it's grinding across the edge before it somehow leaps off, doing a three-sixty in mid air, landing on two of its five wheels. They are hopping up and bouncing off of the walls, each time twisting and turning in a different way, before touching the floor again.

"This is awesome!" Duke shouts and the trick pole responds with colorful bursts across its screens. It harmonically beeps in unison with its wheels smacking and rolling on the floor. Duke's new friend finally comes to a stop. He pops off and stands on the floor next to the pole. "You're incredible!" he says in awe. "Is there anything you can't do?"

The silence that follows answers his question. "Ohh, I get it, you can't talk. Well that's ok… we'll just have to find other ways to communicate!" The screens now turn pink and red, almost as if the machine is blushing.

"Don't worry, I get a little embarrassed when everyone is always telling me how cute I am too. Actually, it's kind of cool being the center of attention sometimes!" Now the pole is swaying back and forth like a little girl that has just been told she's pretty by the boy she likes. The screens are all lit up like Christmas and he can even see hearts being displayed where there were only a long series of numbers before.

"Ohh… I get it! You're a girl robot! I see, I see…Well, I guess that's cool. I've always tried to pretend that I'm not that into girls, but just between you and me, I actually think they're ok."

4

Beep, beep, beep…. Beep, beep, beep…

Duke again notices the sound. He looks at his new friend, but it's clear that the beeping is not coming from her. He looks at the door and then back to her again. "So should we go see what's going on?" he asks.

As he goes toward the door, his mechanical counterpart purposely positions herself in front of him. He tries to side-step her to the right, but she glides across and blocks him. He tries to go back to the left, and he's blocked again. Finally he tries a quick head-fake and a stutter step like he's seen Donny Mack, the quarterback from his dad's favorite football team do to try and avoid a would-be tackler, but she's too quick for any of his moves.

"C"mon! Let's go! What are we waiting for?" he says, exasperated, wanting to go out and see what the problem is. Duke is pulling the plastic tubes harder than he ever has before, but still the pole stands in front of him motionless. As Duke once again tries to push the lightweight aluminum rack on wheels out of the way, he finally looks up and sees what she's been trying to show him.

"What? You want me to open the closet. But why?" he asks.

Without waiting for her screen to illuminate, Duke reaches his hand up and pulls on the handle of the vertical cabinet under the suspended TV. His blue bathrobe and his Bat-man moon-boots are inside, the robe hanging on the door, and the boots tucked behind his dad's shirt which is hanging down from the rack. His folks haven't left this place since they all arrived here, at least not to his knowledge. However, there are quite a few changes of socks and underwear in there, as well as his dad's lucky green 'All-Stars' jersey which he knows his old man wasn't wearing when they got here. After all, he had come straight from work on a Tuesday morning.

Immediately his thoughts go to his life at home, and his favorite pastime, dressing up as Dukey Dude, to fight evil monsters with his robe of invisibility and the Club of Justice. His fat whiffle ball bat with the custom tape job on the grip is used to reign vengeance down on his enemies, and when they lunge at him, he hides beneath his royal blue cloak as it shields him from the sight of his blundering foes just seconds before they catch him and take their revenge. Ha-Ha! He'd have his dragon army poised for battle. They'd be snarling and gritting their teeth, awaiting his orders. Neatly lined in their ranks, they'd wait until his cry of "ATTACK!" could be heard, then they'd take flight, and foil the plans of the evil over-lord Booger Boy, before he can take over the world! Yeah! Take that!

Suddenly, in the middle of his fantasy, Duke's hospital room goes dark. Duke knows the windows overlook nothing more than the Emergency Room, but he none-the-less swears he can make out an oncoming thunderstorm out the window of his room. The darkness that surrounds him now is no different than the kind that swallows Kansas farmhouses moments before a Mid-Western twister tries to rip a house clean off of its foundation. He feels the pressure building and he can almost see the windows flexing in front of his eyes, seconds from exploding shards of glass over everything. As he winces to shield his eyes from the imminent catastrophe, he's pushed into the closet. The door slams behind him. Duke first mistakes the crash for the exploding windows he was expecting, but soon realizes was nothing more than the closet door shutting with a clack, and a ka-chunk-a-thunk-kk as the metal and magnet come together, holding the door shut. The world around him has grown silent, and the darkness is thick in this tiny closet.

"Hello?" he says, but no one answers. The only thing he hears is the sound of a giant fan engaging, winding up to full throttle. He begins to fear that he'll be sucked in and chewed up by the blades. Duke begins to slap at the door, frantically hoping for some kind of handle or hook he can grab onto to keep from being vacuumed up. He finds nothing as he paws around in the dark, but realizes after a few moments that there is no monstrous suction pulling at his meager frame. As he stops his clawing, he feels something start to tug at him. Suddenly, it seems as if ten sets of hands are holding him. They are all grabbing and poking him. He tries again to find a handle on the door that is held shut by no more than a one-inch magnet, but he is pulled back against the wall. His arms are held with force, but, surprisingly, with little discomfort. He can hear the sound of measuring tape being extended and retracted.

Sounds of air-compressed drills and hammer presses

fill the air around him. Whizzzz-Clank-Bang-Screeeee! Twisting metal noises as well as brass and percussion sounds make him feel like he's in one of his folks' old cartoons where the kitty cat is strapped to the assembly line and the mouse is playing Dr. Frankenstein with his parts! However, like the cat in the cartoon, he isn't feeling any pain, just an occasional tickle as a set of mechanical arms yank at an article of clothing before sliding a skin-tight stretchy on in its place. "Stop! You're tickling me! No, Stop! That tickles!" he's saying, while these gentle robotic hands seem to take him apart and put him back together again.

It suddenly smells like an auto-mechanic's garage in the phone booth sized closet. With the smell of fresh paint and engine oil so prevalent and with so many terrible, frightening sounds booming all around, Duke thinks that some nurse or doctor must be on their way to put an end to all of this silliness. If not, he is afraid that the robotic hands might pull him apart, limb from limb. But no one comes wandering into the room, and the hands that are assembling him are as gentle as his mother's hands as she changes her baby's bottom.

5

The poking, prodding, and changing finally stop, and the door of the closet creaks open on its own. The hospital room that Duke sees from the closet is strewn with papers and debris, as if a tornado *had* just come through. He sees his animated IV pole friend, standing outside the closet, just where he had left her. After all, where could she go? She's still connected to him by those thin tubes that constantly carry vital fluids and medications to his bloodstream. Only now, she's gleaming with a brand new paint job. She's sleek blue, but as she turns in the light, a full spectrum of colors shimmers on her. The screens, which seemed to be in the shape of a face before, are now even more personified, with a perplexing, animated expression. Her eyes look real. This is no ordinary IV pole… and this is no ordinary hospital.

"You're beautiful!" he says before adding, "Well, uh-hum, it's not that you weren't beautiful before, you know…" It's been a long time since anyone paid this much attention to her. She feels like a young Helper again, with the way she zipped around and twirled like she used to. Sometimes she felt like she'd never get the opportunity to help anyone again, but now she knows there is another mission for her before she takes her old bag of busted bolts up to that broom closet in the sky.

Duke is standing, in awe, still stammering and fumbling to find the right words to describe the shiny new finish on his IV pole. She tips open the bathroom door with her base to reveal a full-length mirror. Duke isn't really paying attention to this action until he is spun around by his wheeled friend to see his reflection. His bony frame is now covered with muscles. He can see them pressed firmly against the inside of his brand new one-piece body suit. It is a vibrant metallic blue, matching the gleaming coat of paint on his IV pole. He rubs the strange material of his long sleeve against his cheek. It feels like silk, but it's tough as crocodile skin. He gives his forearm a slap with his other hand. Slap! "Oww!" he yelps then whispers, "Amazing," as he does his best bicep flex, admiring his new arms as well as the rest of his cool new physique. The hand that did the slapping is actually what hurt. It is throbbing as if he had smacked a metal bar as hard as he could. It's like he's wearing armor.

The precisely fit, blue onesie has a zigzag line going

up the sleeves that looks like the reading on a heart rate monitor. The pulse stripe is wide and red, with a bright yellow pinstripe going through the whole thing. The stripe comes down from under his arms and goes all the way down to his feet where it creates an amazing sunburst. The shoes are part of the outfit, but it's not like his footie-pajamas back home. He lifts up his right foot and reaches back to give it a tap with his fingertips. The bottoms of his feet feel like his dad's sneakers, but it feel like he's wearing nothing at all. While bending his leg, he realizes that there are thin little pads over his knees. They are hardly noticeable to the naked eye, yet are sturdy, flexible and secure like some sort of futuristic suit of arms. This blows away the hand-me-down get-up he's used to wearing at home.

Next, Duke eyes a yellow belt, which is weighted down with things he's never seen before. Several small plastic canisters are held in a perfect row and on one hip there is a pair of strange looking plastic scissors, which on second thought look more like a bent pair of pliers. His nose and mouth are covered with a mask that he has a hunch is used for more than just concealing his identity. He's seen kids, parents, doctors and nurses alike walking around with paper masks on, and he's heard talk of kids that have no immunities to viruses and infections. Little does he know that, soon, he will be just like them. But for now, he feels invincible in his new super suit.

The last thing he notices is the most astonishing thing of all. The tubes that connect him to his new robotic friend fit perfectly into a tiny hole. The fabric around the hole hasn't been sown in any way.

"How did they get that through there without disconnecting us?" he asks, looking over at the IV pole.

She doesn't answer, so he turns back around and scans the mirror from his feet to the top of his head. 'The Chemo Kid' is written across his chest.

"Who's that? The Chemo Kid... Is that me?" he asks. The silence that follows his question is broken by the sound of the beeping coming from down the hall.

6

"A couple days ago I didn't even know there was anything wrong with me, and now I not only find out I have cancer, but I'm also some sort of super-hero?" Duke asks, leering back at his pole in disbelief. He again recalls the way he used to around his house with a blue bandana on his head, swinging a plastic bat as G.G, Mommy and Daddy run for cover, all the while pretending to not be able to see him under his Gary the Green Dragon bathrobe. That's not real super-hero work. Who is he kidding? He's had about as much practice being a super-hero as he has hair on his chest... none at all!

"I don't know about this. I like to play super-hero, but I don't know anything about actually being one. What if I mess up?" he asks aloud in the direction of his IV pole, but actually addressing something greater.

Duke walks over to his bed in the silence of his disheveled hospital room and grabs onto the rail. He's staring at the floor, not sure what to do or what to say. He shuts his eyes hard. "God, you must be real, because somebody had to make this world. Please help me. I don't know what to do." He keeps his eyes shut for a moment longer, waiting for some kind of response.

When he opens them, he sees the silver dollar that his great grandfather gave him taped to his bed. He pulls it down, turning it around and around in his hand. 'In God we Trust' the inscription says. He slips the coin into a small pocket on his super suit that has no other purpose but to hold something that size. How he knew the pocket was there, he does not know, but he figures there is little option but to accept the extraordinary after all of this.

"I guess we should go check out that beeping noise, don't ya think?" he says as he turns and looks at his robot pole. She stands silently with little expression on her screens. "Well… let's go down there…maybe we can call the nurse or something when we get there."

So, Duke and his wheeled medical sidekick apprehensively start out the door, checking both ways, again, and once more, before they finally roll out into the hall. Duke looks down the hall in the direction of the beeping. He motions with his eyes and the IV pole immediately begins to propel herself slowly down the hall, being careful to keep to the shadows, as to not be spotted. As far as they know, no one sees them, but a mysterious figure is peering down the hall as they quietly make their way. Two white eyes watching for just a moment, and then they are gone.

And so begins the Adventures of the Chemo Kid.

Chapter Five

'Twisted Tubies'

1

He climbs onto the pole, puts one foot on the floor, grips the pole tightly with one hand, and pushes with his foot, like he's riding a scooter.

"Hey, do you have a name?" he whispers. "I thought maybe I could call you Ivy, like the plant. You know, 'cause you're an IV pole... Yeah, I'm going to call you Ivy. You're not poison ivy, are you?" Duke jokes.

She emits a few muffled, yet cheerful beeps which he takes as a good sign. Duke realizes that she is also politely telling him to be quiet. He makes a zipper motion across his lips and pretends to toss away the key to show her he understands.

As they pull up outside the room from which the beeping is coming, he can see there is a nameplate on the wall outside the door. The name Phoenix, Trooper is written in black magic marker on a pink sticker under the plexiglass of this nameplate. Duke hadn't realized until now that his room must be labeled too. That's how everyone always seems to know where to find him.

Well Trooper Phoenix, you're about to meet The Chemo Kid.

The excitement of the moment fades quickly when he peers inside. The lack of light and re-circulated air gives the room a certain swampy quality, as if a fine mist is emanating from the floor. The blinds are all drawn, and the lights are off. The only illumination coming from inside the room at all is radiating from the TV, where the antics of Gary the Green Dragon fall on deaf ears. No one is listening or watching the TV. The television flicker falls on a spider-web of tubes and wires piled on a hospital bed connected to an IV pole. This towering pole has far more apparatuses than The Kid's, but it also has a lot less life. Ivy's thoughts seem to register expressively on her screens and light her up with vibrant colors and text in different fonts. The pole in this room, though containing lots more machinery, stands quiet and still. No colors register on its screens. All that can be heard is the churning sound of its pumps.

The lines and tubes from the IV pole are wound in a neat bundle on the hospital bed, as if a spider had spun a net that would tighten and constrict more with every struggle. The darkness and the stinking haze filling the room would be the ideal environment for a giant arachnid to spin a web around its prey, then to stash the body in the closet for a later snack. The Kid and Ivy peer closer and can faintly make out motion under the heavy pile. Something is wrestling under the weight of it all!

"Who would do this?" The Chemo Kid ponders aloud as he snaps from his inner thoughts to address what is in front of him. He leans in to get a closer look at the web of tubes. Ivy seems to lean over the bed with him. The glow of her monitor and the concerned beeping first surprise The Kid, but after a brief initial shock he doesn't even bother to look back over his shoulder. He's finally accepted his battery-operated friend as his sidekick.

Closely analyzing Trooper's tubes triggers The Chemo Kid's imagination deeper. He can picture the hideous eight-legged monster who spun this web scuttling across the floor, twisting a cocoon between its sticky legs. He sees clearly the evil red eyes bulging out as his armor-plated legs turn into pinchers on the ends. The Kid tries to force down the lump that's built up in the space just above his Adam's apple. Maybe he could wash it down with the beads of sweat that are forming on his brow! As he turns his head to wipe the sweat, he almost jumps right out of his skin. The black extension cord coming out of the wall looks exactly like the outstretched tentacle of the imaginary eight-legged freak.

"Ahhh! Look out!" he screams.

Ivy pirouettes in response. Her evasive action is choreographed perfectly with The Chemo Kid's thoughts. She instinctively understands where his source of concern is and spins in the opposite direction. Like a dancer, she swoops up her partner and glides them both away from danger.

3

"Wait… where are you going?" croaks a feeble, whispering voice from inside the room. At first, they mistake the raspy voice for an arachnid hiss. This sends Ivy into turbo-drive-escape mode. The Chemo Kid, however, wonders if their minds are playing tricks on them. As they spin toward the half-opened door, he squints his eyes to peer into the darkened corner where they thought the eight-legged freak might be hiding.

"Wait," he says and Ivy immediately slows her escape.

"Help!" the voice croaks again from across the room. It is so distant that it sounds like a faint over-heard walkie-talkie conversation from across the hospital complex or simply the wind blowing past the triple-paned window. It was hard for The Kid to believe it was coming from amidst the tangle of twisted tubes on the bed to his right.

Ivy wheels the duo once again towards the bed to listen closer for the cracked and desperate breath that they hear from the jumble of knotted plastic tubing. This time The Kid is on his guard, heart in his throat and hand gripping the pole so tight that his knuckles are turning bright white. Too many more moments like these, and he'll need to make an emergency appointment with his cardiologist!

"Hello…." the tiny murmur comes from the pile of plastic once again. The Kid doesn't answer at first. He and Ivy are now skulking above the bed, where they can see the predicament more clearly. The lines from the IV pole are sticky and moist. They are wound all around this poor patient, and it's clear to see that he's exhausted from wrestling with it. His wrists and ankles are bound to the bed, as if it had been done purposely. The clinging tubes could just as likely be from a spider's spinneret as a leaking IV line. This freaks the duo out even more.

"Who's there?" the tangled tot mutters.

Ivy freezes. Duke Dillan clears his throat to answers the question.

"It's, ah… uh… The Chemo Kid?" is his tentative reply. He really wanted the first time he used that line to be great, but somehow the words slipped out as a mumbling, meager question. The words just don't feel right yet. His cheeks begin to redden, and he's almost about to high-tail it out of there in embarrassment when the voice from inside the bed starts up again. This time The Kid is all ears.

"Did you say 'The Chemo Kid'?" the voice under the knot of tubes asks, wondering if this is real, or if it's his overactive imagination messing with him again. Lonely days and sleepless nights make him think he's seeing and hearing things. The Chemo Kid leans over and cautiously pulls some of the tubes away from his face. Once some of the tubes are cleared away, he can see the face of the child buried beneath.

4

The frightened kid under the mess of tubes looks like it's been a week since the last time he saw the light of day. Trooper Phoenix is covered in sweat, and his face is pale, with two sunken eyes. Whatever heartless fiend could take pleasure in the suffering of a child by tying him up with IV tubes, or at the very least ignoring him long enough to allow the sick child to accidentally ensnare himself like this, lacks a certain component for human decency, lacks a soul.

"Really, who are you?" the exasperated boy whispers, in an almost inaudible breath.

"I'm here to help you. My name is Duke Dillan. I'm not really sure what's going on either, but apparently, I'm some kind superhero or something." Duke's not even sure what to tell this child. One thing he knows is that he's got to do something with these tubes, because something tells him that time is running out.

"What's up with your pole?" Trooper asks. Ivy's screens

are all lit up like the fourth of July. You can almost hear Trooper's teeth chattering in response. He looks as if he's seen a ghost.

"Don't worry, she's with me," replies The Chemo Kid.

5

The daunting task of untangling this jumbled mess of twisted tubes is going to be a real challenge for The Kid. As smart as he is, he's never really been good with knots. He quickly peruses his tool belt to try and find a suitable tool. Looking at the small plastic canisters neatly lined on his belt, he decides to pull one out and see if it's good for anything. It looks like a tiny plastic soda can, but only a fraction of the size. Just smaller than a film canister, but instead of a lid, the top is permanent. It is bright yellow and the only markings on it are a branded logo of a single heartbeat, just like the one that shoots across his chest in his super-onesie.

Trooper and Ivy watch as he twists it around between his fingers. They are both amazed to see the logo on the side of the canister. All three of them stare dumbfounded at the tube.

Snap! It suddenly pops in The Chemo Kid's hand. Trooper squints his eyes and recoils deeper into the tangled tubes as goo flies out of the canister, covering the room and all three of them. The least of it lands on Trooper, since he's now gotten himself covered by even more of the snarled plastic.

"Yuck! Eww, that's nasty!" Duke shouts and asks, "What is this stuff?"

Ivy is completely covered, and it's obvious from her

expressive robot screen that she is not happy about it. The Chemo Kid makes a face of his own as if to say, "Oh, I'm sorry... I'm so sorry." He's got his hands over his face ready to block any surprise punches that might be coming his way from Ivy in retaliation.

"It's sanitizer. Hey guys, it's just sanitizer," Trooper interrupts. The Kid had by now begun dabbing the gel off of Ivy's screens. Their trading of faces continued until Trooper's interruption seeped in. The Chemo Kid turns to Trooper and says, "Wait... What? You mean like the stuff you wash your hands with at the zoo?"

"Yeah, everybody around here uses this stuff all of the time. We all have to keep our hands clean. When you start getting chemo, your immune system gets messed up. Your body won't be able to fight off germs. This stuff helps to get rid of the germs. There are dispensers all over the hospital."

"So why do I have an endless supply of these little things on my belt if there are pumps in every room?" Duke wonders aloud.

6

Now that the sanitizer bomb has all evaporated, and the room has been completely sterilized, it's time to get down to business. The Chemo Kid is facing his first real super-hero challenge, how to untangle Trooper's tubes. He can't disconnect them. He wouldn't have the foggiest idea of how to reconnect them. He can't pull Trooper out, because his hands and feet are secured tightly to the bed. Soon, he remembers the pliers-looking things in his belt. The Kid takes them out and wonders out loud, "What? Am I suppose to cut them?"

"No, don't!" Trooper screams. "Those are my chemo tubies! That stuff is nasty. I know what it feels like when it goes in my tubes. You don't want to find out what it feels like when you get it on your skin!"

"Whoa… what does it do to you?" Duke asks.

"Sometimes it makes you cry. Once, when I cried, my tears were tinted red, like there was blood in them or something. Sometimes it burns when you go, you know, pee-pee. I get sick all of the time. I get sores in my mouth that go all the way down my throat to my tummy and out the other side! And do you know the worst part?"

The Kid and Ivy have both reeled back a bit at his last description. Now they anxiously await the worst part with perplexed looks on their faces. "What could be worse than all that other stuff?" The Kid says as he looks over at Ivy. Trooper rolls his eyes upward, motioning to the top of his head. The Kid digs into the pile of tubes and manages to free Troopers head from the tangle just a little. Trooper raises his head, and they can see that he's totally bald.

"Whoa, cool! You look cool!" Duke says. "Everyone is always messing with my hair. I wish I could shave it all off too." Duke's a really nice kid and he realizes that sometimes you can make someone's day just by being nice. Besides, Trooper really does look cool.

"You really think I look cool?" Trooper asks, not believing him at first.

"Definitely, you look like a tough biker-dude!" For the first time in a long time, a smile registers on Trooper's face.

Feeling good about the fact that he made Trooper smile, The Chemo Kid decides to try and tackle the twisted tubes. He grabs the crooked pliers from his belt and begins to use them to wedge in between the tubes. "I think if I just twist this one like this, and put this foot over here... Now sit still! Wait... Here, give me your hand. Stop, no, wait! Here we go!" The crooked pliers are amazingly strong. The twisting and pinching causes Trooper to do a 360 in mid-air. After he flips over once, he ends up dangling from a hook on the ceiling, cocooned in the tubes ten times worse than before!

"I can't breathe!" the choking youngster gasps, hardly making a sound. Ivy beeps frantically, so much that The Kid has to manually silence the alarm in fear that someone will finally come to see what the commotion is all about.

"Just hold on tight. I'll figure this out!" The Kid shouts. Partly exasperated and totally embarrassed, he knows he needs to do something quick. The entire web cocoon is getting tighter by the second around his new friend. The Chemo Kid is not able to get even a finger under the plastic now. He looks at the scissor/pliers on his belt again and sees the solution materialize before his eyes.

"These aren't scissors or pliers! They're untangulators!" he raves. And, like a genius puzzler seeing his way through the jigsaw maze laid out before him, he starts to, one by one, untangle Trooper's tubes, using his tool to hook the tubes and pull through, similar to crochet, but at an amazing speed. The Chemo Kid works like a whirling dervish careening through the desert in pursuit of a certain carrot-eating 'funny rabbit.' He moves his hands so quickly and unhooks the tubes from the the ceiling so gently that Trooper can't even focus on the action or feel what is happening until all that is left is a skinny kid laying in bed with neatly hung IV fluids and chemo dangling from the pole at his bedside.

"Whoa! That was awesome! How did you do that?" Trooper gushes. Ivy rolls toward the recently freed toddler's pole and emits a series of beeps that remind both kids of an internet connection. Trooper's pole stands quiet and still.

7

"1-2-3, it's the place to be! 4-5-6, now we're pickin' up sticks!" comes blaring out of the TV as Trooper can finally reach the remote, and uses it to turn up the volume of Gary the Green Dragon.

"Aww! I love this one! Mind if I stay and watch a little?" Duke asks, feeling good to be able to be a kid again, at least for a little while.

"Yeah, cool. I have to admit… Gary's not my favorite though. I'm more of a Samuel Steam-Engine guy," says Trooper. He quickly reaches over to the bedside table and opens the drawer. He puts his hand in and comes back with a silver medallion on a shoestring rope. He proudly puts it around his own neck.

"I'm a member of the Little Steam Engines Club. Pretty cool, huh?" He's gloating a little bit, but Duke doesn't mind. He figures the poor kid deserves it.

So it is there that they sit, Trooper Phoenix in is bed, and Duke Dillan, A.K.A. The Chemo Kid, beside him with one foot draped over the arm of the rocking chair and the other leg wrapped around Ivy's pole. Ivy rocks back and forth, almost enough to put him to sleep.

Ivy is plugged into the wall, charging and powered down. Trooper is fast asleep and Samuel Steam Engine is on the TV now. A darkness is forming in the corner of the room. Duke is actually watching himself from the vantage point above the room. He can see the darkness spreading towards the two of them. Out of the darkness creeps the dreaded arachnid and he watches helplessly as the eight-legs creep ever closer to him and his new friend. "Look out!" he screams but they can't hear him. He tries to kick and punch in the air toward the hideous, hairy pest but its deadly glare focuses solely on the two kids in the hospital room. He reaches for the canisters on his belt and flings one at the spider. It goes right through like he's made of a cloud of thick black smoke. The spider climbs its front two legs onto the foot of Troopers bed and begins to ready his stinger; his blood red eyes focused on his unsuspecting prey. He's about to pounce. Duke is screaming his head off, but it's like he's in a sound-proof booth and no one can hear his cries. Alarms are going off in his head. He's got to do something! BEEP! BEEP! BEEP! is sounding off directly into his ear. It feels as if the sound will break his sensitive eardrums. He knows he has to do something to help his friend before it's too late.

"Wake Up!" he screams

BEEP! BEEP! BEEP! He's startled awake by the now all too familiar sound. He springs to his feet in a fighting stance with Ivy right behind him, but the dream is gone, along with the killer spider. He shakes his head and looks back at Trooper's bed where he had fallen asleep, and then back to the dark corner again.

"Just another crazy dream," he says out loud. He looks at Ivy and realizes it was her who was beeping. 'Low Battery' is flashing on all of her screens.

The Kid jumps up quietly, and tries his best not to wake Trooper, who is sleeping comfortably next to him. He hops on Ivy and they start to roll toward the door. Before they can get away, Trooper's voice comes from behind them.

"Wait, you weren't going to leave without saying goodbye, were you?"

Kids around here don't get the opportunity to make friends very often. It's not too hard to see why Trooper doesn't want them to leave. He's even starting to well up a little when he tells them, "I just wanted to get a chance to say goodbye, because I'm not sure how much longer I'm going to be here."

"What do you mean? You might not be here much longer? Are you going home?" Duke asks, hoping not to hear the wrong answer.

"Maybe, but maybe not…. I never know. I've been here for so long that this place has sort of become like a home to me. Sometimes I'm not even sure if I want to go home," he says as the tears start to stream down his face. The Kid is getting misty now too, though he's trying his best to bite his bottom lip like he had seen his daddy doing earlier that day. Even Ivy's screens are blue now. She's heard this tale before.

"Look…" Trooper says. "I don't know what they've told you so far, but cancer isn't like the sniffles. Even though you might not feel that bad, you might be really sick. I don't mean to scare you, I just want you to be careful about getting too close to kids around here."

"Yeah, but I really like you! You're the first person I've even met here, and I was thinking we could come back later to watch some more Gary. I have a couple new DVDs that the nurse in the Emergency room brought." Duke is feeling like a kid again, and he's starting to come unraveled at the notion of losing his only human friend in this place.

"We might see each other again. It's just that none of us ever really know when they are going to send us home. It's all about the white blood cell counts and what our blood work says. My parents don't even know when we're coming and going. You'll probably be leaving soon and then we may or may not be here around the same times after that. It was really cool hanging out with you though. Now, you better get back to your room. They won't miss you as long as you're not gone for too long."

"Ok well, bye then, Trooper. I hope I get to see you again." The Chemo Kid slumps dramatically onto Ivy. She begins slowly plodding for the door.

10

"Hey Chemo Kid! Wait! Wait up a minute…" Trooper shouts. "I've got something for you." Duke and Ivy perk up a bit from their sullen expression and turn back to see what he wants, each with a renewed glimmer of hope in their perspective faces.

"Here, take this," he says as he slings the shining metal object on a string in Duke's direction. It actually took off and sailed, giving The Kid no chance at all of catching it. Fortunately, Ivy is nearly seven feet tall and the string caught on the curl end of her IV hook. The object, which became wrapped up in the string, mid-flight, quickly unrolls until it dangles about a foot above Duke's head, out of the reach of his short arms, but in perfect sight of his inquisitive blue eyes. Ivy does a little shimmy which vibrates the star- shaped base upon which he is standing. He takes his eyes off of the medallion to see what's happening, and as he looks back up to it, it falls into his hand. Its shoe-string necklace follows, covering the medallion in his palm.

The Chemo Kid pulls away the shoestring to reveal the shining medallion, and he sees that it is a likeness of Trooper's favorite TV character. Samuel Steam Engine is a British TV program that occasionally shows up on Duke's Gary DVDs. He's never been a huge fan of the show himself, but this thing is a tell-tale sign of a Little Steam-Engine Club member. This one is even shinier than the one he saw at Blake and Sydney's house. It makes him think that Trooper must be a platinum-club member.

The Kid looks up at Trooper and says, "Dude, I can't take this. This is yours."

"I just wanted to give you something of mine to hold until we see each other again. That way we'll make sure we run into each other soon," he replies. "Now go. I don't want to hear another word about it."

"Alright, but I'm giving it back to you the next time I see you," The Kid reluctantly tells him as Ivy rolls them out of the room, letting the door close quietly behind.

11

The Kid leans back against Ivy's pole and examines the sparkling silver collector's item. It's a perfect mold of

Samuel Steam Engine's world-renowned majestic profile. Set on a steep mountain chugging up to the top, carrying his payload of toys for sick children in his brightly painted cars. For a moment, Duke can picture the train actually climbing the hill, blowing its whistle, Toot-Toot! Thinking about it makes him wish he could just go home. He could sit and just watch movies all day, or go out and play if he wanted to. Most days his mommy would take him with her to work where he'd get to play with his friends. He begins to wonder if he'll ever get to see them again. For now he'll just have to make sure to get back to Trooper's room again as soon as possible. Feeling lonely, and completely lost in the glistening of the shining medallion, The Chemo Kid and Ivy glide through the halls of the hospital towards his room.

The Chemo Kid is jolted back to the present by a sweet little voice coming from the room they had just passed. "Hey," the voice of a girl whispers. "C'mere! Over here. Room 20." Ivy slows her roll and inches them back toward the slightly open door of room 20. The Chemo Kid steps off of Ivy to peer into the room just as she stops in front of the door. Ivy leans into the cracked doorway for a look as well.

The room is completely dark. It doesn't look like any doctor, nurse, or patient have been inside for days. The duo look at each other wondering if they were hearing things. "Whatcha lookin' for?" the voice suddenly whispers into Duke's ear. It sounds like it is coming from directly over his shoulder. He whips around to look up at Ivy and says, "Was that you?" Ivy makes a strange sound that he assumes means she's as confused as he is. She scoops up The Kid and quickly spins them into the middle of the dimly lit hallway to look for the whisperer. Neither of them sees anyone.

"Maybe we should just go back and get some sleep. My mind is playing tricks on me," says The Chemo Kid. The reply doesn't come from his robot friend.

"Hello! What's your name?" asks a little girl with long blonde hair. She is suddenly standing directly in front of them in the hallway. Ivy hops off the floor in shock causing Duke to fall head over heels to the ground as she smacks back down on the linoleum floor.

"Ahhhhh!" Duke screams then slaps his hand quickly over his mouth. "I mean... Hi!" This time this response comes out like a squeeking mouse. Duke is quite embarrassed. He tries yet again, clearing his throat, "Hi." This time in a tone about two octaves lower than the first. The expression on Ivy's screens are priceless, as if she's saying, "Ohh brother!"

It's dark, and Duke can't really make out her face. He leans in for a closer look, but this time Ivy doesn't lean with him. She's leery about this girl and is ready for a quick getaway.

When Duke finally gets a look at her, he's sure she's the prettiest girl he's ever seen. Her eyes are even more blue than his own. Her curly brown hair seems to glow, even in the darkness. She smiles at him and says, "Hi, I'm Angel. What's your name?"

"Well I'm The Chemo K... well actually my real name is Duke. You can just call me Duke."

"Hi, Duke. So was it you who fixed that annoying beeping, or was that The Chemo Kid?" She winks at Duke as she notices the redness filling his cheeks. She's obviously not just beautiful, she's got brains too!

"Well I guess that was The Chemo Kid, but I…"

"Don't worry, your secret's safe with me. I'm just impressed with how well you can ride that thing!" She giggles and points to Ivy.

"Ohh, I'm sorry… Angel, this is Ivy."

Ivy emits a comical series of beeps that makes the two of them laugh. Ivy is clearly not amused, however. Duke senses a touch of jealousy from his robotic partner.

"So, what are you in for?" Duke asks, immediately feeling stupid for having asked it.

"Well. I've been here for a while… neuroblastoma, just like you, right?" she comments with confidence.

"Wait… how did you know that?" he asks, feeling now that this girl may be just a bit too good to be true.

"I just saw your eye and I figured…."

Click, Click, Click

They hear a noise from down the hall. The sound of footsteps gets quickly closer so Angel says, "I gotta go! Here, take this." She shoves an envelope into his hand and plants a kiss on his cheek. Duke feels like he's just been kissed by a real angel. He closes his eyes and just stands there for a minute.

"Wait! When will I see…." he asks as he opens his eyes, but the girl is gone. It's like she's vanished into thin air.

Ivy begins to beep again, and Duke reluctantly climbs on.

"Hey! Watchoo doin' out ya' room?" It's James the

Janitor coming down the hallway. "C'mon... let's getcha in the bed, fo' somebody finds ya' out here roamin' around and we all be in trouble. Watcha doin out here anyway? Sleepwwalkin? Well, c'mon.... cat gotcha tongue?"

Duke looks up at James and doesn't say a word.

"That's alright, don't hafta talk to old James, let me just get ya' back in ya' bed."

James places his hand over Duke's hand on Ivy's pole and rolls them back to Duke's room. He lifts the boy up and gently lays him in the baby hospital bed then quietly checks the protective rails to be sure they are secure. He plugs Ivy's power cord into the wall and heads for the door. "G'night lil' man. Getcha sleep. You gon' need it."

12

Duke curls up with Gary behind the protective bars of his bed. He slips the Samuel Steam Engine medallion around his neck for safe keeping. Duke doesn't even stop to wonder how Gary has made his way back into the bed from the floor where he left him earlier. He also fails to wonder how or when he slipped out of his 'Super-Onesie.' All of his tools have been put away. He's back in his regular pajamas, like it's no big deal. Ivy too has returned to her plain matted façade. Only the expressive screens in the shape of a face betray her deeper purpose.

What he does notice is his Mommy and Daddy, sleeping deeply on the plastic sofa under the window that looks upon the Emergency room two floors below. They sleep seated upright, like statues, perched upon some huge rock, awaiting the return of their son who's gone off to war. Duke swears that if he were to go to them and try to stir them, he'd hardly be able to budge their bodies. They've been frozen in time, dreaming of memories both remembered and those only yet imagined. Memories like those of Duke splashing in the shallow water of the Gulf, the little waves clapping over his tiny little toes, as they sink deeper into the sand. Duke can almost feel the warm breeze on his face as it wafts across the blue-green water past the immense white clouds, and the coarse brown sand crunching under his feet. He hopes they can go back down to Florida. But right now, he's not sure if they will be going anywhere soon.

"Why me?" he asks, momentarily lapsing into self-pity. It doesn't become him, but it's perfectly understandable amidst the current landscape. Duke's not feeling a warm oceanic breeze. It's just the steady flow of re-circulated air wafting into his room through a dusty brown vent, causing the blinds to chitter and clack. There's no blue-green water beneath his tiny little toes. No, there is only the snapping dryness of over-starched hospital sheets and the immense dark shadows suspended above the E.R, just outside his window.

His self-pity only lasts for that long, though. He knows that he has been given purpose through this apparent tragedy. His parents might have a little harder time coming to a positive conclusion, but he'll have them smiling again as soon as they wake up. He knows it.

Duke falls asleep, feeling confident and optimistic. The warm breezes of Florida return in his dreams. The sun beats down, generating enough heat to keep him and his loved ones warm for the rest of their lives: Mommy Daddy, GG and Poppy too. Everyone is together, sitting along the Gulf of Mexico, feet in the water, watching the clouds and the birds joyfully skim the horizon.

Chapter Six

'Family Reunion'

1

When he wakes, Duke is a little groggy, but he feels rested. Actually, he feels better than he has in a while. It's almost like he has been awake for a week straight, then finally got a good night's rest. He hasn't slept so soundly and peacefully as long as he can remember. His dreams have long been haunted.

Since he was a very young boy, no later then two months old, he's been having night terrors. Night terrors are not the same as nightmares. They don't occur during the dreaming part of sleep so the child cannot be woken from the fright. The night terror will induce screams or horror but the sufferer will often not remember the episode. This has freaked Duke's parents out on multiple occasions. They have been be woken up at all hours of the night with inconsolable crying but also with the inability to snap him out of it. At first they figured he just didn't like to sleep, like a lot of other kids, and that it would pass. And it did, but the reasons weren't the ones his parents guessed.

This super-intelligent infant learned to control his outbursts. By the time he turned six months old, he developed the ability to manage his reaction to the night terrors. There were still violent thrashing and crying fits, but he endured them silently. When the struggle was over, however, the nightmares began. As he pushed his unexplained fears deep into his mind, his dreams took shape in the mechanism of his overactive imagination. The nightmare images became more vivid the more he stopped himself from crying out for Daddy and Mommy.

His parents will protect him at any cost, but even they can't protect him from his own nightmares.

First they began vaguely, nothing more than darkness and fear. His mind would race and his eyes would flutter under the skin like he was watching a game of speed-tennis on a screen on the inside of his eye-lids. Then, as his fears developed a little more, so did the vivid imagery that played inside his head, all while the rest of his family lay asleep.

Duke dreamed of a darkness that rolled inward, like storm clouds gathering above the forest. He often followed the same path under this darkness, winding through the dew-covered foliage, covered by a thick mat of pine-needles which cushion his feet as he strolls, unafraid yet unsure. Duke has spent just about as much time on that menacing dream path as he has in what most would call reality.

2

Mommy and Daddy are sitting across the room on the plastic sofa with lots of other people sitting around in chairs. It's like a family reunion in here. People that he hasn't seen in a long time have appeared from nowhere; a regular who's-who of family and friends. There are so many acronyms and hyphenated nicknames in this group that he can hardly remember them all sometimes. Between GG, Mom-Mom and GG-Mom, Aunt Nanny and Aunt NeNe, Uncle Ray-Ray and cousin DeDe, his head is spinning as he peeks out of the covers and listens to his Mommy introduce them all to each other. As he looks around the room, he can see big people, little people, heavy people, skinny people; all apparently here to see him. He recognizes most of them, but there are so many people that he quickly closes his eyes again before anyone sees that he's awake. He needs to get his thoughts together before he has to entertain company the way little kids always have to.

With his eyes closed, he takes a moment to reflect, but, once again, he's a little confused. Was he dreaming when he helped Trooper with his twisted tubies? It felt so real, but here he is, sitting in his bed with Gary, in his regular clothes, and Ivy hasn't made a peep. He's just about convinced himself that, yes, he's been dreaming all of this super-hero stuff, when he feels something inside his pajamas. As he tries to figure out what it is, he gets the same feeling as the time he stashed a twenty in his underwear that he had found on the floor of Chunky Cheese, to hide it from Mommy until he could get it home and into his piggy bank. But this is pointier than money, and thicker too. He quickly grabs whatever it is and stashes it under his mattress.

Duke decides to open his eyes and he sees that everyone has gathered around his bed. They are all staring at him and commenting on his black eye. He feels like an exhibit in the City Zoo. He imagines himself as the magnificent tiger, wounded, but ferocious none-the-less. Or maybe he is in the circus and all of these crazy people before him are clowns. It's not too far-fetched either. Most of these folks are bouncing around, holding balloons and trying to make him laugh or take his picture. They're all making goofy faces as they try to get his attention. The familiar musical clown cadence enters Duke's mind and he imagines them all dancing around him, some on top of balls, rolling around between the rest who are juggling bowling pins or rings of fire. All of them are taunting him with their sadistic painted smiles, and the little tufts of hair on top of their heads.

"ROOOOAAARRR!!!!!!!" Duke cries suddenly! The family reunion rears back on its heels in unison. Duke is proud of the reaction and doubts they will be putting their hands in this cat's cage any time soon, wounded or not.

"ROOOAAARRR!!!!!!!... ROOOAAARRRR!!!!!!!!!... ROOOOOAAAARRRRRRRRR!!!!!!!!!!!!!!" he ferociously growls as if to say, "Back! Back! Baaaaack!!!!!" The crowd of clowns all stand with their eyes wide and their jaws on the floor. He pictures them running around and bumping into each other as they try to get away. Some turn over giant buckets as they try to hide. Some disappear into their whisky-barrel costumes. The rest just run for cover, and the crowd cheers because they all think that it's all part of the show! However Duke's mind is the one playing tricks and his imagination suddenly darkens, as the clown faces begin to twist and distort, melded with the faces of his family. He stumbles back reaching with no avail for his robotic friend. When he turns and looks, it's as if she's on the other side of the world. Turning his eyes again to the darkness he can see the red eyes of his new biggest fear. In his mind grows a hideous choking laughter that echoes in the depths of his soul.

3

Duke is thrashing uncontrollably. In fright so deep, that his parents fear the night terrors have returned once again. His entire extended family regains their balance and stares at him in shock. Mommy and Daddy step to the front of the pack, in a consoling effort.

"It's ok! He's just scared," Jesse tells everyone. "He wasn't expecting to see so many people right when he woke up. That's all. Just give him a minute to wake up."

Jesse is right about Duke being scared, but it's not the new faces by his bedside that struck this fear into his son.

The group is upset. They all feel like they are making this beautiful little boy sad, just when he needs most to be happy. Duke can hear them saying things like, "Ohh, I think we're all scaring him," and "He's frightened!" Some of the ladies are even crying as they watch him.

When Duke notices what he's doing, he calms himself down. He takes note of his entire family, and lots of friends, armed to the hilt with balloons, cards and coloring books. He starts to feel really sorry for being unable to control himself, and he wants to do something to make it up to these people, but the feeling quickly fades. He realizes that he's the one they came to see, and all he needs to do is to flash a pearly grin and they'll be eating out of his hand again. So he does, and they all sigh and talk about how cute he is. He knows just how to work this crowd!

It seems like everyone he knows, or has ever known, is here, and they're all bearing gifts! I guess a kid could get used to this kind of treatment. However, as the nurse walks in, he quickly remembers why he's here, and that sobers him up, and everyone else too. The gaggle of well-wishing onlookers falls silent as the nurse does her routine vital sign check and messes around with Ivy's pumps a little. Ivy doesn't seem to mind. Duke figures the nurses probably have to be wise to Ivy anyway. After all, they have been here a lot longer than he has.

"Everything looks good!" she says to the crowded room. "Ohh!" and "Great!" they all shout. "Even his blood pressure seems to be a little better!" Everyone seems really relieved at that last tidbit of information. Duke didn't even know that his blood pressure was high.

As she finishes her inspection, she's looking at Duke with a great big smile. She talks to him and asks questions about his favorite colors and what cartoons he watches, etc. He doesn't answer her, but he's definitely not shrieking like a prehistoric bird anymore, either.

"Ohh! And look… Somebody pooped!" his mommy says as Nurse Andrea is about to walk out of the room. "Hooray!" everyone hollers in unison.

"Is nothing sacred?" thinks Duke as he looks to his mechanical pal for some relief. Ivy's screens are pink and he can feel her laughing at him. Don't ask him how… he just can.

4

Duke spies Jane from across the room. She and her sister are the coolest girls ever. Jane is the younger of the two. She has straight, dirty blonde hair. She's more into sports and riding horses and stuff like that. Audrey, the older sister is more like a girlie-girl. Her hair is brown and wavy. She plays with dollies and girl stuff. Duke is so happy to see them. His mom notices this and grabs him out of his bed. He walks right past everyone who is bent over for kisses and photo-ops, and goes right up to Jane to say, "Hi."

Audrey immediately runs over to her sister and the two of them giggle and run to the window. "C'mon Dukey, let's paint!" they say as they wave him over. They have the paints that Duke's dad got from the nice lady from the playroom.

Daddy has gone all out and started painting the windows

108

in the room with a big mural. Aunt Ne-Ne is here and she's helping Daddy. Ne-Ne isn't her real name, and she's not really Duke's aunt either, but that's how she's affectionately known by him. Actually, if you ask her, she'll tell you she is Duke's girlfriend, which is just fine with Duke. He likes to think of himself as a lady's man.

Aunt Ne-Ne and Daddy have painted a great big music symbol with the words to one of Daddy's favorite songs. "Don't worry, 'bout a thing, 'Cause every little thing, is gonna be alright." It's by Bob Marley. Duke's not exactly sure who Bob Marley is, but Daddy seems to think he's pretty cool. They also wrote his name on the window and made a big tree with a sun shining down. Now Jane and Audrey, have joined the mural team, adding lots of cool colors. They looked like they were having a lot of fun, so Duke decides to join them.

For a few minutes with paintsticks, he forgets all about his bad dreams and all that other stuff. He is completely absorbed in the reds, the purples and the yellows, so much so that he doesn't even notice as Jane and Audrey retreat during a barrage of flash bulbs and snapshots that the family takes of Duke painting. The only thing that breaks the spell of paint is a quick and rapid tap on his shoulder. A familiar feeling of dread enters Duke's heart. He fully expects to turn around and find his imaginary nemesis staring him in the eye. He hasn't yet been able to identify what or who creates this ever-present feeling of dread, lurking in the shadows.

Before he can bring himself to turn around for his first face-to-face encounter with evil, Duke steals a quick glance out of the corner of his eye toward Ivy. The nurse had disconnected them when she saw so many well-wishers in his room so that Duke could be free to move around with everyone. He hadn't even noticed and now he wishes his partner was at his side for backup. Ivy is standing in the opposite corner of the room, perfectly still. Her screens are unanimated, like a normal IV pole. This gives Duke no reassurance. The entire room has fallen silent. He can tell everyone is still with him, but they seem frozen in time. Duke takes a deep breath. Beads of sweat start to collect on his brow now. Tap, tap, tap… He feels the tapping on his shoulder once again. He closes his eyes tightly and turns slowly to face his nemesis.

"Surprise!" shouts the man in front of him. Duke throws up his arms in fright to shield his face from his attacker. But no one is attacking.

Duke slowly opens his eyes to see what he's confronted with. He sees a familiar face kneeling in front of him. "Popp-EEEEEE," he screams. His Poppy has come up to see him, all the way from Florida. Everyone finally breaks the silence with shouts and cheers as Duke gets a great big hug from his dear old granddad. He feels a little dumb for being so scared, but he lets his joy and smile mask the fear lingering in his bones from the thought of coming face-to-face with his enemy.

5

Soon after Poppy's arrival the nurse returns to reconnect him to his trusty IV pole. She notices that he's a lot happier about this than any kid she's ever seen. But Duke is no ordinary kid, and Ivy is no ordinary IV pole.

Poppy begins to search the room to find something he can get his grandson to eat. "No wonder he won't eat! There's no food around here!" he shouts. They all agree and immediately a search party is sent out to scour the hospital for acceptable forms of nourishment. Poppy sits down for a full-scale discussion with the remaining relatives and friends.

Duke's never been a big eater, but he's interested to see what they'll bring back when they return. Maybe it will be a big banana split! Or maybe they'll bring a big bag of Tortingo's - Dude Ranch Flavor! Or maybe, if he's really lucky, they'll bring both! Thinking of his favorite foods makes him crave food for the first time in a long time. Poppy sees this in Duke's eyes and whips out some candy that he brought with him from the plane ride. When he pulls the candies out of his pocket, Poppy knows he's going to get a lecture from everyone in the room, but Duke's excitement is worth it.

"You're not supposed to be eating any of that stuff!" Maggie says to her dad. "You're a diabetic!"

"Aww! C'mon! I brought this stuff for Duke!" he replies back with a surly grin on his face that makes Duke smile too. Duke's never been big on candy, but it's a little sweeter when it's imported from Florida!

While Duke and Poppy are exchanging sweet treats, an unexpected visitor is walking through the door. Not that he could be much happier to see anyone else than he was when Poppy came in, but he never guessed he'd see his great grandfather, Pop-Pop, walking gingerly through his hospital room door. It was just a couple months ago that he saw Pop-Pop when he was in the hospital. The way he looked then, he never guessed he'd be strong enough to come here to see him.

6

Pop-Pop Chuck and his wife Pat, who Duke always

referred to as Mom-Mom, were both in the hospital at the same time, on the same floor. Mommy, Daddy, GG and Duke were there every day for a week. Mom-Mom had gotten sick one day, when they had picked her up at the retirement home to take her shopping and to see Pop-Pop. No one would have ever guessed that her illness would be the cause of her death just a week later. She had fought Parkinson's Disease for years, but something as simple as the flu was more than her tiny frame could handle. Pop-Pop was in for a lot of reasons. He had cancer, and it had spread all over his body. He was so sick that everyone guessed he wouldn't be able to make it through the weekend. But he made it. Every time they would see him after that, they would all say how he's looking so skinny and sick. That's what everyone is saying about Duke now.

Duke will never forget the long talks he and Pop-Pop would have while Mommy and GG would go grocery shopping for him. Pop-Pop would tell Duke all about his life. He was a millionaire, and he lost it all. He had travelled the world, and fought for his country in World War II. Duke always wondered if Pop-Pop knew that he could understand every word he was saying, or if he just liked talking, and needed someone to talk to. He likes to think that Pop-Pop knows and that he is part of the reason Duke can understand in the first place. He always spoke to him like an adult, instead of all that baby talk that everyone else is always spewing. Pop-Pop had given him a lot more wisdom than he had collected from even Gary the Green Dragon, all because he spoke to him like an equal. And now he is here to see his great-grandson while he sits in the hospital with cancer.

The tears start to well up in Pop-Pop's eyes when he sees his favorite little boy sitting in a hospital bed. He nods to his daughter, GG, winks to his granddaughter, Maggie, then focuses his undivided attention on his great-grandson, Duke. He looks Duke right in the eye and says, "You're going to beat this!" Pop-Pop brushes tears from his cheeks and replaces his hardened face with a glowing smile. The room had gone silent and the sound of his voice was clear and sturdy.

"You're going to beat this!" he says again and everyone starts to cheer. Pop-Pop gives him a hug and kisses him in top of his head, and then GG helps him over to the plastic sofa where he sits down. It looks like it took every ounce of energy for him to come here. It makes Duke want to cry to see him like that, but he won't. Instead, he is inspired. He decides to be strong like his Pop-Pop who came all the way here to see him. He decides once and for all that he is going to beat this monster, no matter what it takes!

7

The search party that had left earlier, in search of edible snacks to fatten Duke up, finally returns with three shopping bags full of food. Apparently if Duke's not hungry, someone else might be. The last item revealed to him is a giant banana split! Just what the doctor ordered. Poppy steps up to be the first to give Duke a spoonful of his favorite treat. Within minutes, Duke's got vanilla ice cream, hot fudge and sprinkles all over his face. After a few bites he says, "All done," then digs his hand into the Tortingo's bag and says to Gary, "Well Gary, things aren't so bad are they?"

Throughout that day, Duke has many more visitors. He even noticed some of his parents' friends with cleverly disguised 'adult beverages' in their hands. It's like a full-fledged party in here. He's gotten more gifts than he remembers from his first birthday, and there are enough balloons floating around here for his next ten birthdays! It makes Duke feel like he is a celebrity.

The day turns to night, and the night had gotten late by the time all of his visitors finally leave. Duke even has to fake sleep a little so that the remaining ones would go. He really wants a moment's peace to examine the envelope Angel gave him.

8

It's after nine by the time the last stragglers leave Duke's room. There's actually still a gang of them talking in the hallway, but he figures he's good to check out the envelope from Angel now. As he pulls it out and looks it over, he realizes that Angel spent some time on this. No glue sticking out the sides, no cheapo crayons or colored pencils. There are pictures all over the envelope, and they are all neatly colored in by hand. The symbols are all different and beautiful, like nothing he has ever seen.

Duke thinks that there is no way a little kid, especially a girl, could have made this. She must have had help from her parents. The envelope is so nice that he doesn't even want to open it. He just keeps turning it around in his hands, almost like he's hypnotized by it. Eventually, he pauses long enough on the back to realizes that it's got a string to untie which opens the flap, so you don't have to rip it.

This is the first time he's ever gotten a note from a girl, even though he fancies himself to have many girlfriends. He doesn't even know what kind of things people say to one another in a note. Once he gave some dragon pictures he made to Mom and GG, but this thing is way nicer than

114

anything he could ever make.

As he unties the string, he feels something deep inside of him, like a flame being kindled. He is actually sweating now, and his hands are shaking. Something about this letter is so powerful that he can hardly even bear to hold it in his hands, yet he can't put it down, or even look away. The sheer beauty of it has invaded his brain.

He hears the letter before he even reads it. The hempen twine slashes through the holes it has been delicately braided through. This causes the flaps to lift by themselves. As it finishes its way through, the envelope actually comes apart altogether causing the entire package to slip out of Duke's hands. It sounds like thunder as the paper falls onto his starch-white bed sheets. He looks back at his folks and their friends in the hallway, wondering if they could hear all of this, and quickly covers the deconstructed envelope with a corner of his bed sheet. He waits an unbearable moment to be sure the coast is clear, then quickly pulls the sheet back, keeping it in a position to be quickly accessed.

The four flaps of the envelope are fanned out on his bed sheet, revealing a brilliant yellow paper in the middle, which has been clipped around the edges with fancy scissors. As it lies on the bed before him, it looks like a newly bloomed flower. It's shining yellow stamen flanked by symmetrical triangular petals, which he now sees are green, blue, pink and orange. Each pie-shaped colored section is precisely tabbed and tucked into the yellow square. The entire five-piece work of art is meticulously covered with precision pen work in an amazing floral design. He's so amazed that he looks over his shoulder to Ivy, who has inched so close to the crib that her main power cord is nearly pulling out of the wall. Duke gently un-tucks the tabs and frees each stiff paper petal, revealing the message on the yellow card.

To The Chemo Kid,

If you are reading this, you may or may not already know that your fate hangs in the balance, as do the lives of all the children who have been brought here. This place is called The Children's Hospital, but here in Sector 3 we are infested with monsters that science has not yet found the cures for.

The horrible disease that has brought you here is known as Neuroblastoma, and it is the deadliest form of childhood cancer. This horrible evil has taken the lives of some of the greatest kids this world would have ever known.

The Nasty Neuro is an adversary worse than can be imagined, but through the years the children have fought back; strengthened by an unseen force that only a child can see. Now we stand united against Neuro and the rest of the monsters that lurk around every corner of this place.

You have been chosen to join our crusade. Before you make your decision, please know that only a few will make it out of here with their life.

If you choose to fight with us, make your way to the 3 South playroom tonight at midnight. The password is "lemonade."

Good Luck,

Angel

As Duke finishes reading the letter, Daddy, GG and Aunt Ne-Ne look back at him from the hall. He realizes that he's been making a little too much noise, so he curls himself in his blankets. He actually goes all the way underneath, creating a little fort of bed sheets. He doesn't understand it all, but he is excited.

Under the shell of his blankets, Duke begins to contemplate the gravity of the message. However, he is distracted by a smell. The letter in his hand smells like a girl! This immediately initiates a gag reflex in the little boy. After the immature instinct subsides, Duke gathers himself, and actually enjoys the rush of emotions and adrenaline. He lets the girly smell and his excitement linger a few moments before shoving the floral invitation between the mattress and the bed.

Laying back he thinks of Angel, still smelling the sweet cinnamon and apple. He pulls the covers up to his neck as he closes his eyes as he rolls to his side, smiling, and drifts gently to sleep.

Chapter Seven

'Finding a Way'

1

"Dah-Deh-Det, Dah-Deh-Det! This is Sports Central!
With your 24 hour sports news!" blares through his
hospital room. If he wasn't awake before, he certainly is
now.

"Hello and welcome to Sports Central! I'm John
Johnson and beside me is the ever cliché-minded Chet
'The Cheetah' Chambers! Ow-Ow-Ow-OWWWWW!"
the brazen duo cackle as they get set to run down the
day's sports news.

"'The Slam-bino' cranked another one out of the park
today, but more speculation surrounds him, as he answers
questions about his alleged performance-enhancing-
drug use... And when we return, we go one on one with
Russian tennis star Natasha Hottieskova. She's never won
a match, but man is she cute! Next on Sports Central!"
the TV blares.

The lights are all off, but the set still shines brightly,
showing highlights of the day's sports action. Duke tries
to shield his eyes as the logo flashes across the screen
in screaming, bold letters: SPORTS CENTRAL! The
television light in the otherwise dark room seems to
illuminate every corner of Duke's hospital room. It is
easy to forget, however, that most of the light comes

from the constant glow of the emergency room below. Most windows look out to the surrounding landscape, but the windows in Dukes' room look in towards a swarm of nurses, doctors, patients and equipment bustling at every hour of the day and night. The occasional glare from the TV just makes it *look* like there is a Chrysler shining its high beams next to his bed.

 Duke has always thought it funny that his parents watch so much TV. He hardly ever watches, but whenever he does, his mommy tells him to go play. If you don't, they'll cover over your eyes at certain parts, and chase you out of the room for others. All because some poor guy is getting his arm chopped off in some ridiculous slasher movie. Duke is amazed that no one in these movies can seem to out-run a guy who is carrying a chainsaw… and walks with a limp! He always laughs when his parents let him sit in on their movies, but they think as long as he closes his eyes on the scary parts, he won't have nightmares. If they only knew what he dreams about at night, they'd probably never let him go to sleep!

 There must be some great thing about TV that no one is telling him. Sometimes it's like his parents are hypnotized by the pictures on the screen, like the people talking are sending subliminal messages through the lights and sounds that are projected from the glass. It seems like they watch the same show, over and over anyway. It's amazing they ever get any sleep. Most of the time, they fall asleep with the volume up so loud, you can hear it in your dreams! But somehow his father and mother lie asleep on a mattress filled with air, forgetting their troubles for a little while. So for that, he is thankful. If he must sleep in the same room as his parents, he's going to have to get used to the fact that the TV is going to be on, and it's going to be loud. For now though, he just gazes over at them and pictures them asleep on a cloud, drifting across a starry sky, watching their favorite shows on TV sets that are mounted in the stars above. He likes to think of them being happy, and he likes to remember the times when they were all happy together.

2

He quickly rises up and looks in Ivy's direction. She is by his bedside, as he hoped, attached via their IV tubes. This time the curtain above the protective bars was half-way down, so he couldn't catapult over like he did before. Most kids would stick their big head and one arm in between there, ending up stuck. That's not the way you want to wake up your folks in the middle of the night. Duke chooses to grab the top bar with is hands, slip off his socks and monkey-toe his feet diagonally up the vertical metal rails. This will leave him balanced horizontally across the top bar of the baby hospital bed. From here, he'll be able roll over the top, letting go of the rail and grabbing Ivy's pole in mid-air. At least that what he plans to do, or else he'll tumble to the ground with a loud CRASH! Mess this up and his parents won't sleep so deeply from here on out. Heck, they'll probably strap him to the bed!

Of course the maneuver is executed perfectly, and Duke doesn't have to worry about waking his parents. This earns him silent praise from Ivy's monitors. He's become quite fond of Ivy's accolades. She always flashes something cool on her screens, this time it is fireworks.

Duke quietly rolls Ivy over to the closet door. Creeeeaakkk. It squeaks as he opens the wooden cabinet. His dad and mom both grumble and roll over, but that's all. Duke slips into the closet, rolling his eyes at Ivy, and whispers, "I gotta remember to put some oil on that thing later." Inside he is once again turned into The Chemo Kid. This time the process isn't so scary. He knows what to expect and is no longer afraid that those mechanical arms are trying to dismember him. His only fear is that his room will be torn apart like it was the last time he got in the closet. But when he opens the door, all he sees is his eager robotic friend awaiting his return. He sticks his head out first to make sure the coast is clear and then steps out of the closet proudly wearing his super-hero outfit.

As he climbs into position onto his IV pole, The Chemo Kid's feet find the same place on her base that they had gone to before, except now it feels like they are embedded in her framework. It's as if someone had molded the metal perfectly to fit his boots. There are tiny little pads in all the right spots. He can feel them cushion and support his balance as he flexes his feet, leaning back and forth. The same can be said for the spots on the pole where his hands go. He's only ridden on Ivy once before, but it feels like he's worn grooves in her aluminum framework.

They coast smoothly to the exit. The Kid anticipates the silver door handle and flicks it down and out with a single motion so that Ivy doesn't even have to slow her roll into the hallway. Duke always thought the handle resembled a silver tongue sticking out of the door, and this makes him smile, even now, as a super-hero. The only sound they leave behind is the faint click of the door as it closes behind them.

"Let's hope Sports Central is on for another couple of hours at least. Mom and Dad'll sleep like babies unless someone turns down the volume!" The Kid jokingly whispers to Ivy.

They make a left down the quiet nighttime hallway. Duke thinks they can get to the playroom quicker if they go right, but he figures Ivy knows best and lets her lead the way. At the very least they'll get the chance to scope the place out a little more, and, this way they'll end up passing Angel's room again.

3

Ivy is thinking the same thoughts, because the first room she brings them to is that of Duke's newest female interest, Angel of Room 20. The door is closed and all the lights are off inside again. Even the TV is off. "Must be nice to be able to sleep in a quiet room," The Chemo Kid mumbles. He's disappointed that he can't see her tonight, but it's late and she probably needs her beauty sleep.

As Ivy lingers in front of Angel's door, contemplating which direction to head, The Kid starts to feel as if someone is watching them. Ivy spins around sensing Duke's instincts. No one is there. They turn back and Duke almost jumps out of his skin. James the Janitor is standing in the doorway of Angel's room.

"You better be careful kid... don't want nobody to see ya' outside your room. They might keep a better eye on ya' for now on," says James as he slips past them and pushes his cart down the hall without looking back.

The Kid watches James stroll away, but he still can't shake the feeling that someone is watching. He has always trusted his instincts, and as The Chemo Kid, they are even stronger and more empowering than ever before. He wonders why James the Janitor suddenly appears every time they are in this area of the hospital and why Angel's room is always so silent. Apparently, this isn't the place to loiter, so he encourages Ivy to roll on, all the while keeping his eyes and ears peeled. He thinks Angel must already be in the playroom anyway, since it is almost midnight.

They make their way through the sleepy halls, and the eerie feeling won't go away. It's way too quiet around here. The Kid feels exposed on every side. The steady marching and buzzing of the hospital is something that Duke found reassuring ever since his arrival. He realizes his parents must feel that same kind of comfort from the constant noise of their TV set. But now, the total lack of sound is completely messing with his head. He suddenly notices that the smell of this place has also changed. The ordinarily antiseptic aroma, reminiscent of the area beneath a kitchen sink, is transforming to a smell similar to the one found beneath a toilet!

The smell, faint and distant at first, becomes stronger as they round each corner. They are cutting across to the other side of the South tower in the direction of the playroom, and the halls along the way are increasingly taking on a swampy quality. The Kid is positive that at any moment his favorite pop icon will rise up from the foggy floor tiles with an army of zombie dancers, all dancing in uniform lines kicking up their decomposing feet and snapping their crusted fingers to the rhythm.

"Deh-deh! Deh- deh-deh!" he starts to hum, remembering the first few bars of that 80's hit.

Ivy joins in the fun, hoping to shake the nervous feelings poking them ever since they checked out room 20. She starts swerving down the hallway, shimmying and shuddering. She's got the entire song and dance routine down pat! Her movements, together with The Kid's shoulder shakes and zombie arms, look just like the famous music video. Ivy snaps her IV latches at all the right times. Duke jokingly rolls his eyes back in his head. If anyone were to catch the two of them now, they would think they were dreaming. It is not unusual to see children skulking through these halls like zombies, dragging their IV poles behind them, but it's much different to see a child dancing down the hall, riding on an IV pole, acting like a *super-hero* zombie!

They dance right around the final corner before the playroom. There is an invisible wall of stink waiting for them when they get there which halts them in their tracks. Ivy stops her shucking and jiving without a single word from The Kid. He feels like someone has shoved a heavy hand onto his chest, making it increasingly hard to breathe. He unhooks his mask to help, but the thick chewy stench clogs his lungs and causes The Kid's eyes to water. He pulls the mask back over the bridge of his nose. Its purpose, before now, seemed to be steadily pumping fresh, filtered air to his lungs, but this newfound odor is giving his super-charged ion-filtering mask a run for its money.

Ivy won't even go more than a few feet past the corner before she stops. This makes The Chemo Kid wonder, "Can she smell too?" Then he realizes what has held her up. He peers down the hall to see some strange-looking characters blocking the way. Ivy is backing them up now.

The weirdest looking creatures Duke has ever seen are standing outside the entrance to the playroom. It seems that Angel is not the only one who knew he'd be here tonight. They don't look like they are much in the way of brains, but they make up for it in sheer size… and smell.

4

The Chemo Kid and Ivy slip back around the corner, out of sight of the stinky grizzly monsters. "What are those things?" The Kid asks Ivy in a whisper. Ivy rolls the two of them over to a sanitizer pump hanging on the wall. He reaches his hand up and squirts a bit onto his hands. He rubs them together and rubs all in between his fingers. Lastly, he shakes his hands dry while going "Hah-Hah-Hah-hah." It's the little game his folks play with him to get him to wash up.

Mommy had taken Audrey, Jane and him to the zoo one day. After petting the llamas, she insisted they all wash up with this funny smelling green goo. Actually, it wasn't green at all once you started to rub your hands together. It had such a strong smell, and all three of them had wrinkled their noses when she put it on their hands. It smelled just like the stuff The Kid was using now and had used before untwisting Trooper's tubes. It's funny how smells can recall memories.

When The Kid finishes washing up he expects Ivy to head back down the hall in search of an idea on how to get these guys. Instead, she stays put.

"C'mon, Ivy, let's go," he says.

Ivy stands her ground to make a point, then starts hopping around the sanitizer pump. It is obvious that she is trying to communicate something. The Kid doesn't figure it out at first. "I washed my hands already, Ivy! Plus, I have all these canisters full of that stuff right here on my belt!" Just then, it hit him.

He points his finger back toward the corner. This time, Ivy doesn't hesitate. She knows he's figured it out. Together they peek around the corner to the entrance of the playroom. The funny looking idiots are actually over-sized germs. Of course! They look just like those cartoon germs in the TV commercials.

Duke had just recently seen one of the ads where a family of germs set up a campsite in the nasal passages of some poor guy, and, as they drive their tent-spikes into the ground, he rubs his head, like he's got a headache. The father of the mucus family says; "I could stay here all summer!" Just then, the announcer chimes in with, "Should have used 'Boog-Eze'!" in his most 'used-car-salesman' voice. And then the over-zealous chorus sings the jingle, "Boog-eze, Boog-eze, Whenever you're sick, pick Boog-Eze!"

This song playing in his head helps The Chemo Kid piece his current mission together. He's in a hospital, using sanitizer to fight germs. It's that simple. Not so crazy, right? It's just a little surreal is all, considering these particular germs are as big as he is.

"Well, at least these guys won't be camping out in my nose!" he jokes to Ivy. She beeps questioningly. Apparently she doesn't watch very much TV.

<h2 style="text-align:center">6</h2>

The Kid knows he'll need to get a lot closer to the playroom in order to wage a successful attack.

Ivy quickly starts in the opposite direction. She's moving fast, and it's everything The Kid can do to hang on to her without tumbling off and soaking himself with his sanitizer cartridges.

"Wait, you're going the wrong way!" he says.

She ignores him, cruising through the hallways of Sector 3, flying under dimmed fluorescent lights, zipping past the Nourishment Room. That must be where Duke's dad ran earlier for his sippy cup of milk. Before he knows it, Ivy brings them back to the hall where Duke's room is. They slow down as they pass Angel's room. Again, the room is dark and silent.

As they roll by, Ivy has to swerve to keep Duke on her base. He's craning his neck as far as he can to try and catch a glimpse of his new girlfriend through the small glass next to the door. The fear of getting caught wakes The Chemo Kid from his daydream about Angel as they pass his own room. Duke had forgotten that his daddy and Aunt Ne-Ne painted pictures on the door and the window to the hallway, so the glass is now opaque. There are flowers, a big sun and lots of colors. There's no chance of anyone spotting him in the hallway from the inside as long as the door is closed.

Just down the hall from Duke's room, Ivy makes a hard right swerve, then a left, then a right. The surprise changes in direction, almost send The Chemo Kid sprawling. "Whoa!" he says, as he struggles to keep his grip. Ivy is dipping and diving with excitement and the robot equivalent of adrenaline as she remembers the thrill of action. The Chemo Kid senses this high and just holds on tight, enjoying the ride.

Ivy has slowed down and is now creeping toward the corner at the other end of Duke's hallway. She leans her pole diagonally so they see around the bend. There they are! Once again, they see and smell the bad-guys loitering in front of the 3 South playroom. This time they are just a few paces away. The vantage point from here is much better than that of the other side. Ivy's extensive knowledge of the hospital layout has given them a clear advantage, and The Chemo Kid plans to use it wisely.

They silently slink around the corner, just a little bit further, and hide behind a trashcan. They are even closer than he thought! Without his super air-filtration mask's auto-silencer mode engaged, the germ monsters would surely have heard The Kid's frightened gasp as they rolled into place. He had no idea how close they would be to the grotesque colorful creatures guarding the playroom.

Chapter eight

'Battle for Chemo Cove'

1

Since the day of Duke Dillan's birth, October twenty sixth of the year two-thousand and six, he had always been a mild-mannered, loving boy. Never short-tempered, never quick to fight, Duke brought smiles to the faces of all that he met. Though he has mouthed harsh words on occasion, and has even back-talked his mother a time or two, he has never raised a hand in anger or hurt someone intentionally. Tonight, however, this will all change. Sweet Duke Dillan will step aside, and his alter-ego, The Chemo Kid, will have a whole lot of fighting to do.

At this moment, in the hallway of Sector 3 South, The Chemo Kid crouches behind a trashcan, ready to move on the goons who stand guard in front of the playroom. His robot partner, Ivy, stands perfectly still, disguised as ordinary hospital equipment left for the night. The Kid has been sent here for answers, by his new girlfriend, Angel, and he is prepared to do whatever it takes to honor her invitation.

Before he makes his move, The Kid wonders if this is a set-up. His heart tells him no. Angel wouldn't be a part of any of that. But he can't know for sure until he takes action. He has come upon these vile creatures on their blind side, and he knows that set-up or not, he can now successfully rid this hospital, and even more importantly the world, of six nasty bugs. Ordinarily, he would not approve of a sneak attack like this, but he realizes that these are the type of scum-bags that will get you when you're sleeping, so, therefore, in this instance the Dragon Rules do not apply. A blind attack is necessary and fair. Besides, he would much rather get them before they can get him… or any of the other kids on this floor… or in this hospital.

Ivy is suppressing her excitement because she can't crouch down completely behind the trashcan that obscures The Chemo Kid from the germs. She struggles to stay still and keep her screens from turning every color of the rainbow in anticipation of the upcoming battle. The Kid can see that she has already silenced her beeping mechanism, because all he can see an icon of a speaker with a diagonal line through it on her screens. Other than that, they are blank. It is amazing to him that he has only known this robotic IV pole for a couple of days, and already he can understand her speechless expressions and emotions.

2

He has decided that he will throw one sanitizer grenade toward the center of the semi-circle, where the armed guards wait, in order to see what effect the sanitizer will have on them. He crouches with the canister cupped in both hands between his feet, his knuckles almost touching the floor. He then brings the thing up quickly and tosses it over the trashcan in the direction of the milling guards, as if he is shooting a free-throw granny style. His intention is to put enough arch on it so that they will not, at first, be able to tell which direction it came from. He's hoping this can cause a little confusion among their ranks.

His aim is true, and the plastic canister almost touches the ceiling before it begins its descent, just inches from the center of the group. The guards that stand close to the falling object have their backs to it, so even they do not see what is about to crash down. And as it hits the floor with a SNAP, the thing explodes goo all over them. It's payload of disinfectant sprays the three primary colored germs first, red, blue and yellow. The goo bomb does not disappoint. Upon impact the alcohol smelling stuff starts to evaporate the brightly hued foes with a surprisingly loud HISSSSSSSSS! Their screams are much more of shock than of pain. This element of surprise is what allows The Chemo Kid time to toss two more disinfectant canisters into the fray.

The Kid had been certain that his blind-side attack would leave his conscience heavy with guilt once he heard the cries of pain. He actually thought he would feel too bad to continue. However, the germs apparently don't feel pain, which makes him want to put an end to their hideous lives even more. He thinks about the pain they have caused the children of his new home for as long as this place has been here. These thoughts send the first wave of furious anger through him. Now it's personal.

The two monsters on the side closer to The Kid's hiding spot still have their backs to him. As they spin around to see what the problem is and to try to figure out its source, they get their own soaking. The second and third bombs come crashing down directly on their heads. Ivy is shaking with adrenaline now. She can barely contain herself. The Kid can see why she turned off her sirens and beeping mechanism.

Five of the six guards are now badly injured. They are running in circles, screaming hysterically. Their cries are not from physical agony, but are more like whines of a child who has been made to clean his room as his friends are outside playing in the sun. The purple germ is the only one who is not wounded. Ivy, who can stand still no longer, scoops up The Chemo Kid so quickly that he almost fumbles one of the two grenades. He almost falls off of Ivy trying to catch it.

When he regains balance, the purple germ is no longer in the vicinity. He has apparently turned tail and ran, no doubt tattling off to the big boss, or whoever his stinking superior might be. Red, Blue, Green, Yellow and Orange, for lack of their proper names, are all hit now, the latter three seem to be taking it a lot worse than the first two.

Blue and Red have enough energy left to dive over the puddle of hissing goo on the floor and wage a counter attack. They set their sights on Ivy and her blue-suited captain and begin hurling menacing clumps of blue and red globs in their direction. Most of the mucus flies past Ivy and The Kid without touching them as the agile IV pole darts left and right, spinning and jumping, to avoid a direct hit. The slimy gunk that does splatter on her aluminum frame is mostly from ricochets off the wall, but even that little bit makes her screens go red. The muck sizzles as it takes its toll on her pristine wax job.

Orange and Green, obviously the two weakest links, finally scramble to their feet. They are confused and run smack into each other with a THUD! Ivy turns hard left, and is momentarily riding on only two of her five wheels. This positions The Kid perfectly to hit both dazed germs at the same time with another one of his anti-bacterial bombs as they collide. SPLOOSH! The cleansing goo swamps them both and their orange and green hides meld together into a rather unsettling shade of brown. Their decomposition emits a smell that reminds The Chemo Kid of the Port-O-Potties at the orchard during the Apple Festival. He hurls a second bomb on top of their heap, just as much to disguise the smell as to finish them off. It works on both counts! They sizzle until there is nothing left but a puddle of bubbling brown goo, speckled with orange and green pellets, which will most likely remain until a janitor's mop finishes the job tomorrow morning.

Red, Blue and Yellow have by now scattered from the battle zone and can't be seen. Ivy decides the safest path is a retreat past the trashcan around the corner to where they launched their sneak attack. She makes sure The Kid is secure, then dashes in that direction.

3

As Ivy and The Chemo Kid turn the corner, Blue is waiting for them. He lunges in for the tubes that connect the super-heroes, but the fleet IV pole avoids the attack by quickly making a brilliant half-spin stop, like some mechanical ice hockey star, spraying imaginary snow in the face of her opponent. Blue fires a round of mucus at point-blank range. It hits The Kid right in the chest, splashing a few drops on his cheek. The steaming shrapnel burns hot on his face like lava, but the stuff that lands on his chest disappears almost immediately. His suit must be booger-proof!

The Kid grabs two grenades and snaps one in his hand, spraying sanitizer all over Ivy and himself. This friendly fire cleans the stray mucus off of them both. A rejuvenated Ivy zips backwards and The Kid tosses his second sanitizer bomb right in the face of the blue bean-bag chair look-alike. It lands right between the eyes!

The overgrown blue bacteria stumbles backwards as he

slaps a pair of fuzzy mitts over his burning eyes. The staggering germ reminds Duke of Bo-Bo Tubby-Tubby, one of the psychedelic characters from the show that's on after Gary the Green Dragon. "Bo-Bo go bye-bye!" shouts The Kid.

He is dizzied by the acrobatics and the thought of fighting the infamous, pudding-eating, Bo-Bo-Tubby-Tubby, but The Chemo Kid still has the presence to nimbly reach down to his belt for two more germ-killers. Ivy swings him back around to striking distance. The Kid uses his ammo to cymbal crash over the ears of the slimy blue fiend, sending showers of hissing blue goo all around. There is nothing left of Bo-Bo the Blue Bacteria, except for the odor of decay and burning plastic. It causes The Kid to gag and instinctively sends Ivy in search of more germy foes.

4

Their initial attack was swift and effective, but there is no way of telling how resilient these gross guys are. They don't want to leave themselves open to a blind-side counter-attack, so they cautiously peek back around the corner toward the playroom. The hallway is silent.

By the look of the yellow stain on the floor and the red footprints leading away from it, The Kid and Ivy figure that Red is tending to a wounded Yellow somewhere nearby. Yellow's left side was liquefied by the original rainbow toss that landed in their circle. Red had been hit too, but not nearly as bad. There are no traces of Purple, which again makes The Kid think *that* disease has left the building.

They decide it is safe to move cautiously closer to the playroom. As they move forward, they see the entrance is littered with congealed goo of every color. A thick splotch of violet on the door at first makes The Kid doubt his analysis of Mr. Purple. But then he remembers a little book GG used to read to him. "Red and blue make purple, too," she would say. On either side of the violet splotch, he sees red and blue splashes. It wasn't the purple germ who left this stain. It was created by a mixing of Red and Blue's wounds. One green blotch on the opposite wall shows him more about their original formation.

"How did I miss that?" The Kid asks himself. "We saw their circle from two different angles, but I never took notice of how they were lined up."

So now, using his skills of rainbow color combinations, he finally deduces that his enemies were lined up in a circle that went like this. Mr. Purple was the guard who stood the closest to where Ivy and The Kid waged their sneak-attack. Moving clockwise from there was Mr. Green, then Mr. Orange. Orange had been standing to the left of the playroom door and Yellow guarded the entrance from the other side. The blue and red footprints leading away from the sunburst of yellow along the floor and the right side of the doorway show that the circle was completed first by Mr. Blue, then Mr. Red. Judging by the splatters on the wall, Mr. Green, Mr. Orange and Mr. Yellow sustained the most damage from the initial bombing.

The Kid's offense had produced an ominous, abstract painting, both beautiful and terrible. Yellow blends perfectly into orange, creating a multi-dimensional sunset centered on the playroom doorway and falling beneath a vast mountain range. Green hills breathe life just beneath the threshold of the doorway, yet fall to the ground in a heap of brown sludge as its vast swampland unravels on the hallway floor. Beneath the brown muddy ooze sits a vast ocean of blue whose waves quickly churn into a blood-red caldron of damnation from which these vile creatures have risen in order to prey on the weak and the helpless. The colors finally puddle together in the center of the hallway creating a black, infinite abyss. The pearly translucence of the hallway tiles lend a misty quality to the mosaic. They outline a dark river whose lifeless banks extend the black nothingness into eternity.

The trajectories and sheer power of The Kid's arsenal have created an unsettling landscape. A casual onlooker might think it was etched by a disturbed, savant graffiti-artist who has emancipated the tortures of his soul, visually, in the halls of Sector 3 South. Some poor custodian will certainly be shocked and awed when faced with the challenge of cleaning up this mess in the morning.

5

Lost in the beauty of this accidental masterpiece, The Kid and Ivy don't even register the threat of the red and yellow footprints, which carve a bright line down the blackened hallway. Mr. Yellow and Mr. Red have circled the third floor hall, just as Ivy had done earlier, and are painting themselves back into the picture behind The Chemo Kid. Their artless placement is missed by our boy hero, but his faithful and wise sidekick sees the reflection of the attackers in the window of the playroom door.

Ivy whisks The Kid away from the Daliesque epic sunset just as a pair of red and yellow stink bombs crash on the door. She starts spinning faster and faster in the middle of the painted hallway. The Kid takes his queue and grabs four cans of sanitizer from his belt, two in each hand. He concentrates hard on his balance. Ivy is whirling around like a tornado by now. The Kid spreads his arms out like an airplane and unloads a swirling stream of sanitizer everywhere. The startled germ-monsters fall down as they try to avoid the propelling spray. They get back on their feet too quickly because The Kid's cans are still sending a strong stream of anti-bacteria round and round. Red and Yellow are whacked by a turbine of rapid liquid slaps. Their two fuzzy, germ-filled bodies disintegrate under the spray, and the last of their stink-bombs, fully intact, is released from Red's rotting hand. It rolls around like a top on the floor. Ivy and The Kid reel back as it arcs around in a circle, steadily slowing down. After a few moments, the vial stops its cyclonic motion, and The Kid picks it up for examination.

The stink-bomb's strange hourglass shape reminds him of the containers that potions would come in, in his favorite fairy tales. "The Common Cold," he reads aloud to Ivy as he looks over the label on its side. It seems even the germs are a little bit more organized in this place. The Kid is angered when he thinks about these creeps tossing this stuff around the hospital like jelly beans. No wonder everyone is sick around here!

6

"You saved my bacon back there, Ivy! I'm starting to think you're the real hero!" The Kid tells his companion. They are both watching the remains of Mr. Red and Mr. Yellow sizzle and melt in a brilliant orange puddle. The boiling disintegration looks like a distant planet or star that is moments away from implosion.

Both Ivy and The Chemo Kid, sense that this wave of

danger has passed even though they cannot visually account for the purple germ from the gang of playroom guards. They are convinced he has run away as fast as his stubby legs will carry his blob of a body. That means that there is nothing left standing between them and the midnight playroom meeting, save for a multi-colored puddle of goo at the entryway. As they stand there, The Kid wonders just how he'll cross this mess, which might as well be a lake of lava, for all he knows of this stuff. Ivy, however, is not made of flesh and bone. She wheels the two of them right through the swampy stuff to the door.

Standing outside of the playroom door is like standing on the brink of destiny itself. The hot stench of germs mixed with the pungent alcohol smell is enough to bring tears to The Kid's cool blue eyes. This smell, together with the eerie beauty of the explosive splatter-marks on the floor and walls, would bring more than just tears to a normal child. Even Duke's head is spinning, and it is no surprise that he has a difficult time motivating himself to open the door. How could one so small, become the key figure in a war against foes who have taken down men, women and children since the beginning of time?

The picture in the midst of which he stands, tells a story of a battle. At first glance one might think that the battle is won, and that our young hero stands upon the precipice of his prize, having vanquished his enemies. However, this tale has only just begun, and The Chemo Kid is about to embark on a whole new adventure, one where his mettle will be tested, and his senses will be sharpened to a point.

Chapter Nine

'Stepping Inside'

1

The Chemo Kid stands outside the playroom hoping to find answers behind the door to at least some of the questions that have arisen over the course of the last few days. He feels so small set against the background of something so big, the magnitude of which he can't seem to grasp. He is a child, suddenly thrust into battle with one of mankind's greatest enemies. If he were able to grasp this, his mind might have overtaken his innocent passion. He might, at this exact moment, have just turned around and given up.

Men and women of all ages have tried to defeat this monstrous evil. Many found themselves unable to cope with the mental stresses that came with their diagnosis. Many of their minds became unhinged at the thought of what was growing inside them, and what they'll have to endure. Some have succeeded in ridding themselves of these nasty tumors, which come in every variety, every shape and size. But cancer always remains. The ones who are blessed enough to have survived the disease stand on platforms for the rest of their days, fighting from the outside for men, women and children who are still on the inside waging an epic battle against forces that grow stronger as they grow weaker. The ones who have passed are their inspiration, because they are the ones who have paid the ultimate price. They paid with their lives.

The Kid makes up his mind to move ahead. The handle of the door is cold in his tiny hand as he begins to raise the flat metal lever toward the ceiling. The door opens with a subtle click. It swings inward to reveal an unlit room filled with toys and crafts. A square table, half the height of any he's ever seen before, stands in the center of the room with multicolored paint splatters along its edges. On any ordinary day his eyes would fill with childhood delight, and he would go racing in to find a plaything. Playtime is one of Duke's few respites from his advanced consciousness. But today is not like other days. He will not find even a second's peace from his thoughts here.

The Chemo Kid and Ivy skate through the doorway into the dark playroom. They look at each other with fear after the door swings shut automatically behind them with a loud CLICK! Ivy reactively wheels them around to check the handle. Duke tries to lift it, but it won't move an inch. He starts to panic. Surely he and Ivy will be trapped here, and then discovered in the morning by the doctors, or even worse, his parents. Maybe they will even separate him from Ivy, ending their ability to do good and heroic deeds together. He will certainly be stuck with some other pole that doesn't have the slightest idea how to help him. His panic continues to grow with thoughts like these until he notices something peculiar on the inside of the door. It's a computerized keypad. Its lighted screen makes him think that this little gadget could be a distant relation to his nimble sidekick.

"Hey, is this thing like one of your cousins or something?" he jokes to Ivy. The Kid's smile quickly turns cold when he sees the cross expression lit on her screens. She practically bucks him off of her at the thought of that. "Sorry! I didn't mean anything by it! Don't go blowing a circuit or anything!" he says.

Ivy makes a beeping sound he hasn't heard before, which The Kid assumes is a robotic cuss word. Actually, it even sounded a little like one he'd heard his old man use before. He can tell she's not really mad, although he now knows not to make jokes about her computerized lineage. Blood is thicker than water, and apparently the same applies even when there is something more like engine oil involved.

3

The Kid is right. Ivy is quickly over the insult and turns them around to quietly inspect the room. The quantity and the quality of the toys and games in the room are astounding. There is surely something here to suit everyone's tastes. Duke momentarily forgets about his cancer and the mission they are on to enjoy the thought of playing with such an amazing array of playthings. His imagination runs wild with the possibilities of being a normal kid again, for just a little while at least.

Ivy glides over to a shelf with several Barbie dolls in a few pink bins.

"Hey, no offense, but I'm not really into dolls," The Kid says with that furrowed look boys get when they're being cheeky little know-it-alls. Ivy just turns away without any audible response. "You just hang out here, and I'm going to go check out these dragons," he asserts.

The dragons are lined up on a nearby shelf, which also includes a cardboard castle, with little mosaic tiles all over it. There is even a cool battery-powered Gary the

Green Dragon toy towards the back of the shelf that towers above the rest of the toys. Duke thinks it probably talks and might even have the ability to dance around the room, as long as its batteries are still charged. Excitedly, he steps off of Ivy for a closer look.

"Ow!" cries a surprised Chemo Kid. He felt a sharp twinge in the back of his neck. It's as if he'd been bitten by a mosquito, but from the inside. He slaps his hand to his neck. It's not the first time he's felt the strange tingle at the top of his spine since he's been here, but this time it has a little pop and it seems to linger like an echo.

He looks accusingly up at Ivy. Her screens are pink, which tells him that she might just be acting a little cheeky herself. She must be zapping him like that, as if she were saying, "We have a real dragon to slay, Duke Dillan!"

The Kid stares at Ivy as the sting echoes in the base of his head. With each repetition, a bit of the pain subsides and is replaced with a word: real – dragon – slay – Duke. He suddenly realizes that she is actuality communicating with him, verbally! She just told him to stop playing around with toy dragons!

He is shocked! Before now, The Kid has used Ivy's body language, the symbols on her 2-D screens, and her beeping alarms to interpret her thoughts. But her linguistic ability goes further than that. He now realizes that the beeping and churning of her pumps have gradually faded in his mind over the last two days to reveal an actual voice. She's speaking to him, like on a cell phone, however, the bluetooth receiver is in his head. All he has to do is focus on it to turn up the volume.

As he turns his head upward, he can see that the cheeky

grin that Ivy had been displaying on her monitors has been replaced by a beautiful smile. Her screens are lit in a way that shines soft light down on his face. She knows that he can hear her now, but she says nothing. All she does is smile.

<h1 style="text-align:center">4</h1>

"C-c-can you really talk?" The Chemo Kid asks Ivy as the realization flashes across his young face. For a boy so young, he has had his share of these moments of realization. A young life that has been affected by more unexpected and horrifying events than some people will ever see. This time though, he can share the poetic moment with someone. Finally not having to hide his epiphany from an adult or peer seems to make all the struggles worthwhile. They have brought him to this moment. The Chemo Kid and his noble steed, his new best friend, are now truly linked.

He has only been with her for a couple of days now, and the bond between the two has strengthened exponentially over that time. The most obvious connection between them is the multiple tubes that carry fluids and medication, sometimes even food, to his body. Dispensed by Ivy's many beeping pumps, these vital medicines and hydrating supplements give his tiny, weak frame a chance to withstand the abuse his body will endure, as the cancer fights with the chemotherapy deep inside. But the thin, plastic tubing that connects them physically is only the shallowest part of a deep pool of intuition that they now share.

Ivy's language isn't exactly proper English as we would know it. Sure, she tries her best to emulate the dialect she has heard spoken in these halls, but she is an IV pole none-the-less. If others were to hear her communicating with Duke, it would simply sound like a series of beeps coming from one or more of her monitors at a time mixed with the sound of her moving pumps. They might notice that her beeps seem a bit more organized and strangely harmonic than those from her less intelligent counterparts hooked to each young patient in this hospital. But Ivy is careful, and self-aware enough, to prevent the average bystander from questioning the patterns. Duke is certainly not the average bystander. He has formed a cosmic bond and a deep trust with Ivy that have allowed him to internalize her language without even realizing it, until now. He understands her so clearly it is like having an interpreter translating her words directly into his brain.

"Yes, I can talk. I am IV model 3S19. They call my kind a Helper," she says. Duke hangs on her every word. Every syllable chills him to the bone.

"So your name is Ivy?" Duke asks. He is confused that he may have given his pal a nickname that turns out to actually be her real name.

"No. You are the first to give me my own name. Before everyone always called me '19' or '3S19,'" she says with a hint of sadness wrinkling on the aged face of her blue-lit screens.

"That's what friends are for," The Kid says, as if it should be common knowledge. "My dad has so many nicknames for me I'm not even sure what my real name is sometimes!"

The expression on Ivy's screens has now turned from blue to pink. She twists back to him and scoops him up, doing a little spin on her wheeled base to wedge beneath his feet and land him on her base without any effort on his part. Before he knows it, they are spinning around the room diving past obstacles and laughing. This is the first time in all of Ivy's years that she has made a friend who has cared so much about her.

"So what do you mean by a Helper?" asks The Chemo Kid. He can't imagine anyone else having this type of friendship with their own medical equipment. "How many other kids are on speaking terms with their IV poles?" he adds gingerly, but with humor.

"There used to be more, but few remain. The monsters have systematically taken us down. We help those who we feel can help others. You were chosen by the Searchers at the time of your birth, and I was brought to Sector 3 specifically to help you," she replies.

The words cut through him like a hot knife through butter. Before now he thought there was a chance he could be dreaming all of this. All this information is starting to overwhelm him. He wants to wake up now, but pinching himself doesn't seem to be working. Is this possibly all a dream, or can Ivy really communicate with him?

Ivy notices Duke's tender state. It is powerful, even to her, that they have been connected, in some form or fashion, since he was born. Slowly and gently, Ivy tells him what she knows of his story.

5

Maggie, Duke's mother, had taken all of the steps necessary during her pregnancy to deliver a healthy baby boy. She had not eaten tuna fish, too much mercury. She had not eaten hot dogs, too many nitrates. She hadn't allowed herself even a drop of alcohol. She even stopped drinking caffeine. The pregnancy proceeded without complication and her labor began exactly as expected, with induced labor at the end of her fortieth week.

As the contractions increased in frequency and strength, his family gathered in the room around his beautiful, young mother. She was glowing radiantly as the anticipation grew to that final moment, when Duke would arrive. She and her husband had waited for the better part of a year to see the miracle of life come to fruition in the form of their beautiful son.

After a few hours in the delivery room, Maggie was ready to push and the family members went to the waiting room. Daddy and GG remained there to watch. The delivery also went exactly as planned. A doctor was not needed until the very last moment, when a charismatic young obstetrician, singing like some lounge-act crooner, came bounding into the room. He sang to Maggie, "You are so beautiful… to me!" His antics were appreciated by the young couple. Within minutes, Duke Dillan was born into this world, screaming and wonderful. Soon the room filled again with extended family, and four generations sat together, enjoying the perfect beauty of new life. Duke was the first son, and grandson, born unto the family.

Two hours later, as the family sat together, joyfully celebrating a new life, the first in a laundry list of issues presented itself. A nurse came in to read Duke's vital signs, and the look on her long face scared the daylights out of the ones who could see it. As she turned her pale face to the family members that did not see her initial reaction, she tried desperately to hide the horror that was racing through her mind. With poise, she delivered the news. She'd be taking Duke away from them, to see why his tiny heart was beating too fast. And just like that, he was gone.

In his place, a cold silence filled the delivery room. The look of dread invaded the family's faces, and their down-turned eyes tried desperately not to make contact with those around them. Duke's mother, who had given over to the love and devotion she felt upon first seeing her new son, sat motionless and blank. This room, that had previously been filled with laughter and tears of joy, with the musical lyrics of a well trained obstetrician, and the unparalleled sense of happiness that engulfs people when the miraculous has taken place, was now as dead and barren as an abandoned pathway leading into the deep dark woods.

Not knowing what to do, or what was happening, their stillness was finally broken with a terrified cry from Mom-Mom Jo-Jo. "He just has to be OK!" she screamed.

And she was right. He had to be ok. Soon the fate of an entire generation's sickest kids will rest on Duke Dillan's shoulders. But as for this day, he is not OK. The doctors struggled to slow his rapidly beating heart for hours without even daring to pause to inform the family of his condition. Every moment was critical. It turns out that Duke was born with an additional and, until now undetected, electrical connection inside his tiny chest. His malfunctioning heart was pounding out a beat almost three times what is considered normal. Supra-ventricular-tachycardia is the fancy word for it, but the simple fact is that his heart was beating way too fast.

To the family, it felt like an eternity between the moment the extremely frightened nurse took their new baby boy away until the doctor finally arrived with the diagnosis.

The silence had been broken, but the new mood which prevailed was worse. The nervous and frightening shock made it hard for anyone in the room to see anything but violent and painful images of their beautiful new boy in their minds. The fear wouldn't give them a moment's peace.

Lips moved and heads nodded, but the ones who were there that day heard only the horrified ticking of the mind's clock as it counted down to zero. Prayers were uttered to God, whose name hasn't been spoken by some of these people for years. They've been told that God should be like a steering wheel, but seldom do any of them go looking for him until they are in need of a spare tire, or a jump-start.

The doctor finally returned. "SVT is not common, but it happens," she told them. "We're still working with him, and he's not out of the woods yet. We got his heart rate down, and we're just trying to keep it there. We've notified Dr. Gleason from The Children's Hospital cardiology. She'll work with us until we get everything under control."

The doctors finally did get his situation under control. After an eternity, everyone exhaled. Everyone except for Mommy and Daddy that is, they aren't going to breathe easily for a long time. It is not easy to relax after a few days of standing like ancient gargoyles perched over a crib in the NICU, amidst incubators containing preemies and babies with other unknown issues, praying that your baby will be OK. But Duke's folks were finally able to take him home.

Life for him began with an asterisk. The proud parents were able to take their beautiful, blue-eyed boy home, but not before he was forced to confront his first life-or-death struggle. The records of this battle were sent to The Children's Hospital to prepare for a follow up visit a few days later. They served as his entry forms into the complex and mystical system of that medical complex. The data that filtered through the network and the blood-work that was processed in the labs were all that was necessary to mark Duke Dillan as a potential hero to those who search. One day he will fight for the lives of others, but for now, going home to his loving family is joy and victory enough. Bless his sweet little, rapidly-thumping heart.

6

The Children's Hospital is more than just a place where sick kids come to try to feel better. This is a world-class medical complex, unequaled in this or any other country. Its doctors and nurses are the cream of the crop. It would be difficult to find a facility anywhere with more modern and cutting edge technology. These are its obvious outstanding features. The subtle characteristics of this place are even more awe-inspiring.

Deep in its hallways, encoded in the rhythms of daily activity, and hidden in its internal communications exists a supernatural nervous system. Comprehension, sharing, and action take place in a realm where science cannot reach. The Children's Hospital prospers on the plane of accepted reality, but it lives and breathes with glowing energy on a much deeper metaphysical level. Information is its spectral life-blood, pumping through well-oiled veins. This is not the kind of information that ends up on the desks of doctors and nurses.

It is said that one hundred fifty years ago, this place was

a hospice for children with rare and incurable diseases. It was the first of its kind on the continent. Small pox, typhoid and scarlet fever had quarantined practically the entire city and countless dying children had no place to go to for care. Those in their final days were received at the new facility and treated free of charge. It was a dark and sad place, but its reputation grew and its patients multiplied because of the quality of treatment and the stories that began to circulate. It was a place of miracles.

As the hospice grew into a fully functioning hospital for children, patients and staff alike often reported strange occurrences and paranormal phenomenon. Brightly colored monsters were reported roaming the halls. Strange sounds were heard coming from empty rooms. IV poles were said to have come alive, and even speak with patients. The deep loving care that was offered the innocent children of the hospital had, for the first time in history, slowed and stymied the forces of death and sickness to the degree that their dastardly deeds were no longer confined to the shadows. The fight for life and health had migrated to the conscious world.

The unparalleled friction between life and death, health and sickness, love and evil created an energy that was absorbed by the walls of the hospital. This energy is neither good nor evil. It simultaneously aids both sides of the battle by providing them the sustaining power to exist on a higher level. Germs are personified. Superhero technologies are developed and tested. Disease armies are created. Dreams are infiltrated. Helpers and Searchers are recruited from previously inanimate objects.

Ivy knows the energy in the walls, and she has even met a few Searchers in her time, but this energy merely sustains the complex nervous system of the hospital. The unexpected life that Ivy and a few select machines enjoy was bestowed by the touch of God. As occurs in more places than credit is given, God answered the prayers of the faithful children and caretakers of The Children's Hospital. It was not really even an option. Otherwise the forces of darkness and grief, who had begun to feed off the growing energy in the hospital, would have overtaken this promising facility and eventually reigned over all refuges for the sick and helpless.

Ivy was one of the lucky ones, touched by God, granted life, and ushered into the society of Helpers. Her consciousness was awoken, her intelligence was developed, and her iron was reinforced. She caught onto the lifestyle quickly and passionately, ultimately developing a legendary reputation in the underground community. Her claim-to-fame is surely her string of victorious battles with The Heart Attack Man. No Helper has had more success in the cardiology sector reversing his treachery and mayhem. During her one hundred years of war with this cardiac villain, Ivy remained the greatest obstacle in his mission of death and pain, even considering she has maintained a cover of silence for the last twenty-five years or so.

Some people say she went into hiding. Others fear her dead, or worse, captured and enslaved by the very filth she has devoted her life to fighting. The truth is that her status began to make it harder for her patients to fight these diseases of the heart. The Heart Attack Man and his henchmen were so focused on her demise that they often killed patients who would have normally recovered. So, she decided to disappear… until now.

Duke was initially a cardiology patient himself, due to his mild heart condition at birth. This was his link to The Children's Hospital and to Ivy. When he made his first visit to the facility, Ivy was already waiting patiently outside the room where he would stay. As soon as they decoded his supra-ventricular-tachycardia documentation, The Searchers convinced her to come out of hiding. It wasn't much of a struggle to convincer her. She had missed the action for quite some time and the case made for this new patient with an overactive heart was very compelling. It was there, in Sector 6, the Cardiology wing, on an unseasonably warm night in December, that Ivy first met Duke Dillan.

Duke was two-months old. She was connected to him for just one evening, but she quickly loved him more than all the others she had helped. All the kids here are heroes, and they all need help, but a few have that certain genetic make-up which allows them to be a hero for the heroes. Duke had this trait to an extent never before seen. On that night, through their intravenous connection, Ivy impregnated Duke with all of the knowledge and skills that she possessed, most of which would be stored away in the deepest reaches of his mind and body until time or circumstance chose to extract them. She wasn't sure if she would ever see him again, but she knew that no matter where he went, Duke possessed the ability to utilize these gifts in the fight for health, love and life. She trusted he would rise to the challenge. Passing on her experience was in her opinion, justification enough to come out of retirement.

Ivy was as surprised as anyone that Duke Dillan's destiny brought him back to The Children's Hospital so soon after his release from the Cardiac sector. It was only a year and a half later that he was readmitted, this time in Sector 3, Oncology. She decided this was calling to return to action full time. She put in her transfer immediately. The fighters in Sector 3 were happy to have her. Their numbers had been dwindling in the Oncology sector because of public enemy number one, The Nasty Neuro.

7

As Ivy tells the story, The Chemo Kid stands with his mouth open. Her account of his life leading up to this very moment, of how his destiny is shared with the legendary Helper from Oncology, is inspiring. It shows him that his life is more than a series of mishaps and torment. He is an essential warrior in the battle against disease. This very mission in the playroom is part of a much larger war whose magnitude is immense.

He stands there for a long time with a glazed look in his eyes. More questions had been answered here than he ever could have imagined, more than he ever wanted to know. He now knows how he came to possess knowledge unseen in other children his age. He now knows who he is, what his purpose is, who and what he is up against. All this doesn't surprise Duke. It is more like he re-learned everything he already knew.

Ivy lets Duke digest her story. She knows that it is a lot for him to comprehend. It would be a lot for anyone to comprehend, let alone a kid.

"So, you've known me since I was two-months old?" Duke asks her. However, he is not really looking for an answer because he already understands. Ever since she started beeping and illuminating for him, he knew she was an old friend. Duke's mother has always said that when you meet someone who you will be eternally linked to, like a spouse or a best friend, it always feels like you've known them your whole life. That's how you know when love is real.

"I wanted to tell you sooner," she says in her robotic voice. "But it took you a while to understand me."

"I knew that you were trying to speak to me. I could interpret your body language. But today is the first time I could understand your words," he responds. "I feel like I've known you all of my life."

"You have known me almost all of your life. We will always be connected. Since that night in December, you have carried my knowledge with you and I have faithfully followed reports of your status from the Searchers. I always knew you would be doing great things someday, but never in my worst nightmares did I wish we would be reunited like this." Ivy's monotone, semi-robotic voice speaks to him with a true sadness that makes Duke turn away from her. He doesn't want her to see him tear up.

"It's not your fault, Ivy." he says as he gathers himself and wipes the salty wetness from his cheeks. His comforting voice makes her draw a little closer. "There's no way you could have known, and there's nothing you would have been able to do to stop it anyway."

"But it makes me feel so angry. I wish I could just take everything back!" says Ivy.

"I don't!" proclaims The Chemo Kid. "We are here now and we have each other. There's no way I would change my life, and there is no way I would ever be able to help these kids without you."

The Chemo Kid and Ivy stare at each for a long time. Sometimes a little quiet says more than a long speech ever could. They smile with the confidence of a great friendship.

"Well Kid, are you sure you're ready to do this?" she finally asks.

"I guess we won't know until we find out!" he replies with a snicker. "I have the password, if you know where to key it in."

Ivy winks with half of her screen and turns once again toward the shelf with the Barbie dolls on it. The Kid blushes. He feels like such a dork. She had tried to show him the secret spot behind the Barbies earlier, but he was too busy thinking about dragon playtime. Duke won't doubt his robot friend anymore, especially now that he can understand her language in his head. But Duke and Ivy will need a lot more than good communication skills after they enter the secret password that Angel told them.

Chapter Ten

'Cove of Wonders'

1

Tucked neatly behind the Barbie dolls on the middle shelf, is a toy laptop computer, the kind that would suit most kids his age. Duke is insulted. He knows how to use a real laptop, thank you very much! However, he's not about to second guess Ivy again so soon, so he puts his pride aside and pulls it off the shelf. He opens the cover and presses the power button. Nothing happens. He tries again. No power. The batteries must be either dead or missing.

"Anybody got any AA's?" he comically questions the Barbie dolls on the shelf.

After his joke is answered by silence, The Kid realizes he was asking the wrong playthings. The battery powered Gary the Green Dragon on the nearby shelf should be of greater assistance. He thanks the talking dancing green toy for its sacrifice as he turns it over and pops open the plastic cover its belly to reveal two AA's.

"I owe you one, Gary," says The Chemo Kid.

Quickly and smoothly, The Kid shakes out the batteries from the belly of the green dragon and slips them into the back of the Baby's First Laptop. Before he even has a chance to press the power button, the toy laptop lights up in his hands. Sssssssssssssss. It starts to hiss and glow, red-hot. He drops it to the floor just in time. If he had held on any longer, he would have suffered serious burns on his soft and sensitive hands. Even his fancy gloves wouldn't have protected him from the heat now radiating from the boiling and glowing laptop on the floor.

Darkness falls on the room. The dull light which had been casting into the room from the hall windows is now gone. The fiery red radiation from the toy laptop in the middle of the room takes its place. The Kid clings to Ivy's pole, frozen with fear. A slow hum builds around him and sounds as if it's coming from every direction at once. It reminds Duke of the time he was on an airplane with his mommy, just a couple of months ago. The engines sounded a lot like the constant and terrible whirrrrrr sound he's hearing now.

WHIRRRRRRRRR…. KSHHHHHHHHHHHH… KSSHHHHCHUNGGK!

The whir transitions to a crash. Red smoke fills the room, light from below by the glowing toy laptop. Ivy sweeps The Kid onto her base and wheels them quickly back to the doorway, but it is gone!

"Where did the door go?!" cries Duke.

He again begins to panic. Surely they will be trapped here. Maybe the janitor will find them in the morning and tell his parents that he's been sneaking out of his room at night. Or maybe, since doors are disappearing and airplane engines are whirring and smoking all around, no one will find him… until it is too late!

The Kid hugs Ivy's pole tightly and squints his eyes in an effort to see through the smoke. The noise is gone now but the air is thick and impenetrable. The first sense that regains its focus from the confusion is The

Kid's sense of smell. Suddenly everything is a whole lot sweeter. The foul stench of decaying germ-warriors has been lifted, The Kid's nose and lungs are filled with fresh cool air. When the wintery air blows away the smoke, The Kid and Ivy are more confused than ever at their surroundings.

2

With a rush, the smoke is gone and the lights come back on to reveal a completely transformed playroom. All the toys, all the games, all the shelves with construction paper and glitter are gone. The Chemo Kid and his faithful sidekick, Ivy, are standing in the center of an empty room with no windows, and no doors. The only other objects in sight are a huge computer monitor on the wall where Barbie and dragon shelves formally stood and the toy laptop cracking and cooling in the middle of the floor.

In unison, they look up at the giant computer monitor. It must be the size of a plasma screen in a sports stadium. The screen on the wall is blank except for a blinking blue cursor. A cursor on display of the Baby's First Laptop precisely mimics the color, shape and rhythm from the mega computer monitor. Obviously, they are connected.

The two heroes look at each other, and The Kid can hear Ivy's voice in his head.

"Enter the password," she says in a strong a commanding voice. It's the voice you'd expect to hear if you were being knighted by a queen, proud and resolute. Then she adds, "if you're ready."

"I'm serious, Duke," she continues. "You have a battle to fight for yourself, you know. I won't think any less of you if you choose to go back to your room and try your best to deal with your own personal monster instead of taking on the burden for everyone else."

"Ivy," he says, "as long as you're with me, I feel like I can take on the world. So let's go, and from now on, call me The Chemo Kid!"

3

The Chemo Kid's confidence begins to fade as he strides over to the toy laptop in the middle of the floor. He doesn't know if it will burn his hands, transform the room into another smoking cauldron of hell, teach him the cure for cancer, or what. The Kid's optimism wins out, and he slowly kneels to the floor, saying a silent prayer before hitting the first letter:

L

There is no whirring engine or smoky cloud this time. The capital letter on the screen of the Baby's First Laptop throws a blue light on the left side of his face. The computer monitor displays the same letter, in the same font, and lights up the entire left side of the room, Ivy included. The cursor blinks in unison on both screens two more times before The Kid quickly types in the rest of the password:

E-M-O-N-A-D-E

For a moment, nothing changes except for the tiny word now displayed on the toy laptop and the same word, as big as a Ford sedan, now on the huge wall-mounted monitor.

"Lemonade," says The Chemo Kid out loud. It reminds him of summer. He looks back at Ivy to see if the password inspires an association on her screens too. Instead of nostalgia, he sees a brief reaction of fear followed by a focused stare to the right. He snaps his gaze to the wall across from the large monitor to see a growing light blooming through the façade.

The place on the wall where the entry door to the playroom was previously located is transforming. An outline of a rectangle reveals itself through the drywall. It looks as if the light of the sun is shining through it. Actually, it's as if the light of a thousand suns is shining through it. It's as if the whole world is on fire on the other side of a new doorframe. The light forces its way through a minuscule rectangular crack. It is a color neither of them has ever seen before and is broken only by what appears to be new door hinges. The Kid and Ivy both retreat without even looking at each other, out of fear, and out of curiosity about what is blazing its way through, like a portal in time. The radiant heat is hot enough to make The Kid's eyes water. A fine mist steams up from beneath the place where the door comes just short of touching the ground.

"What's this?" The Kid asks his sidekick. "You've been through all of this before, right?"

"I...... do not know." she replies in a distant voice. This time her voice, which had just a moment ago seemed in total control, is full of fear and hesitation. "All I know is Cardiology. I was only moved here to help you."

"But I thought... I mean... how did you know about the laptop?"

"I can sense when machines have been touched by God for a greater purpose, like myself... but I had no idea what would happen once you typed in the password."

Until now, The Kid had counted on Ivy's understanding of the elaborate maze that is The Children's Hospital. He begins to sweat, from the heat of the portal, and the realization that she is as lost as he is. They are going to have to help each other more than he previously thought. He gathers himself, with a new sense of responsibility, and approaches the door. Ivy follows, peering suspiciously at the door over his right shoulder.

The shape of a doorknob has appeared by now, engulfed in the same mysterious light as the doorframe. The Kid takes a deep breath and reaches toward the glowing knob. It's brass, like the ones at his house, not at all like the other door handles in the hospital. He also notices that the door is made of wood.

The radiant heat has dissipated by now, so he is not surprised that the brass knob is cool to the touch when he places his hand on it. He turns the knob, and it clicks as it reaches its desired rotation. The wooden door slowly rocks on its hinges and pulls itself away from the boy's hand. There is no sun on the other side of the door. There is no burning world. There is no blinding heat. There is nothing. It is as if the fire was ignited when the entryway had been forged, and then it was snuffed out when the door was opened.

The space on the other side of the doorway has no feeling at all. Astronauts must have the same feeling of emptiness that The Chemo Kid and Ivy now feel when they open their hatch and look outside to the barren waste of space. Now all that is left for them to do is to step through. So with one foot in front of the other and one slow rotation of her rubber tires after another, Duke Dillan, A.K.A. The Chemo Kid, and his IV pole, Ivy, step into nothing.

161

After a brief feeling of weightlessness, lightheadedness, and deep black emptiness, The Chemo Kid and Ivy find themselves back in what they think must be the hallway from which they entered the playroom. The scenery has changed significantly since they left, just minutes ago. The most glaring difference is the total lack of stinking, steaming, rotting germ warriors and their picturesque splatters. Duke figures the Environmental Services staff must have been out here scouring while the two of them were still in the playroom.

The Kid starts back toward the door, to see if maybe they had made a wrong turn or something. As he approaches, it slams shut before he can get a hold of the knob. He claws at the space between the door and its frame, but before he can get a grip, the doorway disappears altogether! He is stricken with a sharp fear, like the feeling he gets during his dream walk on the forest pathway, but much more concentrated. Is this a dream? How else could rooms transform and doorways disappear?

The Kid and Ivy are speechless. They both feel their confusion and fear will be manageable if they aren't articulated. So, with silent trepidation, The Chemo Kid hops on Ivy. Together they head in the direction that their room would normally be.

The lack of splattered opponents is not the only difference from the hallway they left behind. As they roll down the hallway, they notice the lights have changed from ten-thousand watt fluorescents, to crafty mood lights and ambient table lamps. Cozy corners decorated with little armchairs and coffee tables with magazines and coasters are illuminated in a soft glow. Duke figures they landed in one of his mom's favorite home-living TV shows. He is just waiting for some metro-type guy to come out and start explaining the fabulous combination of mauve and taupe that they've put together here. The smell of disinfectant and hand sanitizer has been replaced by the sweet smell of vanilla and maple syrup. GG's pancakes couldn't possibly be nearby, but this combo definitely makes him crave his favorite dish for the first time in a while.

"Uh... Ivy? I don't think we're in the hospital anymore," he whispers to his companion. He knows they must be, but he can't figure out how they came to this place where the smell and sights of home have become so prevalent. When they round the next corner, the one which would lead them to their room, they find their answer.

The hallway is bustling with a full hospital staff, working in perfect unison, slipping past each other, absorbed in their thoughts or checking their clipboards, weaving in and out of rooms all the way down the hall. This could be any ordinary hospital setting, in any ordinary hospital. At second glance, however, The Chemo Kid and Ivy realize that the hospital staff is comprised of children in little lab coats and scrubs, most of whom are bald and malnourished, being assisted by robotic pieces of hospital equipment. They look like they should get back in bed, and maybe get about 300 mls of IV nutrition. The skinny juvenile hospital staff all notice The Kid and Ivy in unison. The bustling hallway freezes like someone scratched the record and the music suddenly stopped. All the children's eyes and the robot's monitors stare at the two outsiders.

The Kid and Ivy match the stillness and shocked faces of their newfound counterparts. A full minute of silence passes before some of the kids start to murmur amongst themselves. The Chemo Kid can hear what they are saying, even though he and Ivy are still standing a good distance away. All of his senses have become refined since the moment he entered the hospital.

"Is that him?"

"Is that the new guy?"

"He looks so skinny. What's so special about him?"

After about ten seconds of this, The Chemo Kid sees a commotion brewing behind the staff of mini-doctors. A boy, who is definitely a couple of years older than him, makes his way through the pack with little effort. They all step out of his way and shut their mouths as they realize who is coming through. He's obviously the one in charge.

"What's going on out here?" the boy yells. He stares down a few of his subordinates, but they each give him the old shoulder shrug as if to say, "Don't look at me." The boy then looks down the hallway to see the new faces for himself.

"Who are you?" he barks.

The Chemo Kid is startled by the boy. His tone of voice is remarkably commanding and angry. Plus, he's wearing a full baseball uniform and carrying a bat which is slung over his shoulder like he's waiting for his turn to hit.

"I... I... I... My name is... uh... D, D, Duke Dillan. I

mean... The Chemo Kid!" he stammers in response.

"Well, Well, Well... Duke Dillan, huh? The infamous Chemo Kid is finally here. I guess the rumors were true."

Everyone in the hallway immediately starts to stir and make a racket as they turn to each other in disbelief.

"Your reputation precedes you, Mr. Dillan. But you have to prove yourself around here! We're not the kind who blindly believe the hype," puffs the older boy.

Some of the mini-doctors chuckle and snort a little in order to get brownie points from the apparent boss, but the excited look in their eyes makes it clear that most of them at least find hope in the hype. The boss's direct approach and confidence have The Kid on his heels though. He can't seem to find the right words to respond. Soon they all start to talk amongst themselves, and he can hear them starting to question whether he is the one they thought he was. This is all the ammunition that this older kid needs, and he goes in for the kill.

"You're nothing but an impostor, aren't you!" he shouts. "Answer me! And do it quick, before I get one of the Hodgkins Kids out of bed!"

Duke doesn't know who the Hodgkins Kids are, but he can definitely tell he isn't ready to find out just yet. He better do something quick before he loses this crowd and gets tossed out of here.

6

Before he can figure out what to do, Ivy takes over. She scoops him up and they whirl toward the stunned onlookers.

"What are you doing?" he asks her.

"Just trust me. I know how to handle these kids." And apparently she does.

Ivy flies straight to the mob of mini-doctors at the other end of the hallway. First she swerves past the boy-boss in the baseball outfit. His mouth is open wide in silent shock. No bold threats are coming out of it now. Next Ivy dips and dives through the rest of the crowd. Duke does his best to look like he's not scared, even though Ivy tore off before he was ready. It is difficult for him with the sharp and sudden maneuvers she makes through the crowd.

Ivy glides them deftly through the crowd and back again. On her way past the little slugger for the second time, she does a 720-degree double leaping spin before she skids to a halt in the middle of the hall. The older boy can't be any more dumbfounded. He's now joined by another kid who is wearing the same uniform, but this kid is holding a glove and a ball instead of a bat. Their uniforms are from their favorite team, the Philaburbia All-Stars.

"Wow!" says the new kid sarcastically, "You know how to ride a helper pole! Whoopty doo!" His macho routine doesn't quite work next to the first boy's silent, stunned expression. "Look everybody, The Chemo Kid can ride an IV pole!" He continues to mock The Kid and turns toward the crowd causing them to chuckle a forced laugh in unison. It's clear that these guys are a couple of big-hitters around here, and they work as a team. The rest of the kids are probably just brown-nosing.

"This isn't just any IV pole, you know," retorts The Chemo Kid. "Her name is Ivy, otherwise known as 3S19."

"Yeah right!" the first boy says, regaining his voice and bravado. "3S19 is just a silly legend. Plus, even if this is him, he'd have to be 125 years old by now!"

The Kid feels like he is getting the upper hand again. "First of all, *he* is a she! And she is 3S19!" he tells them and then continues, "And I would be careful asking a lady about her age, if I were you. It's not very nice!"

The first boy thinks this over for a second, and then says, "You expect me to believe that the legendary 3S19 is not only alive, but is also a girl! 3S19 has been dead for at least 25 years, and besides... 3S19 is a Cardiac Helper anyway! Brandon, look at her tag. We'll see who this thing really is."

The second of the older boys starts toward The Chemo Kid and Ivy. She starts to pull away, but The Kid gestures for her to stay still. He trusts they will understand the truth.

The one named Brandon comes around Ivy's backside and bends down to look at the silver plate on her base. It's worn, but he can make out the engraved numbers and letters as he gets a little closer.

"Tommy, it says, IV Model 3S19. There is a date of manufacture, but it must be scratched, because it looks like it says, October 1883. That can't be right, can it?"

This time the second boy is speechless. Without a word he barges past Brandon and shoulders The Chemo Kid out of the way. The one named Tommy is not yet ready to accept the truth. But when he gets down on his knees to look for himself, he sees all of the same numbers and letters etched into the worn metal name-plate that Brandon reported. He also sees a serial number: 00-000-

0001. This makes him jump to his feet. He looks over at Brandon and the rest of the slack-jawed onlookers.

Tommy's face changes from one of arrogant doubt, to one of enlightened reverence. The rest of the kids know what he's going to say even before he says it. Despite this, he takes a moment to clear his throat, then addresses the crowd.

"This is the legendary helper: 3S19."

No one makes a sound. The staff of mini-doctors, together with Brandon and Tommy, instead do something even The Kid would never have expected. Each and every one of them falls down on one knee, and bows.

7

Duke has never seen anything like this before. Even the few times his parents have taken him to church, he never saw such a complete act of reverence as this. He always got the feeling at church that at least some of the people were just doing it for show.

While thinking of this, he feels a hand pull on his shirt. It is Tommy, one of the little sluggers. Eventually, he pulls him so hard that The Kid too is on one knee. It was necessary to complete the act of honoring the most famous IV pole ever to have rolled through the halls of The Children's Hospital. Finally, after about 3 minutes of silence had passed, everyone stands up and a familiar voice comes from the back of the room.

"I tried to tell you The Chemo Kid is real!" the voice calls out. "But none of you wanted to listen."

The two boys who had given The Kid and Ivy such a hard time before, are now standing side by side, waiting for their punishment. The crowd is rustling in front of them, making way for the owner of the voice. The mini-doctors are stepping aside, one-by-one, looking down at the ground, not able to make eye contact with their leader. Finally, a small hooded boy in slippers and a blue robe with cartoon trains makes his way to where they are standing.

In a cracked and dry voice he asks, "Do you know who I am?"

Ivy gives no response. She is still in awe after just having all these kids bow down to her. The Chemo Kid can't see a face past the oversized hood which is hanging down past the boy's eyes. He thinks the voice is very familiar, but he can't place it. If it weren't for the cartoon robe and tiny slippers, The Kid would have guessed this voice belonged to a man of eighty years old.

He finally replies, "No."

"Who told you about this place?" the boy then asks.

Not wanting to get his new girlfriend in trouble, The Kid stammers some, then blurts out, "I found this letter in my room!"

"Why are you lying to me?" the voice asks.

The Chemo Kid doesn't know what to say now. He doesn't want to get Angel in trouble, but he knows this guy is seeing through his lies. He finally replies with a question of his own. "Who are you?" he asks.

The little kid under the hood begins a slow laugh. The others all join in and the laughter becomes louder and louder until the whole group sounds like cackling thunderstorm. They are all leaning backwards holding their stomachs. It looks like some of them are going to fall over. Some of them are grabbing at each other's shoulders in order to stay on their feet, while others are bent at the waist looking like they had just run a marathon. They continue to laugh until the boy raises his hand up then sweeps it down quickly. They stop in unison like as if the boy was the conductor of an orchestra. Most of them had their eyes closed or weren't even looking up at that moment. They just knew when to stop, like they had practiced it a million times.

The conductor looks at his orchestra of children. They once again stand humbly stone-faced, eyes to the floor. He then turns to The Chemo Kid and removes his hood.

It's Trooper Phoenix.

8

Duke stands looking into the eyes of the friend who he had just the other night rescued from the twisted spider web of IV tubes. He can't believe it.

"What are you doing here?" he shouts.

Instead of replying to The Kid's question, Trooper makes a motion with his thumb over his shoulder. Immediately, the crowd returns to their original duties, hustling and bustling, from room to room.

"What is this place?" Duke asks Trooper. He is astounded at Trooper's ability to control his followers without saying a word.

"It's Chemo Cove," he says as he throws a hand on Duke's bony shoulder. "Sorry about those kids before."

"Who are they?" Duke asks, obviously unable to concoct

anything other than a question of just a few words.

"That's just Tommy from the City and his buddy Brandon. They're still relatively new, but they are good to have around for the heavy lifting. Tommy came in with AML a little while back, and I found him using a light-saber that he got for Christmas as a baseball bat in the hallway. I figured I could put him to work as security around here. Brandon came in soon after Tommy, and they play ball together in the halls with their parents. They do everything together. That's why their folks got the matching baseball uniforms. They NEVER take them off!"

Duke chuckles thinking about those guys running around in their stinky outfits. Just then a beautiful young girl walks over to them and whispers into Trooper's ear. She never takes her eyes off of The Chemo Kid though, so he chokes the laugh down. Her baby-blues are locked onto The Kid's, and he is mesmerized. He'd never admit it, but he always found girls kind of cool… even though they are girls, you know? This particular one is making eyes at him like never before. She has been finished relaying her message for a couple seconds now, and she's still staring at him.

Trooper just rolls his eyes as he looks at the two of them with their eyes locked on each other. "Ehh-hem!" He pretends to clear his throat. The two immediately look away from each other.

"That will be all, Avery." he says.

She looks at him and says, "Ohh, right."

As she begins to walk away, she looks back over her shoulder in a very flirtatious down home way and says,

"Bye, bye Chemo Kid. See you around." Duke's cheeks are glowing bright red now as he raises his hand in a wave. When Trooper looks back at him, they both burst out in laughter. It seems that news of The Chemo Kid is spreading quickly.

9

Trooper motions for another girl to come over. When she does, she takes an alcohol pad out of her back pocket, and begins to wipe The Kid's tubes, right where he and Ivy are connected. Duke remembers the nurse doing the same thing in his room earlier that day when she un-hooked the two of them. The Kid starts to pull away from her, but Trooper once again puts his hand on Dukes shoulder, and tells him it will be ok.

"She's going to take Ivy to charge up, and get a quick tune-up. Don't worry. She'll love it, and in no time she'll be twirling you down the halls of 3 South in style with a fresh waxing and crystal clear screens!"

He is hesitant at first, but The Chemo Kid finally gives in. Ivy is disconnected. He puts his hand on her and says, "I'll see you in a little bit." Without their physical connection, he can no longer hear her in his mind, but he can read her like a book none-the-less. She looks sad, but he can see her winking at him on her screens. Then, the same girl who un-did their link slowly walks Ivy away until they are out of sight completely.

"Are you alright?" Trooper asks Duke. He can see his friend's eyes welling up with tears. Trooper actually has to fight off a couple himself. He too can remember the first time he was parted from his pole.

"I just feel like I'm never going to see her again," Duke

says as he wipes the wetness from his eyes.

"Everything will be fine. They are just going to give the old girl a tune-up. Besides, you and I my friend, have some things to talk about!"

Chapter Eleven

'Q n A'

1

Before The Chemo Kid lets Trooper lead him too far away for their talk, he looks around to try to catch a glimpse of Ivy. He scans the hallway and luckily sees her briefly as she is shuttled between rooms by the nurse who did the alcohol swabbing. Ivy looks deconstructed and vulnerable to The Kid, and he starts to worry. Has she been taken away to harvest spare parts or something? He wants to run over to her and hook up their tubes once more. He can't stand to see a woman sad. First it was his mommy, GG and Mom-Mom Jo-Jo. Now he's worried about the emotions of his robotic IV pole… no, make that his robotic best friend.

"It's alright. Hello?… Over here!" Trooper is saying when Duke's attention finally draws back in his direction. "They do this all the time. Don't worry about a thing. Everything's gonna be alright."

Trooper has seen it all here since his diagnosis day. He was diagnosed at Christmas-time last year. That makes it eight months now that he's been on this journey. Eight months is no short amount of time to be hanging around these halls, and fighting these bad guys. Trooper Phoenix is only a little bit older than his new friend, Duke, but he's seen much more. He's the kind of ally The Chemo Kid needs to defeat the Nasty Neuro.

It is surprising though, his choice of words. Don't worry

about a thing. Everything's gonna be alright. They are almost the exact words that everyone has been singing back in Duke's room! It's the song that his dad sings practically every time he comes home from work. It's the words that Duke's dad and Aunt Ne-Ne painted on the window right next to the huge music symbol. It must be an omen. Hopefully, it's a good omen. At the very least, The Chemo Kid has now figured out his what his theme song should be.

He just can't shake the uncanny coincidence of Trooper's language, though. Has Trooper been spying on his family this whole time? Is he luring The Kid into a false sense of security only to be double-crossed? It is impossible to tell just yet. In this position, The Kid only has his own instincts as a guide. He remembers the Samuel Steam Engine medallion that Trooper gave him after rescuing him from the spider web of twisted tubes. That gesture has allowed The Kid to trust the leader of this secret section of The Children's Hospital so far. He'll have to continue to trust him, because, now that Ivy is no longer by his side, Trooper Phoenix is the only one who can show him how to get back to his folks.

2

As they start down the strangely lit hallway The Chemo Kid sees that things are even more different than he had thought. The place where the fleet of kid doctors and nursing staff stood before looks more like the inside of a high-tech air traffic control tower than a nurse's station, which is what he thought it was before. And now that he can take a closer look, he realizes that these kids aren't dressed as mini-doctors at all. They look more like scientists, complete with oversized glasses and pocket protectors. The Kid doesn't know if he can believe his senses or his instinct anymore. Nothing is normal. He wishes he would just wake up from this strange state of consciousness already and find himself in his bed back home with no sign of a black eye, no remnants of an IV needle in his veins, and no burden of a super suit, legendary sidekick or evil nemesis.

"Where are we?" The Kid asks Trooper, hoping his word will pull him back to reality with some sort of plausible, detailed explanation.

"I told you," replies Trooper. "This place is called Chemo Cove. It's our secret headquarters. The doctors and nurses know nothing about it. They do their jobs better than anyone in the whole world, but they don't even know how much they rely on our help to succeed."

The Kid decides to get a look for himself and darts over to one of the groups of children gathered in the hallway. Trooper reluctantly follows. They peer over the shoulders of some of the shorter mini-scientists to see what they are doing. They all are gathered around strategically placed computer screens, discussing lighted pictures of the insides of other kid's bodies. They are focusing most of their attention on the large image of a boy on the center screen. The boy's organs are clearly distinguishable, if a little blurry.

"Whoa! What are they looking at?" The Kid asks. "It looks like the inside of somebody's guts!"

"Well, that's exactly what they are doing. They are looking at the results of someone's MIBG scan. This test shows us where the cancer is in someone's body. It detects neuroblastoma by tracing a radioactive dye that has been injected into the patient. That's how they could see mine." Trooper says.

"Wait, you have NB too?" Duke asks. "But how come you don't have a black eye like me?"

"Well I did. Actually, I had two black eyes. They were kinda cool if you ask me. I didn't even wear sunglasses when my mom told me to. But the black eyes were the least of it. There were many other places that the NB had started to grow inside me. The tumors behind my eyes were just the first outward sign. They are how my folks found out…"

Trooper wouldn't normally ramble on about his personal NB case, but he is nervous. He doesn't know how much Duke understands the disease that has invaded his tiny body. These are things that are normally best to hear from the doctors. They know how to explain it so that even without a medical degree people can understand, and can prepare for the battle ahead. Trooper is not quite sure if The Kid is ready to fight through the inevitable self-doubt and depression that all warriors must overcome.

"So wait, the areas that are glowing on these screens are the tumors?" The Kid interrupts. He is catching on quicker than Trooper had hoped he would.

"Well, not exactly… but pretty much. Some things glow no matter what. But the spot up by this kid's eye and the ones in his chest are all NB."

Now Trooper is sure that he'll have to be the one to spill the beans about the severity of Duke's cancer. But Duke just shrugs his shoulders and shakes his head slowly back and forth. Trooper sees in his expression that The Chemo Kid is more concerned with the health of this anonymous little child, than he is concerned with himself. This kind of compassion would normally be just the weakness the Nasty Neuro would exploit to defeat his foe. But, if half of the potential that Trooper sees in The Chemo Kid is fulfilled, he is confident that the nasty one won't be able to rely on his old tricks of hate and fear and greed. The Chemo Kid could be the one to eliminate the need for these mini-scientists to analyze a MIBG scan for neuroblastoma ever again.

3

The Chemo Kid and Trooper turn away to continue down the hallway. "Where are we going?" asks The Kid. "What happened to the old hallway?"

The Kid is starting to sound frantic. He is upset about the little boy's cancer scan that he just saw baby-scientists analyzing on a big screen. He has no idea where he is. His parents are probably worried to death looking for him. He hasn't gotten any sound sleep since he's arrived in the hospital. It all is starting to catch up with him. He starts bubbling over with questions for Trooper.

"What is happening to me? Why was I chosen for this? Have you been spying on my family? Where are my parents?..."

Trooper interrupts him, "Slow down a little, Kid. Not too fast. Let's take it one thing at a time."

But by now The Kid has retreated into his own mind. His immense lack of understanding is overwhelming. He doesn't even know what questions to ask anymore. Trooper sees the confusion and exhaustion settle in The Chemo Kid's expression and he decides to stop tiptoeing around. If this kid is going to make a difference in the

178

fight with The Nasty Neuro, then Duke Dillan has to win his own internal battle of determination.

"Look, Kid. I like you. You're pretty cool, but are you sure you can handle all of this? I mean, I'm not so sure... this is all a lot of responsibility for someone our age, and you are kinda puny if you ask me."

Trooper pauses briefly to see if The Kid will react to that last comment. Nothing... so he continues, "You have to learn to be in two places at once. You have to find a way to be there when you're needed, even when you are so sick that you don't even want to get out of bed." He is subtly insulting The Kid to test how he faces adversity. Trooper needs to know if he can pick himself up even in the most overwhelming of situations.

Trooper takes a deep breath, looks The Kid right in the eye and says, "I didn't want to be the one to have to tell you this, but you're going to find out anyway. You're sick. You're really, really sick. You have neuroblastoma and it's bad. Tomorrow you are going to have a CT scan and an MIBG scan. That's when you'll find out how bad it is. You need to understand that it's going to be really hard on you... and your parents. I wonder if you have the nerve to overcome this." He stops here. The accepting of a neuroblastoma diagnosis is difficult for anyone, let alone for a little kid. Considering the additional layer of bullying he's been piling on, Trooper needs to give Duke his space.

Trooper's tirade has chipped away at Duke's confidence. He has known that he's been sick for a while now. He even figured it must be something pretty bad when he couldn't even force himself to eat his favorite foods anymore. He had lost so much weight, but his belly still looked the same. His parents even said, "He's not eating, but he doesn't look like he's losing weight." Little did they know that the thing that was filling out his frame was cancer.

Even though he knew something was wrong, Duke never complained. He didn't want to worry his parents. Then the black eye happened. He didn't even know what to make of that. He figured, since he never had a black eye before, that you could get one without feeling any pain at all. But now he thinks that maybe he is just a weak kid.

Trooper sees the bully tactic has pushed his new pal to the edge. The emptiness in The Kid's eyes as he recalls his last couple of months betrays the inner battle he is fighting. This wouldn't be the first time that a kid froze up when he heard the news. Even some of the kids who have had a special set of skills, like Duke, have cracked and crumbled when the severity of their diagnosis was pointed out to them. Of course none of those kids had even a tenth of the potential of The Chemo Kid. That is why this confrontation is more important than ever. Trooper needs to be sure that The Kid won't go through his inevitable battle with self-doubt at the wrong time.

The Chemo Kid is still standing quietly, staring into space, so Trooper decides to push him a little more. He makes his best effort to sound genuine and gestures to an innocuous looking door behind him in the hall. "Look, Bud," he says. "I shouldn't have laid this all on you so quick. You are obviously not strong enough to handle it. Here, right behind me… all you have to do is go through this door, and you'll be right across the hall from your room, in the Soiled Utilities closet. From there, you can just walk across the hall to your room where your parents are waiting for you, and you can forget all about this."

Trooper stands, holding out his hand, presenting his friend with an escape from all this craziness. Duke barely turns his head in that general direction. He's still standing motionless and speechless. The silence is starting to bother Trooper. He thought that The Chemo Kid would be able to see through his charade or at least take the heat better than this. As he opens his mouth to push him further over the edge, The Chemo Kid finally speaks.

4

"There's a reason I'm here," proclaims The Kid. With these words, the look of shock leaves his face and confidence and strength return. His silent meditation was like a hypnosis session. The Kid was able to approach the dream state without entering. He could see the dark forest, the pathway and the dark figure as if looking through a foggy window from the outside. The dream will never end peacefully and happily if he were to give up now.

Trooper can tell that The Kid has found his determination, but he doesn't yet know how. He starts to smile as The Kid continues, "I've known ever since I got here. It's what all of my crazy dreams have been getting me ready for."

"Dreams?" Trooper asks with a slight turn of his head. The smile has left his face. "What kind of dreams?" His eyes open wide as he asks the question. He doesn't worry anymore about The Chemo Kid's ability to overcome his self-doubt. Simply being able to gather himself for a response after being bombarded with such devastating news is all the proof that Trooper needs to put his mind at ease. Instead, Trooper's completely eager to hear about The Kid's dreams.

"I don't even know how to explain them," replies The Kid. "I fall asleep, then I wake up in the woods, or at least I always thought it was the woods until the other night. Now I'm not so sure. When I wake up in my dream, I walk toward the clearing in the trees. I've never made it there until the other night, but when I finally did, everything changed. There has always been this feeling that I have when I'm dreaming that I've never been able to explain. It's like there is someone watching me. Some nights I think it's someone bad, and other nights I feel safe, like it's God watching over me. The night I showed up at the hospital I dreamed that I finally came to the end of the clearing, but once I got there the vines and the weeds of the forest started to pull me down, and the ground turned into mud. I couldn't get out! Before I knew it, I was almost sunk. Then all of the sudden a blinding light shined through…."

"And the vines and weeds suddenly just let go. When you wake up, you are still a little scared, and you feel like your life has been saved by the light, right?" Trooper finishes Duke's sentence.

"Yeah! How did you know that?" Duke asks. "How did you know?"

"I've had the same kind of dreams since I was a baby. When I was just a couple months old, my parents were so upset, because I was having night terrors, or something, and I would never sleep. One day I was at the doctor's office, and a really sweet girl doctor gave me an IV in my arm. At first I cried, but I stopped suddenly and felt at ease. When we got home that day, everything had changed. I could all of the sudden understand what my parents were saying. I knew the answers to all of the questions they were asking, even the ones they didn't know the answers to! The craziest part was that I never cried at night again. My parents were so relieved. They could finally sleep. Little did they know that instead of screaming, now I was just dreaming the most vivid dreams you could imagine. They were epic. Good versus evil, and all that. The night I ended up here, I had the same dream you did."

The Chemo Kid wonders how it could be that they both had the same dreams, even though they lived a hundred miles away from each other. He's not sure if it's because of this thought or the heavy news that Trooper just shared but he feels like he's being pulled back into the hypnotic waking sleep. First, his feet go numb, like the vines are back, wrapped around his ankles, cutting off his circulation. His knees start to buckle causing him to sway back and forth. This grabs Trooper's attention and he grabs The Kid's shoulders. The Kid doesn't even notice because by now his head is light, his eyes roll back in their sockets and he passes out cold.

5

"….he's really shaking now. We might have to sedate him if he doesn't calm down. Come on now… Why won't he wake up? Isn't there anything you can do, Mr. Dillan? I thought you were his father." a female nurse says to his dad. When Duke sees his reaction, he realizes that his daddy is not too thrilled with this particular health care worker's bedside manner. Actually it looks like he's ready to rip her head off!

"You're the doctor! You do something!" Jesse Dillan snaps back at her.

Duke is watching this whole exchange like he's a fly on the wall. He doesn't know if he's dreaming, or if he's like one of the ghosts from the Christmas movie that his parents watched last year, observing himself from above. Mommy and GG are talking to a nice man dressed in a white coat. This guy is being very gentle with the little Duke he sees below. He walks over to the shaking boy and whispers something in his ear. It doesn't wake little Duke, but it calms him down. Amazingly, even from above, Duke can hear clearly what the man is saying.

"You are a hero, little guy, everything is going to be OK," he says then winks at Dukes dad.

The Duke below must like this male doctor. The Duke above remembers him. It's Dr. Houston. The room is silent for a moment until the female resident doc, who has a strip of white through her midnight black hair, interrupts the calm.

"That is so funny! It looks like his eyes are looking in two different directions at once," she cracks.

Everyone else in the room stares at her with furrowed brows. They are each thinking that she would probably be looking in a lot of different directions too if five different people were shining lights in her eyes while she was having a nightmare! The looks inspire the wise cracking nurse to shrug her shoulders and saunter out of the room. She has planted all of the seeds of wisdom that she has to offer. Immediately the rest of the people look at each other, and Dr. Houston says, "Good, now that she's gone, we can get back to business!" They all smile briefly, but quickly remember poor little Duke below and focus their attention on the boy. They are no longer trying to rouse him. They are monitoring him and applying cool compresses to make sure he doesn't start another fit.

Watching from above, Duke simultaneously feels a

sense of cool comfort. He is happy that there are so many people in the room who love him, but he is confused as to why he is watching from above and hasn't really figured out what is going on below. The relaxation dissipates with a jolt. It looks like everyone in the room is yelling at little Duke but strangely they are no longer calling him by name.

"Hey! Kid! Hey"

The figures blur and below become difficult to see. They start to look like completely different people. Darkness is overtaking the room. He can hear them yelling in his ears as if they were standing directly above.

"Are you OK? Kid!"

"Hey…"

Before the room goes completely black, Duke swears he sees the evil figure from his night visions standing over little Duke where Dr. Houston used to be. The room is in complete darkness now. All that he can see are the glowing red eyes of the dream creature. They are no longer looking down at the scene below. They are looking directly up at The Chemo Kid, burning a red hole in his soul.

6

"Hey Kid! Hey Kid! Wake up!"

The Chemo Kid starts to come back to his senses.

"Hey Kid!" he hears once again. Then, "Wait, wait… I think he's coming around. Give him some room!"

The Chemo Kid opens his eyes to see that he's not in

a hospital bed surrounded by his family and caretakers. He is lying on the floor in the hallway surrounded by a bunch of kids. The first one he recognizes is the girl who disconnected him from Ivy. He can't see clearly, but he guesses that she's re-connecting him to his robotic friend.

"Just relax. Everything is going to be OK. You two are back together again," she says, confirming The Kid's guess.

Trooper takes one hand and Ivy swoops around for the other, and together they lift The Chemo Kid off the hallway tiles. Without even thinking, he shifts his body onto Ivy's base and rests on his comfortable perch.

"Are you alright?" asks Trooper.

"Yeah, I'm alright," he replies. "I don't know what happened… but I think I just had some sort of out-of-body experience… or a flashback or something. That resident with the skunk haircut sure is mean!"

With that, the entire group of bystanders busts out laughing. Apparently he's not the first one who's had a problem with her!

"Don't worry, Kid. They're not all that bad!" shouts Trooper and everyone howls with laughter. Trooper quickly gets back to business, however. He is concerned about The Kid's health after witnessing him faint like that, just when he appeared to be regaining his strength and confidence. "What you need to do is tell what you saw when you fainted."

7

Avery, the cute girl from before runs over to The Chemo Kid and interrupts his conversation with Trooper. She looks at him with tears in her eyes. "Are you alright?" she asks.

"Yeah, Yeah… I'm cool," replies The Kid. He even tries to lower his voice as much as he can when he says it. Trooper whacks him on the arm. Shaking his head, he mocks, "Hey, Kid… you alright?"

The girl ignores Trooper and says, "I'm glad you're alright. See you later." She turns away and sort of skips back to the other side of the hall to a giggling pack of girls. As Trooper tugs on his sleeve, he sees her sneak a quick back peek over her shoulder. His eyes meet hers and he quickly darts them away, with his cheeks turning bright red. Trooper shakes his head again, this time making a 'tisk, tisk, tisk' sound with his teeth. Ivy sends the signal to The Kid that she'll kick Trooper's butt whenever he wants her to, but The Kid just smiles. "Maybe later… I think I can handle this one," he says with a wink.

"The Kid has a girlfriend… The Kid has a girlfriend… Na-Nana-Boo-Boo!" Trooper jokes as The Kid's cheeks return to their normal shade. He furrows his brow and looks at Trooper with the eyes of an ultimate fighter staring down his opponent during the weigh-in. He balls a fist and nudges his pal with it. Trooper is excited that The Chemo Kid is fight ready and, at the same time, scared that he just might use him as a Trooper punching bag. He quickly adds, "Ok, Ok, Ok… I'll stop, I'll stop! Just don't hit me, loverboy!"

8

The moment settles, and everyone feels confident that The Kid is over his fainting spell. Trooper decides to address the blackout later and returns to his bully game to

187

be sure he read The Kid correctly. "So are you in, man?" he asks the boy in the blue superhero suit mounted on his legendary IV pole. "Or do you want to go back to your family and forget about all of this. Remember, the choice is yours." He points his finger toward the door that he showed him before he fainted.

"We're in, right Ivy?" says The Chemo Kid, tapping the pole of his robotic friend. She replies with a series of beeps and flashes of light that no one else but he can understand. "We're definitely in, Trooper. But I want to know one thing. Do you believe I can make a difference in this fight? You were pretty harshly doubting me just a minute ago."

"That was a test of will, Kid," Trooper replies. "All cancer patients go through moments of self-doubt and depression, even a patient as special as you. I wanted to be sure you didn't have to fight that internal battle at the wrong moment. You proved to me you could climb out of the darkness all by yourself. I think you are the one we have been waiting for."

All of this was true. Trooper just left out one small detail. He thinks it was independent of his test, but he is silently worried about The Kid's fainting spell. Any time Trooper has seen a cancer patient faint, especially one who otherwise seemed confident and strong, it was bad news. For the next few nights, he'll just have to be sure the mini-doctors and scientists are tuned into the data and vitals coming from Duke's hospital room to see if they catch any new insights or cause for further alarm in his medical diagnosis.

His other hypothesis would be even worse. Trooper hopes that The Nasty Neuro hasn't already developed the ability to roam freely inside Duke's dreams. This would mean he could pull The Kid back into a dream state whenever he wanted. The Kid would never again find peace in his waking or sleeping hours.

The Chemo Kid senses Trooper's worry, so he reiterates his commitment. "If we're going to do this, Trooper, we are going to do it all the way! We are going to beat this Nasty Neuro... him and all his friends!" He opens up his hand like he going for a high five, wiggles his fingers into a fist and holds it out for a response. Trooper forgets his worry for the moment and returns in The Kid's fist-bump. Reverse Fireworks Fist-Bump they'll later name their new secret handshake. Soon the whole world will be doing it, but for now, it will be the symbol of the elite cancer-fighting task-force in Sector 3 of The Children's Hospital. Ivy is a little upset that she's left out of the secret handshake, so she plays fireworks in reverse on her screen and adds the appropriate sound effects to the action. The three of them look each other in the eye with a sense of purpose.

"Well... what are we waiting for?" asks The Chemo Kid.

Chapter Twelve

'The Crew'

1

Trooper escorts Ivy and The Chemo Kid around the hall to see all of the important people and places that they'll need to know about. He first introduces them formally to the Sluggers, Brandon and Tommy. He explains to The Kid that they'll be the ones on duty when he's unable to work.

"I can tell The Chemo Kid is looking forward to kicking some butt, but don't try to be a hero and tell us you'll be here when you can't," Tommy says to The Kid. His tone is a lot less confrontational than their first encounter. "Brandon and I both have AML, which is a form of Leukemia. We get chemo too, but our cancer is in our blood and bone marrow. You'll probably get to go home when your rounds of chemo are done. We'll have to stay until our counts come back up. So when you're not here, all you have to do is let us know and we'll be able to cover for you."

"Especially during scans or surgeries..." Brandon adds. " What's your schedule look like, Kid?"

"I-I-I'm not sure. I haven't heard yet," he says sheepishly. Trooper sticks his hand up in the air, snaps his fingers, and a little baby girl, no more than a year old, scurries over. She tugs on Trooper's pant-leg to let him know she is there. Trooper leans down and grabs a piece of paper out of her hand. She quickly hurries away. "Thanks Soapie!" Trooper calls after her with a smile.

"You're welcome, hun!" squeaks a small voice as she scuttles back to her cube.

"That's Sophie, my personal assistant. She's great with all of the logistical stuff, and she makes a mean apple juice too!" he jokes as he turns around and gives her a wink. "Well, let's see here... Ohh yes, you've got a big day planned tomorrow. MIBG-Scan, CT-Scan, Bone Marrow Biopsy, Tumor Biopsy. It looks like you might be out for a couple of days," Trooper says.

"What? Let me see that!" Duke says as he rips it from his buddy's hand. "I can't believe this... It's going to take forever! I'm ready to get started!"

"Listen Kid, don't sweat it. Go take care of what you need to do. The first week is really busy with tests and all that. Trust me, your parents are going to be acting like total Looney Tunes for a while anyway. I'm surprised you've been able to get out as much as you have. Take it slow till you get through the scans and then we can really get down to business." Trooper has been through this all before. Duke has a lot more medical issues to overcome before he can get down to fighting Nasty Neuro. The Kid might not want to hear it now, but he'll have to juggle all of these tests and treatments with his new life. That is the only way he will be able to rid himself, and the world, of the nasty malignant monsters.

"Don't worry, Duke. I'll be with you the whole time. I can let you know when there's trouble. We'll get through it together," Ivy says.

191

"I know Ivy, I know," he warmly replies.

2

"Come here, you guys. I want to show you something!" Trooper says from halfway down the hall. The Kid and Ivy roll down the hall toward a set of double doors at the end. Trooper stands with his back toward the doors. "This is the gym," he says as he turns and opens the doors. "This is where you'll learn how to use your powers." The Chemo Kid's face lights up as he scans the room, looking at all of the different stations, each populated with kids in training. They are doing flips, stretches, exercises and some even seem to be flying through the air.

"This is even cooler than Chunky Cheese!" says The Chemo Kid.

"You can say that again!" Trooper replies. "Here, let me introduce you to some people."

Trooper leads them to the first station where a kid, no bigger than Duke, is doing target practice with sanitizer grenades. The kid is diving through obstacles and launching bombs at wooden cutouts that resemble the germ warriors. This kid is splashing each one with precision. Every once in a while, one of the wooden cutouts pops up in the shape of a doctor or a sick child. The practicing kid uses those moments to dive behind a wall and peek around the other side to prepare himself to drop another enemy when it pops up.

"Whoa! That kid is good!" Duke shouts.

"That's another new guy... Aiden... just showed up about a week ago. They call him Nickles, because he whooped up on some germ warriors by disguising some sanitizer grenades as loose change. He had the things on a remote and when the greedy scum bags ran over to grab them, KABOOM!" Trooper shouts as he makes an exploding gesture with his hands.

"That's the first training everyone around here has to go through. Protection against germ warfare is the most important thing in The Children's Hospital. When patients get chemotherapy, their immune system gets totally wiped out, sometimes for a month or even more. Something as simple as the common cold could make a cancer child really sick... or worse. It's important that you get used to washing your hands with sanitizer whenever you can, in addition to perfecting your grenade skills. It'll keep you from getting sick." Trooper points to the sanitizer pumps which are located on the walls, about every fifteen feet from each other.

"Wow! What's that girl doing?" Duke asks, pointing to an older girl who seems to have the ability to jump ten feet in the air.

"That's Jenny Springfield," Trooper says. "Jenny lost her leg in a battle with The Sarco Monster. It almost killed her. She couldn't get out of bed for a month. But then one day, she showed up back here with that." He points at the metal spring attached to her hip, where her leg used to be. "She can jump higher than anyone I've met. She's one of our top fighters. We just call her Springs now."

"Hey, Springs!" he yells. Jenny crouches down, and in one motion bounces into the air, landing right in front of The Chemo Kid. "Springs, this is Duke Dillan, also known as The Chemo Kid, and this is his Helper pole, Ivy."

"It's great to meet you, Duke," she says as she bounces

around the three of them. "Your Helper is really cool!" she continues, "I've always wanted one, but I got a chair instead." With that she points to a chair in the corner of the room. "I haven't even used it since I got my springs!" She giggles as she bounces away.

Duke and Ivy roll over to the chair. It's dusty and covered with sweaty towels. Duke starts pulling the towels off and finds the charger. When he plugs it in, the chair lights up. Ivy inspects the chair closer. "This is not just any old chair," she tells The Chemo Kid. "He's a Helper! I can't seem to establish a wireless connection with him so I think he's a really old one. With a little work, though, he could be back to his old self again!"

3

"Trooper! Ivy found something!" Duke shouts as he finishes removing the sweaty towels from the chair.

"What is it?" Trooper asks as he runs over.

"It's a Helper! Ivy says he just needs some work and he'll be good as new. I'm sure there's someone around here who needs one, right?"

"There's a lot of kids around here who need one, but Helpers are only meant for kids who have the ability to help others. Only the Searchers can tell us that."

"Who are the Searchers?" asks The Kid.

"Before you were admitted to this hospital," responds Trooper, "and even while you are here, more often than not, if you have the feeling you are being watched... it is the Searchers. They monitor and seek out information that will identify potential members of our fighting force. They work behind the scenes and rarely show their faces.

I'm sure they have already noted the discovery of this old Helper. We'll just have to wait to see who will get to use the chair. For now, I'll have Wyatt check him out. He's our mechanic. If anyone knows what to do, it will be him."

Trooper touches his ear and begins talking as he walks away. In seconds, a team of grease stained children in overalls pour in through the double doors. Wyatt is the last to come in. His hand is up by his ear like Trooper's.

"Somebody call for a mechanic?" Wyatt shouts, peering over a big pair of cowboy sunglasses. He takes off his green and yellow trucker hat and scratches his head. Then he walks right over to the chair without waiting for a response. "This thing?" he muses and gives it a shake. "Feels solid enough. Who says this thing is a Helper?" he asks.

"We did… well, Ivy did," answers The Chemo Kid. "This is my helper Ivy, better known as 3S19."

Wyatt saunters over and looks Ivy up and down. "She's a beaut'! They just set you up with this thing?" he asks popping a sunflower seed in his mouth.

"She's been with me a lot longer than you might think," The Kid answers. He gives Ivy a wink.

"I like your style, partner," Wyatt says as he shakes his head in approval. "You two are going to fit in real good around these here parts." He turns around and puts his hat back on his head. Before snapping his fingers to summon his crew, Wyatt makes a production of tipping the brim down in Duke and Ivy's direction. In a flash, they all hustle out the door with the newly discovered Helper chair.

195

"This is something you'll be very interested in, Kid." Trooper says as he thumbs over his shoulder to a door that reads, Shooting Range. Ivy rolls Duke over and the three of them look through the window. They see kids holding guns of various sizes, shooting all different types of ammunition.

"Look to the right, over there," Trooper says. They see a child with a gun that is bigger than he is. The gun is firing a liquid that sizzles down the wall, burning off the image of a terrible monster that had been painted there before. "That's the Chemo Cannon 5000. It will become you're best friend. The secret to this weapon is the more rounds of chemo you get, the more powerful it will become."

"Do you have one?" Duke asks Trooper.

"Yeah, I have one… and it's powerful. I have other powers too now. Check this out."

Trooper steps through the door and shakes hands with a couple kids inside. Then he points toward the target area. Through the windows, The Kid sees a few new targets appearing on the far wall. The other children step back as Trooper puts his hand to the side of his head. A beam of blue light shoots from his eyes and destroys the targets, leaving a smoldering mess. Trooper high-fives the other kids and walks back through the door.

"Well, that was fun!" Trooper says with a smile. Then he winks at Ivy and adds, "Sometimes people call me Firebird." He looks proud, but The Chemo Kid can see a bit of pain and exhaustion behind Trooper's smile.

"Are you alright?" he asks.

"Yeah, but I should probably sit down. Whenever you use your powers like that, it really takes the energy out of you. At first it's not too bad, but after a while, it gets worse. You have to learn to use your powers wisely, or else you won't be strong enough when you need it most," explains Trooper. "That leads me to my next point. Follow me."

As they continue on, Trooper places his hand on Ivy to steady his balance. She feels his clammy hand holding tighter and applying more weight than she would expect. Something tells her that Trooper has used his powers quite a lot.

5

"The Chemo Cove Café," Trooper announces as he pushes open another set of double doors. The Chemo Kid sees an array of snacks and goodies that would make anyone's belly grumble: candy, cupcakes, chips and pretzels in bowls surrounding platters of sandwiches and cheesy pizza, warm bread with dips and jellies… even stacks of pancakes with syrup and butter are piled high on this buffet table.

"Whatever you want, whenever you want it, it's yours!" Trooper says. "If we don't have it, our chef's will make it! We have to keep our strength up any way we can during treatments. Otherwise you'll have to get a tube." He says all this as he walks around the table grazing and grabbing a couple things for later.

The Chemo Kid looks to the mountain of food on the table. There's something there for everyone, but he's still not really hungry. Instead he asks, "What do you mean by a tube?" although he's pretty sure he doesn't want to know.

"Let's just say that you don't want one. Make sure to eat, even if you don't feel hungry, so you don't have to get one, OK?" Saying this, Trooper pops a mini muffin in his mouth and closes his eyes with a smile. The Kid follows his lead and grabs one too. He's still not hungry, but he isn't trying to find out about this tube thing either, so he takes a nibble.

6

Trooper leads The Chemo Kid out of the Café, into a little area where he sits down on a nice chair with a groan. He sets his lunch down on a finished wood table in front of him. The Kid sits down next to him and they look out to the main area where all of the others are hard at work.

"Who are all of them?" asks The Chemo Kid. "Do they all have special powers too?"

"Some of them do, but most of them are just kids who want to help because they are tired of seeing all of their friends get sicker and sicker. They might not be super-heroes, but they all work well together. It's kind of cool to watch the synergy."

Seen through the observation glass, their synchronized movements are like a Broadway show. With dramatic twists and turns, the dancers weave and waltz through a series of near-misses and close-calls through the computerized laboratory. Papers are flying through the air, inter-mingling in a way that suggests that they are magically possessed. IV poles are swinging to an unheard beat, and mini-acrobats are hanging off of them deftly slipping files in bins held by other kids who slip off stage in their own syncopated wave. The complex choreography reminds The Kid of the daily rhythm of

198

the hospital routine. It has intoxicated him for these last couple of days in so many ways. He is also starting to realize it is this machination that drives the engine of this hidden under-hospital.

The clanking and whizzing of IV poles, printers churning and telephones ringing in the Broadway show has built to an amazing climax. Everyone is singing together, the orchestra is sustaining a thunderous chord, when, suddenly, the music stops, the door swings open, and a bright light shines in revealing the silhouette of a tall, slender… bunny rabbit?

7

"Well? Isn't someone going to take my coat?" rings a strong female voice from the open doorway. She steps forward for everyone to see. The whole place erupts in cheers and the music starts again. Two young bald-headed kids with tubes in their noses slowly make their way over to her, sharing the duty of carrying her coat. She puts a hand on the top of each of their heads, and they both start blushing. They scurry off more quickly than they had come. It seems that this girl has a way of making the young ones feel like they have a little extra hitch in their giddy-up!

"Who is she?" asks The Chemo Kid. "Everyone seems to like her a lot!"

The answer comes from a mini-pediatrician holding a clipboard with a dinosaur sticker underneath. The Kid hasn't seen this child before. "She's pretty much queen bee around here. Word has it she's going to be on TV pretty soon… Good Morning Philaburbia, or something like that. Her name is Starr Powers. Supposedly she kicked the Meddullo Monster's butt a couple of weeks ago. I heard when she gets mad, she turns red and then shoots radiation from her hands!"

After a pause, the wide-eyed mini-pediatrician, who looks to be about 8-years old, continues, "Let me be the first to introduce myself. My name is Mario Genioso. Please feel free to ask me anything, and I will find the answer. Should I call you Chemo Kid, or do you prefer to be called Duke, or Mr. Dillan?"

"How did you know my name?"

"It's my job to know everything there is to know about you, Mr. Dillan. You were born to Maggie and Jesse Dillan on October 26th, 2006, in Suburban Hospital. Your grandmother's names are GG and Mom-Mom Jo-Jo. You still like a binky, which you prefer to suck upside-down, and you're obsessed with Gary the Green Dragon. Your diagnosis is Neuroblastoma Stage IV and you formerly visited here at the age of two months for Wolfe Parkinson White Syndrome. This is where you first made contact with IV Model 3S19, and where most of us assume you received your powers."

"Mr. Chemo Kid I presume?" a voice interrupts Mario's jabbering. Mario immediately stops talking and shyly filters back into the crowd, not before he gives a little bow in the direction of where the voice came from. The Kid turns around to see the tall girl wearing a bunny rabbit eared hat. "Welcome to the club," she says as she walks past him. "Trooper, bring him in my office so we can all get to know one another." Her back is now turned and she is heading through a doorway where two more youngsters wait eagerly to push in her oversized desk chair and to slip pink fuzzy slippers on her feet.

"Here we go," Trooper says to Duke, and they head into

her office.

Starr Powers is chiseled on the brass plaque on her door. The Chemo Kid looks at it twice as they walk through the doorway.

"She must be a big-shot if she gets her own office," he says to Trooper.

"Shhh!" he whispers. "She's a little bit of a diva, so if you want her to be cool with you, just follow her lead." The Kid thought maybe Trooper was top dog in this place. Now he can see that Starr has him out-ranked for sure.

They cross over the threshold to Starr's office and enter a mahogany library fit for a king. Inside are the most extensive wood workings and carvings he's ever seen. Duke is not a novice at carpentry appreciation. His father is way into wood-working, and he's always got magazines and catalogs with cool pictures laying around the house. Jesse would be drooling in this place.

"Have a seat, Mr. Chemo Kid," Starr says as her underlings escort him and Trooper to a couple of folding chairs in front of a massive desk. Apparently the amenities stop with Miss Powers. Not until they are seated for a full minute and start to squirm in their seats does the tall skinny girl, with a tube in her right nostril and a tattered bunny ear hat, break the silence.

"Mr. Chemo Kid... Well, well, well... It truly is a pleasure to have you in my office. You've become quite the legend in the short time since we've heard of you.

I have a feeling that the artistic expression you created using Neuro's Germ Warriors will be talked about for generations." As she says this, she points a remote control at the wall behind her. The panels of the wall slide open exposing a dozen television screens. She uses the controller to rewind the image on one of them. When she gets to the part she's looking for, she presses play. They all sit quietly, watching The Chemo Kid race around atop Ivy's base. He is fully engrossed, watching himself splash sanitizer grenades over the heads of the dumbfounded guards when Starr pauses the screen. The image left frozen on the screen is of a fierce-looking Chemo Kid, mounted firmly on Ivy, who is leaping high over their confused enemies.

"Pretty impressive Mr. Dillan. Your ability to think on the fly and improvise will get you far in this place," comments Starr. "And you, 3S19! We are honored to be in your presence." With this, Starr's two awestruck young assistants bow their heads to Ivy. It's becoming more and more obvious to The Chemo Kid as they encounter more and more characters in the underground world of The Children's Hospital, that Ivy hasn't told him everything there is to know about her history. She certainly is garnering immense respect from everyone, and the focus and determination on her screens that he just witnessed on the surveillance video was like nothing The Kid has ever seen.

Ivy beeps and churns in response to the adulation. The Kid translates for her as her words come to his mind. "She says, 'Thank you, but please, it's not necessary. I merely fulfill the duties assigned to me as a simple Helper pole."

"You can speak to her... What is it like?" Starr asks. The

expression in her eyes reveals the she has momentarily left her diva aside. It's the first time anyone in this place has seen the child side of Starr Powers since her arrival. Trooper is surprised, but holds a respectful posture as she leans her bony frame over the table to get a better look at Ivy.

She has forgotten everyone else in the room. She's too busy examining the lightweight aluminum alloy pole with the freshly oiled wheeled base. Underneath the fresh wax, Ivy's metallic blue finish shimmers and sparkles. Ivy pulls away a little as Starr, now crawling on her desk, gets a little too close for comfort. The tall girl flinches, but it doesn't stop her from leering down past the edge of her desk for one final good hard look.

Ivy sees Starr's eyes pause momentarily on her monitors. She takes the moment to show off, suddenly displaying a colorful array of stars and fireworks. Starr suddenly bursts into a huge laughing smile and scurries back to her seat. The rest of the kids applaud and Starr just sits grinning from ear to ear. She is jealous of the awesome connection that Ivy and The Chemo Kid share.

"It's kind of like getting electrocuted a little bit every time she has something to say," says The Chemo Kid. He then looks over at Ivy expecting her to answer with a spine-tingling charge. She instead simply winks using her screens and lets out a quick series of beeps, which has them all cracking up again.

The Chemo Kid looks back to the television screen, which has slipped out of pause by now. He sees the paint-splattered entranceway as it looked just after he and Ivy slip into the playroom. The Kid can't look away from the multi-colored, terrible landscape that they created. Even after he sees the door to the playroom sliding shut behind himself and Ivy, his focus remains on the television screen.

10

Ivy drifts into a daydream of her own. She remembers the beginning, when her special talents were first used to help others. The doctors were confused and alarmed when she charged through the doors of an operating room three stories underground. She burst through the doors with the limp, lifeless body of a small boy slung on her base. The first doctor ran out the door to see the nurse or orderly who pushed this IV pole into the operating room, but found no one. The rest of the surgeons grabbed the young boy and began to give him CPR, while frantic nurses hung bags of IV fluids on her hooks.

Thanks to Ivy's quick transportation, they were able to stabilize the child who she had found wandering the halls of the basement. The little boy had been left alone after an extensive surgery which left him weary and disoriented. The boy stepped into the hallway to look for his family, and was overwhelmed by the terrible sounds he heard of doctors and nurses scrambling inside crowded rooms trying desperately to save children whose lives haven't even had the chance to begin yet. In his feeble state he could hardly steady his body. He ricocheted back and forth down the hall until he finally fell flat.

At that same moment, Ivy was standing in a quiet corridor of the same hallway. She had been recently purchased by the Cardiology department, but one of her wheels was askew. There she stood, waiting for the handyman to come and tighten her crooked caster when she saw a little sick boy in need of assistance. IV Model 3S19 was never one who liked to wait for help, especially when it was someone else who needed it. That maintenance man looked up and down the hall for her the next morning, but found no sign of a broken IV pole. Instead, she left the scene on her own volition, embarking on her extraordinary mission.

IV 3S19 has saved thousands of kids since that day. She has also seen many Helper friends come and go over the years. Today, there are few that remain, and those few are spread over the hospital so thinly it's as if they aren't here at all. That is why she was so excited to discover Springs's abandoned Helper chair. Ivy is afraid that there aren't many left who, like her, possess the gifts to change the world.

11

"Let's get down to business then, shall we?" Starr says as she sits back down at her mahogany desk. The other youngsters fall into line quickly as it becomes clear that Miss Powers is ready to continue the meeting. They've clearly been trained to do exactly what the Onco-Queen says... and fast. She addresses Trooper directly.

"Mr. Phoenix, you obviously know that The Chemo Kid has not been granted full clearance yet, judging from the fact that you haven't left his side since you've arrived. Isn't that right, Mr. Phoenix?" she asks with the comical voice of a well-trained actress, adding a little southern drawl to her phrase and raising her eyebrows to complete the charade.

"Look, I know I should have asked you first, before I started showing him around, but I woke up all twisted in my tubes. It was crazy. The more I struggled with it, the more I got twisted. Finally I was wrapped up so tight that I couldn't even get my arm free to hit the call button. The next thing you know this kid comes riding into my room atop his very own Helper and I hadn't even heard that there had been any new NB diagnosis! I thought I was dreaming, but they managed to free me and they even hung out for a little while watching Gary! Look… I'm sorry I didn't ask first, but Tommy and Brandon found him in the hallway and I knew this kid was the real deal. He's gotta be… um… ahhhh" Trooper realizes he is uncharacteristically rambling again, so he lets his voice trail off without finishing his thought. He stands silently, with a stern look on his face, preparing himself for a tongue-lashing and complete embarrassment.

"Sit down, Firebird," she says, then clears her throat. Trooper does as he's told, happy for now at least that he was able to escape without complete embarrassment.

"I'm not angry with you, Trooper. As always, I wish you would have come to me first. We don't hand out letters containing secret passwords to just anyone…"

"Wait, what? I didn't give him a letter… I don't even have any. I gave my last one to Aiden," Trooper chimes in.

All eyes shift to The Chemo Kid.

"There are only a couple of other kids who aren't in this room that could have given him the letter, both of whom are home right now!" Starr's face is scrunched like she just bit an apple and got the worm.

12

"I don't know anything about any letter," interjects

206

Duke without prompting. He desperately wants to protect Angel.

"We need to know who gave you the letter, Mr. Dillan." Starr commands. "We need to know if our security has been breached."

"It's not her fault, I swear!" he blurts out, realizing that he can't hide the truth. "I'm the one who vandalized the hallway. I'm the one who entered the password and snuck into this place!" The Kid doesn't want any of his friends to take the fall for him, but he knows he has to come clean.

"Listen," he continues. "I was coming back from Trooper's room when this little girl poked her head out of her room. Man… she was cute. She told me to come over and so I did. She wanted to talk to me. Look, I don't want her to get into any trouble over any of this…"

"What is her name, Mr. Dillan?" Starr asks again!" Duke hangs his head dejectedly. There's no better way to start a new relationship than to stab your new girlfriend in the back!

"Her name is Angel, but please... I don't want her to get in any trouble!" Duke pleads.

"Angel, you say?" Starr has an inquisitive look that tells Duke that she's interested but if he's making this up he's in for it.

She snaps for one of her assistants. The one closer to her shuffles over to Starr's seat. He's only two and a half feet tall so he doesn't need to bend down for Starr's message to be whispered into his ear even though she is seated. As she pulls away from his ear, he turns and quickly scurries out of the room, making a silent gesture to his counterpart with his eyes. The other kid immediately runs behind Starr and begins to massage her shoulders.

"Ahhhh…" Starr groans. "This place is like a great big ball of stress wrapped in anxiety. You'll have to really be careful, Mr. Chemo Kid, if you don't want to end up in Dr. Lyncap's office after all of this… She's the resident head-shrinker on this unit. I see her twice a week myself. You know, just to keep my sanity."

As Starr finishes her tangent, the infant messenger returns with whatever information Starr had requested. He whispers into her ear, and the expression on her face becomes sad. The Chemo Kid and Trooper can see the tears welling up in her eyes. The emotion seems so strong that they both feel the urge to stand up and give her a sympathetic hug. However, they hesitate too long. Starr's eyes roll back into her head and she slumps into the chair. Ivy reacts quickly. She wheels around to her chair just in time for Starr to slide off onto her base. Ivy does her best to contort her frame to comfort Starr's limp body, though she usually needs a good night to conform her metal base to the liking of a new rider.

The two personal assistants rush together in fright as they watch their queen lying helpless on the Ivy's base. Trooper finally rises to action and hits the emergency call button to order a medic. Within 90-seconds, two older kids rush in and everyone backs away to give them room. Only Trooper stays by Starr's side, continuously saying things like, "It's going to be alright," and, "You'll be OK, Starr." The Kid follows suit by gathering the little assistants close and trying to comfort them.

Starr's eyelids begin to flutter. She's returning to

consciousness. The first thing she sees is a teenage boy hanging a bag of IV fluids on a spare pole. She is confused but lifts herself off of Ivy's base and begins to look around the room to see what happened. The other medic takes her hand and helps her to her feet. Starr looks at him and stops cold. She thinks he's a real looker.

"Hey, my name is Tom. I'm the head of the EMT's," he says.

Starr hangs on his every word. She knows the rest of the guys on the Emergency Medic Team, but she's never seen him before.

"I'm new to the Team. I'm a firefighter and EMT on the outside, so they asked me to take over after the last guy finished his treatments."

The Chemo Kid and Trooper look at each other. They begin to giggle. Ivy gives The Kid a shock for being so inconsiderate. Trooper keeps chuckling, but when he sees the six-foot tall pole looming over him he knocks it off quickly.

"What's your name?" Tom asks Starr.

She is blushing so badly that she turns away and shyly says, "Umm... Starr Powers..."

"Whoa, you're Starr Powers? I've heard all about you. You're some kind of hero around here," the bald seventeen year-old says to her. Totally embarrassed now, she forces herself to regain her composure.

"Uh-humm!" she clears her throat. "Whew! Wow... well thanks for all of your help, Tom. Maybe we'll see you again sometime."

Tom can see that this is all making the normally well-put-together Starr Powers very uncomfortable, so he decides that now would be a good time to make a polite exit. The other boy rushes to finish hooking up the fluids so the two of them make their leave. Tom takes one last look back at Starr before disappearing out the door. She starts blushing again, then laughs it off while shooing him out.

13

"Wow Starr, you really had us worried. What happened?" Trooper asks. He tries as hard as he can to not let her notice his jealousy of her obvious affection for the EMT.

"It's just... when you said Angel... I... I," she says as she tries to keep the tears down again. "She was my best friend. We spent so much time together before she... she..." Now she can't stop the tears and The Chemo Kid hands her a tissue. "Thank you, Duke," she responds.

After a rather un-lady-like blowing of the nose, Starr quietly speaks again. "Angel and I were inseparable when we were in together... she practically took out all the germ warriors on the floor in one battle, but Neuro made it his pet project to get her back. Her stem cell transplant and total body irradiation really took its toll on her body, and Neuro did the rest. I almost gave up when she went." Trooper and The Kid have to bite their bottom lips to keep from crying now too.

After a quiet and awkward moment, The Chemo Kid finally speaks. "I'm so sorry, you guys. I don't know what to say. She sounds like a great girl. I wish I could have known her. This must be a different Angel though, because she's in the room right next to mine."

"We better look at the tape," Starr says as she wipes tears away from her eyes. She motions to a boy who is sitting at a computer and he clicks the keys until the TV shows The Chemo Kid and Ivy leaving Trooper's room. They all lean in close to try and see who stops the duo on their way back to their room. They see them stop and peer into a dark doorway. Then suddenly, they whirl around in the middle of the hall. The Kid is leaning off of Ivy and almost falling, but she scoops him up and steadies him before James the Janitor appears from the opposite side of the hallway. He wheels The Kid and Ivy away. The tape doesn't show anyone inside the dark room. It never displays anyone handing The Chemo Kid a letter. The only figures in the hallway during that time period were Ivy, James the Janitor, and The Chemo Kid.

"Mario... can you come in here dear?" Starr calls into a black box on her desk. Mario comes scurrying into the office and perches himself in front of her desk before The Chemo Kid can even process what he just saw. "Mario, can you please tell me who is registered to the room next to Duke Dillan?" she asks. Mario's right hand types with blazing speed on the handheld device in his other hand. He then mumbling, "Well, according to the official hospital log, that the room is empty and has been for four days, fourteen hours and thirty-two minutes."

"That's impossible!" yells Duke finally. "I'm telling you... a beautiful girl with blue eyes and brown curly hair stopped me. She gave me that letter! She even kissed me on the cheek! It had to be real... it just had to!" Duke is starting to cry. His emotions are getting the best of him.

"It's alright Duke," Starr says as she comes around the desk and hugs him. "You may have been dreaming all of it… but that doesn't mean it wasn't real. We all have dreams and they are very real. All of our enemies can get to us whether we're sleeping or awake. As for Angel, I wouldn't put it past her. She was one of the best in life. I know she's still with us in spirit, so maybe she has found a way to communicate."

Starr takes a framed picture off of the windowsill. She raises it in front of Duke's face. He take a long moment to focus on the picture, then looks to the floor.

"That's her. That's Angel," he says.

14

Duke is more than a little shocked. Did he really get a kiss from a ghost? It felt so real. Starr said it could still be real, so Duke decides to hold on to that notion. Even if Angel is only a dream, he still wants to see her again.

First, he picks up his head, then he stands up to address the room. With a far off stare, The Chemo Kid says, "I know I haven't been here for very long, but I feel like I have known Neuro my whole life. I've always felt like some creep is lurking around every corner waiting to jump out and get me. This fear is even stronger in my dreams. It doesn't matter whether it's my usual nightmare where I'm slowly walking down a wooded path toward the sunset, or whether it's a fun dream like surfing in California… there is always something in the back of my mind that keeps me from feeling comfortable. Someone's always watching me. But no matter where I look, I can't see anyone."

"I guess I always knew that it would come to some kind of showdown. However, I never guessed that I had cancer. You know what the funny thing is? I'm not even scared of the cancer. I'm a little afraid of needles, and I don't think I want to get one of those tubes up my nose, but the thing that really scares me is the thought of losing my friends. I never really had too many friends before, but over these last few days, I've met the most exciting and amazing people. I don't officially know you guys that well… but I feel like I do. I feel like you are my friends. I want to fight for you. I want to help every kid in this hospital, and beyond. I want to beat Neuro for all of them…" The Kid pauses for a single breath. He looks Starr in the eyes and continues, "… especially Angel."

The other kids remain silent for a minute. Then Trooper sets his hand on The Chemo Kid's shoulder in a show of support. He looks over at Starr, and she nods. The Chemo Kid has cleansed both Starr Powers and Trooper Pheonix of any doubt that may have been lingering in their minds. The Chemo Kid is for real, and they are going to join him in the biggest war this, or any, hospital has ever hosted.

The Kid lets the moment linger, then says, "I think I want to go back and see my mom and dad now."

"Sure thing," Starr responds without hesitation. "Trooper, will you show Mr. Dillan how to get back?"

15

Trooper escorts The Chemo Kid and Ivy back to the doorway that leads to the Soiled Utilities closet across from his hospital room. "Dude, I know this is a lot to take in," he says. "It will be best if we all just take it slowly, OK? You've got a big day tomorrow. You'll be out of commission pretty much all day with tests and family matters. Don't worry about it. We got your back. Come back only when you're ready. We'll map out our game plan then." Trooper then initiates a Reverse Fireworks

Fist-Bump. The Kid responds in kind.

He turns around to grab the door handle, but pauses. He turns back and says, "We're gonna beat this creep… me and you… for Angel." Then he turns back, and opens the door. Before he steps inside, he adds, "God help us."

Ivy waits for The Kid to fully breech the threshold then rolls through, just before the door closes. It is pitch black in this tiny room. Neither The Kid nor Ivy can move more than a few inches without bumping into some kind of equipment with a clatter. They don't even have time to panic, though, because the door is quickly reopened behind them. The Chemo Kid looks back over his shoulder to see James the Janitor.

"Welcome back, Mr. Dillan…" he says with a wink. "Let's getcha back to bed."

Duke climbs out of the cluster of brooms and mops by himself while James clears a path for Ivy. "Your room's right there," James says, pointing across the hall.

Duke stares at James. He wonders how much he knows. James just smiles and gently opens the door to his room. Duke takes his cue and shuffles quietly though the doorway, getting more and more sleepy with every step. He doesn't even look back to thank James or be sure Ivy is following him. He just climbs back into his bed and falls asleep. James shuts the door silently behind the little superhero and his robotic friend. He then walks briskly around the corner to report Duke's return to Dr. Houston.

Chapter Thirteen

'Scan-xiety'

1

When Duke wakes up in his hospital room the next morning, he can tell that today will be different from the first few days of his visit here at The Children's Hospital. He tries to keep his eyes shut for as long as possible, but the day is already in full swing. The room is filled with sunlight. His parents are striding around the room collecting themselves. Nurse Andrea is standing above him, cleaning the end of his tubes with little squares of antiseptic that smell similar to The Chemo Kid's sanitizer grenades... but not exactly.

"I'm just cleaning your tubies, OK sweetie?" she says to him as he gives in to the morning rustling and opens his eyes. "We're going to get you ready for your tests today."

"Ugh! The tests! I totally forgot! I can't believe I slept this late!" he thinks to himself, fully expecting a calming response in a sweet monotone voice. He even falls back to his pillow in dramatic fashion to show off for Ivy. When there is no response, he bolts upright to see that his five-wheeled friend is sitting alone, in the corner by the computer.

Duke's eyes are still adjusting to the light so he blinks a few times to see more clearly. He can see Ivy, but she is too far away to still be attached to him. She is plugged into the wall. Her monitors are dark and her pumps are silent. She must be completely shut down!

He hasn't even realized they were separated for more than ten seconds, but he already misses her badly. A tear falls down his cheek and he feels a burning, dull pain in his heart. He doesn't even cry this way when his mom drops him off at Aunt Shelly's house anymore. This is the first time in months that he is actually crying out of despair and not just to get what he wants.

"Ohh sweetie, it's OK… don't cry…" Nurse Andrea says as she puts her hand softly behind his neck.

"Thiiii-hi-hi-his…" struggles Duke loudly, as he points his tiny index finger at his pole on the other side of the room. His high-pitched whine has everyone passing by in the hallway scrunching up their faces and covering their ears as if there was a fire engine in there. The family members and attendants inside the room don't mind the volume as much, because they can see the sadness and disappointment in Duke's face. Their instincts tell them to do whatever they can to him to feel better.

"What's wrong, sweetie? You don't have to worry. You'll get hooked up to another pole down there," Andrea says with a genuine smile as Duke's mother and father rush to his side.

Duke strategically builds the volume and pitch of his response to create the perfect crescendo. He doesn't want another IV pole. "Nooo-OOOO-OOOOO," he wails then abruptly cuts the siren short by holding his breath. Everybody in the room knows that the longer a kid can hold their breath, the louder the battle cry once the breath is let out. They can see Duke is prepared to hold out for a long time on this one.

"It's OK. It's OK," proclaims everyone in the room at the same time.

"We can hook you back up to that IV pole if you want, sweetie. OK?" Nurse Andrea interjects. She hopes to be in time to prevent the breath-holding outburst, but she squishes her face in preparation for another wave of screaming because she is not quite sure.

"Yeeeeaaaah!" replies Duke. His voice bursts from his mouth gleefully. "Dat my ivy pole!" he continues in the cutest voice ever. This sends the girls in the room into a fit of hysterics all their own. They're jumping around making faces and saying how cute and smart he is. Nurse Andrea is even blushing and commenting that he's the most adorable thing she's ever seen. She then re-wipes his tubes with alcohol, and re-connects him to his mechanical friend.

When the task is completed, with the ceremonial twisting and wiping of the plastic caps for fifteen seconds, Duke's dad grabs him under his twig-arms and hoists him up. "Whoa," he says, "I never realized how skinny you were getting. I can feel your ribs! We're going to have to get you fattened up."

"I'll have them page Elizabeth Wallace to come and see you when you come back," says Nurse Andrea. "She's the nutritionist on the floor. She'll give you guys lots of ideas for how to get some weight on his bones!" The nurse then walks over to Duke and pinches his cheek. "You are just too cute! Do you know that?" she asks him. He just smiles and buries his head into his dad's shoulder.

Andrea unplugs Ivy from the wall and she lets out an involuntary bleep signifying that she's fully charged. She wheels over the pole that Duke was so adamant about staying connected to, and Jesse takes a hold of it. "Ohh, I can see why he likes this one so much. This one is so bright, and it looks really sturdy," he says as he looks at the colorful monitors.

Just then, Ivy turns to him and chimes a bit. Duke quickly chuckles and says, "Funny, Daddy, you funny!" in an effort to disguise the extraordinary actions of his IV pole. Everyone else cracks up in response to Duke's comment, but Duke's father is suspicious. He feigns laughter, but Duke and Ivy can tell the distraction didn't quite work by the look on his face. Maybe he is starting to catch on that there is more than meets the eye when it comes to his son's IV pole.

2

Now that Duke is content, everyone has time to gather their things and head out for the day of testing. On their way down the hall, they walk directly past the room that Duke now knows for certain belonged to a beautiful girl named Angel before she died. He's still not sure if he dreamed their encounter in the hallway or if he was awake. Either way, he is convinced that it was real. With an innocent kiss and a magical note, that beautiful little girl gave Duke the motivation and information he needed to fully commit to the responsibilities of being The Chemo Kid.

He peers inside and catches a glimpse of the freshly scrubbed room. He's not sure if Angel's parents painted the windows in her room like his have, but the three giant panes of glass are now polished to a streak-free shine. The bed is stripped down to the plastic liner over the mattress.

Jesse sets Duke down, right in the doorway of the vacant room. He turns and watches Nurse Andrea, who is on hold on the hallway phone for a confirmation from the sedation team that they are ready for them. Duke takes this opportunity to take a closer look at Angel's room in the daylight.

He nudges Ivy slowly through the doorway, hoping his father doesn't notice them sneak away. Inside, he focuses on the sun-glare shining from the skylights ten stories above the Emergency Room. It's throwing an eerie haze across the floor. The effect is so mesmerizing that he imagines he can see Angel's silhouette standing in the corner of the room trimmed by a sunny glow.

"She was one of the best, you know..." says the silhouette.

Duke and Ivy simultaneously gasp in surprise. Duke throws his hand over his mouth and Ivy quickly turns on her mute function to keep from alerting his father with any more unexpected noises. They peer deeper into the shadows.

"I knew that girl fo' a long time... most of her life," continues the figure as he steps into the filtered sunlight. It's not Ivy. It's James the Janitor, pushing a wet mop in front of him. He pauses and leans his chin on the handle of the mop. Duke can see a tear forming in the corner of James's eye. It's clearly been preceded by others, evidenced by the trails down the side of his weathered face.

Duke closes his eyes, shakes his head, and decides to accept James's habit of appearing unexpectedly from the shadows. When he opens his eyes, he sees something beyond James's wet mop on the floor. "What's that?" he asks as he shuffles over to pick up a small object under the bed.

James wipes his nose with a handkerchief he pulled from his back pocket and asks, "What'd ya find?" Then he stuffs the kerchief back in his trousers.

"It's a star," Duke replies. He holds the pink plastic trinket up to the light from the skylights. As he turns it over, he can see that Angel's picture is inside. "It's a picture," he says and hands it to James.

"Ohh my…" James says. "Weren't she a pretty little girl?" He has the hankie out of his pocket again wiping his nose and then brushing away more tears with the back of his hand.

"You keep it," Duke says, seeing the joy that the locket has brought to James's face.

James smiles. "No, no kid… This one was lef' here special for you. I seen it before. Now you hold onto it good." he says returning the star back to Duke then using his huge hand to close Duke's over it.

Their moment is broken by the sound of Duke's dad rushing into the room. "C'mon Duke…" says Jesse. James turns his face away to hide his emotion. "I'm sorry, this little guy keeps bothering you," Jesse says to the custodian who quickly returns to his mopping.

"He ain't no bother to me!" James replies without looking up from his work.

With that, Jesse sweeps Duke up in his right arm and pushes Ivy into the hall to where Maggie and Andrea wait. Duke watches over Jesse's shoulder as James turns to look at Angel's empty bed. His head is hung low and his hand rubs his jaw and the mop falls to the floor with a single crack!

Nurse Andrea swipes an ID badge across a black box on the wall. It beeps, the door clicks and then swings open without assistance. Out into the bustling halls of the main hospital complex they walk. For Duke, it's his first time off the floors of 3 South in days. It's loud, and even though they are well within the building, he can almost feel the fresh outside air.

In the Oncology wing, the air is super-filtered, dry, and sterilized to the point of static-electricity. If you take too deep of a breath you might get zapped on the nose. Out here, in the public halls of The Children's Hospital, the air is wet and thick. Duke immediately becomes aware of the coughs from across the hall. He can smell stale cigarette smoke on someone's clothes. Most of the outsiders look down at the floor once they've gotten a look at his black eye. He wonder's what's up with them.

"Don't worry about them, Duke," Ivy tries to tell him discretely.

Andrea stops in the middle of the hallway and presses a few buttons on Ivy's pumps in response to the beeping. Then she re-establishes her quick pace for just a few more steps before she swipes her ID card on another black box. With another beep, another door swings open, leading them to another brightly lit hallway. This one is empty. The sign says, 'Radiology.'

They walk through empty halls until they approach a bigger doorway. This one doesn't need an ID swipe. It swings open like magic. Andrea doesn't even have to slow her gait. She nods to the woman sitting behind the desk, and without a word or a moment's hesitation, a new nurse appears from behind the seated woman. She leads the group to their room.

The group enters the new room. Jesse lays Duke on the bed. His mommy and GG immediately climb in on either side of him. This is routine has become commonplace lately, so Duke doesn't say anything. It embarrasses him to no end, but he can tell that the two leading ladies in his life are at their wits end. If all it takes to keep them sane is a little cuddle time, then he's obliged to cuddle.

Nurse Andrea walks around to the side of the bed opposite of Ivy. She pulls a TV toward her new favorite patient. She tunes it to his favorite show without even having to be asked. Duke puts both hands behind his head and just watches TV. This pose starts another chorus of "AWWW!" from the ladies. Duke has perfected the art of cuteness. He pretends to be ignorant of his charm and crosses his feet nonchalantly to complete the picture for them. He looks more like he's sitting on the beach somewhere rather than in the hospital waiting for sedation and a CT-Scan. All he needs now is a pair of shades and some flip-flops!

As Jesse shuffles around the room trying to be useful, different nurses and doctors come in and out. Duke just lies there watching Gary the Green Dragon, with two fussing and loving women at his side. He has decided to let the grown-ups in white coats do what they have to do without incident. He thinks it is the best strategy to get these procedures over as soon as possible. He is acting cool about it, but Ivy can tell he is anxious about both the tests and getting back to help Trooper & Starr in their imminent war with The Nasty Neuro.

A friendly male nurse approaches Duke and tries to rouse him from his TV induced trance. "Hello Duke, my name is Mike," he says. Mike had been in and out several times already with the doctors. Duke responds with one of his ear eardrum piercing-pterodactyl screeches.

"Aaaawkk!" he calls, looking away from the TV for just a split second directly into Mike's eyes. Mike steps back and blinks. Dr. Houston warned him about Duke's dinosaur cries, but he didn't think it would be so intense. He feels like he just looked directly into the eyes of a real flying lizard!

Mike takes a moment to gather himself, shakes his head, then re-addresses the little boy. "Ummm, Duke? May I please take your blood pressure and put this pulse/ox on your finger? It's just a hug on your arm, and a band-aid on your finger for a little while. What do you say?" Then he adds, "It's nothing a dinosaur can't handle." He has obviously done this before. Even though he was caught off guard, he still knows just what tone to take with the boy-pterodactyl. Duke appreciates his effort and lifts his arm up for him without taking his eyes off of his show this time. He's seen the blood pressure cuffs and pulse oximeters a hundred times since he's been here. It's no big deal to him, but he's not going to let the nurse know that so easily.

Mike finishes this round of vital signs. He pulls on Jesse's sleeve and whispers to him that he'll be back in soon with the sedation team. As he walks out the door, he thinks better of keeping a secret from the boy with the impressive dinosaur scream. He turns back and says, "I'll be back in a minute, Duke." Duke raises his hand to say goodbye, once again not letting his eyes leave the TV. The nurse smiles and then slips out the door.

When he returns, Duke's nurse, Mike, has a tray full of syringes and alcohol wipes. He is followed into the room by a doctor that Duke hasn't met. Duke opens his mouth to squawk at the doctor, but decides to remain silent as the man tells his family about the procedures and drugs they will be using on their little boy. Duke can't decide if wants to listen or ignore what the new doctor is saying. Ultimately, he decides to keep his focus on the TV while monitoring his nurse with his peripheral vision.

Mike is preparing different saline flushes and sedation medications on a rolling metal cart, which he slides over the foot of the bed. Duke sees him grab a non-generic syringe, scrub his tubes with alcohol and attach them to each other. He pushes about three-quarters of the solution in the syringe into Duke's tubes. Duke feels nothing at first, but after the nimble-fingered nurse sets up the next one and presses the plunger, he begins to feel very happy.

Gary the Green Dragon suddenly seems a whole lot bigger than what could fit on the thirteen-inch screen just moments ago. All the adults chuckle as Duke, whose eyes grow bigger and fixate completely on the TV set, nestles back into his pillow. Mike infuses the boy with a couple more doses, and Duke's eyes soften. He drifts off to sleep.

(Polka-style music playing)

> *ABC-123, we're a great big family!*
>
> *Everything is alright, don't worry,*
>
> *It's you and me and our pal Gary!*
>
> *We're tra-vel-lin' through history!*

(Music changes to hip-hop)

> *It's your super-funky-fresh-alistic half-hour program.*
>
> *Stupendous, momentous, it's your favorite show, man!*
>
> *The prehistoric, host from a far and away land.*
>
> *So everybody clap your hands for the Dragon!*
>
> *It's Gary the Green Dragon!*

Applause and cheering from a large number of children grows in volume as the funky rhythm continues. Flames are blowing out the tops of makeshift volcanoes and sweet-smelling red goo is floating down the sides of the mountain.

"Hey everybody, it's your favorite pal, Gary the Green Dragon!" *proclaims a voice off-stage.*

Gary runs on-stage, followed by a group of elaborately dressed kids. The crowd erupts again. This time the camera scans the crowd. Each of them is wearing so much branded paraphernalia that it's no surprise Gary drives a Lamborghini! Dragon tails on sticks are waved high, and kids in Gary costumes have set up a conga line to re-enact one of his classic skits. It looks more like a pro football game than the set of a TV show.

*"Hey kids… today we're going to learn about cancer!"
exclaims Gary cheerfully. "Can anyone tell me what
cancer is?"*

The live studio audience lets out a long, "BOOOOOO."

*The kids on the set behind Gary look at each other with
forced smiles, shrugging their shoulders as if to say, "I
don't know, do you?" Then they turn to the audience
and freeze. They stare into the cameras with emotionless
smiles plastered across their faces.*

*The Chemo Kid watches all of this, mounted on Ivy,
from the shadows behind the audience's bleachers. He's
not sure why he's lurking this way, but he knows that he
doesn't want to be seen.*

*"Well kids… cancer is a terrible disease that attacks
innocent children without warning!" Gary loudly
pronounces while gesticulating wildly with his arms. His
movements morph into a bizarre dance that is replicated
by the awkwardly smiling group of kids on stage. The
energy is quickly passed to the studio audience. They
scream louder and start to jump up and down on the
bleachers.*

*In their excitement, an audience member kicks over a
huge cup of soda right in front of Duke and Ivy. The Gary
branded plastic cup explodes at their feet. They jump
back, trying to avoid the sticky splash, but are amazed to
see that the soda doesn't splash them at all. It goes right
through them.*

*The Chemo Kid and Ivy look at each other perplexed.
Just then, another kid swings a foot back that would*

surely have smacked Duke right in the head... but it goes right through too. Ivy decides to roll them out of the shadows into the lights to get a better look.

They are practically onstage when they realize that no one can see them. The Kid steps off Ivy and waves his arms directly in front the face of the only audience member that isn't jumping up and down wildly. The fat boy looks straight through The Kid, continuing to suck on his Gary lollipop and stare at the dancing green dragon on-stage. In an act of frustration, The Kid tries to grab the lollipop from the boy's grasp. His arm passes right through the apparition causing The Chemo Kid to lose balance. He spins around and stumbles in a circle until Ivy sweeps him securely onto her base before he can fall to the ground. They catch their breath together and watch the crazed faces of the holographic Gary fans bounce on the bleachers as the over-stuffed dragon prances around the stage.

6

While their son lies fully sedated and dreaming, the Dillan family silently fear the worst for their little boy. Images of pain and thoughts of helplessness have been common lately, but sitting in this room labeled Nuclear Medicine, watching as Duke's emaciated body is scanned for cancerous cells is the darkest moment yet. Even noticing that his black-eye has started to subside fails to break the heavy spell of sadness. In other contexts this might inspire optimism, but, each in their own way, they can't help but think what life would have been like if Duke's eye had begun to heal on its own at home.

Maggie Dillan is taking it the hardest. She's been living her worst nightmare for the last few days. Her baby boy, whom she loves so dearly, has been diagnosed with a deadly form of childhood cancer. She is living in fear of every word uttered from a doctor's mouth at this point. The anticipation of what they might say to her later this afternoon after these tests is almost too much to bear. As she sits in that room with the image of Duke's tiny body appearing on the screen, she is silently screaming. When she can't take the stress anymore, she walks away from the monitors, pacing the room and trying to strike up a conversation with whoever will talk to her. Anything is better than her own thoughts.

Jesse Dillan is focused on the scan. His anxieties are buried deep beneath this skin. Judging by the doctors' tones over the last few days, and from over-hearing their conversations, he's fully expecting the worst possible scenario. Even though no hint of surprise surfaces when he sees the glow of a golf ball shaped tumor above Duke's eye on the monitor, the painful reality of it still hits him like a hard blow to the gut.

The scanner continues to do its work, making the image on the screen increasingly easier to make out. Clearly displayed is a picture of Duke with a large tumor on his left side, which Dr. Houston already told them could be stemming from the Adrenal gland. Also obvious is the spot above his right eye. The area inside the chest and abdomen are obscured because various organs and glands glow on this scan as well. Therefore, Jesse can't truly make an accurate assumption about the results there. The last thing he sees before walking over to put his arm around Maggie is a glowing spot below and above the knee on both legs. They stand there in the observation area until Duke is wheeled back into the sedation room, silently looking at the ground. They need to be near their son, but they just don't want to see his disease lit up on high definition computer monitors anymore.

7

As Duke is carted back to the recovery area with his family in tow, his vivid dreaming continues.

"Well today kids, we have a special guest!" shouts Gary. "Everyone give a great big Gary welcome to my pal, Mr. T-Rex!"

The audience jumps to its feet. Thunder crashes, and the on-stage volcano spits out a burst of steam while more red goo melts down the side. Gary has the same super-duper excitement in his voice as he does when he introduces guests like Larry the Left-handed Llama and Percy the Penguin.

Out steps a character that Duke has never seen on his favorite show before. He climbs onto Ivy and skates around to the side of the stage. A huge Tyrannosaurus Rex is now roaring at center stage, sending the crowd into an even more furious uproar. Even though Duke has always liked dragons, he is scared to death of dinosaurs, especially T-Rex. Even Duke hasn't been able to explain why. In tandem with his gasp of fear, the volcano erupts again, this time showering the first two rows with steaming muck. Youngsters in Gary brand ponchos scream with delight. The Kid is certainly not echoing their excitement.

Ivy wheels the two of them to the front row. The Chemo Kid is still not sure why they're here, but he wants to get a better look at Mr. T-Rex from as close as possible none-the-less. In this dream environment, he seems able to control his fear of prehistoric meat-eating carnivores. As they reach the edge of the stage, Ivy feels The Kid suddenly squeeze his grip and shake even more tension than when he first saw the dinosaur.

"What is it?" she asks.

The Chemo Kid is mesmerized. He doesn't answer, so Ivy looks to where his eyes are now locked and sees what has drawn his attention. It's Angel, sitting Indian-style on stage, with the rest of the junior dragons. Ivy decides to snap The Kid out of his trance by abruptly scooting backwards, almost allowing him to fall forward, then catching him again with a quick hop toward the stage.

"It's her!" shouts The Chemo Kid. At first he's afraid he'll be heard, but then he remembers that no one can see them. "What is she doing here?" he exclaims.

Mr. T-Rex is on-stage with Gary, and they are doing the 'Pterodactyl Tango' together in the middle of the junior dragons. Pterry the Pterodactyl is hovering overhead and a repetitive and annoying song about flying lizards is playing loudly. The audience is cheering louder and louder as the two massive characters do their dance on-stage.

Something is not quite right with the terrible lizard alongside Gary. Mr. T-Rex's costume doesn't seem to fit him right. It keeps flapping open in the back. As a matter of fact, his costume seems to be disintegrating as he shakes his tail and stomps around. It only takes another moment for The Chemo Kid to realize that under this shabby costume is the shadowy figure from his nightmares. The Kid now knows this creature is none other than The Nasty Neuro!

On-stage, Gary continues to dance and smile ear-to-ear. The Nasty Neuro mimics him with a false grin that stretches the folds of his oily, pimple-covered face, exposing teeth that look like Stonehenge. The whites of his pinpoint eyes hardly appear as he laughs and spits out gobs of slime and nasty stuff.

"What is Gary doing with him?" The Kid quietly asks Ivy.

Instead of answering him, Ivy pulls The Kid to the back row, away from the lights, just in case Nasty can see them. The Chemo Kid fights Ivy to look over the crazed audience toward Angel again. He's worried for her and the other kids... but she's gone. He darts his focus around the stage to find her and catches a glimpse of a small tail heading behind the curtains on left side of the stage. He convinces Ivy to follow her.

"Why are these kids cheering for Neuro? They need to get as far away from him as they can!" exclaims The Kid as they rush through the crowd to stage right.

"They probably can't see him for what he really is," Ivy answers. "No one can see Neuro unless they actually have cancer. All they see is Mr. T-Rex out there, with his fifty gold chains and mohawk, stomping his feet and roaring."

On cue, Mr. T-Rex bellows from the stage, "RRROOOOAARR!" The audience goes to their feet again with a thunderous applause, momentarily cutting off The Chemo Kid's view of Angel. It takes a few moments after the crowd calms again for Ivy's keen eye to reestablish Angel's pink dragon tail as it wiggles behind a curtain. Ivy sneaks The Kid backstage in pursuit.

The two of them follow the tiny dragon as she works her way around the back of the stage, finally stopping directly behind Neuro. She empties a surprising number of sanitizer bombs from her costume before pulling it off completely, revealing a pink body suit, with more ammunition strapped across her chest. The Kid's eyes grow wide, seeing her in full battle mode. She's even more beautiful than he remembers as her curly brown hair unravels down her back.

Just then, a fire alarm sounds, and an army of germ warriors flood the sound stage with a surprise attack. Sprinklers rain down cold water on the whole scene, completing the disintegration of Neuro's Mr. T-Rex costume. He lets out a menacing laugh and bounds off-stage before The Chemo Kid can even get a good look at him. Kids scream for their mommies as others sprint around the room looking for an exit unguarded by bacteria monsters. It's a hopeless effort because the multi-colored germ army has the scene completely surrounded.

Gary has been running around in circles on stage. In his hysteria, he slams into the make-shift mountain of lava and drops to the floor. The massive paper mache volcano dumps its bubbling red slime over him. He is out cold! The stage has been crawling with germy fiends, and they descend on Gary in an instant. There are too many shades of colored monsters to count.

Blue, Green, Red, and Purple jump on Gary's big belly. A menacing rainbow of troops then form a ring around the lead attackers. Shoulder to shoulder they stand, on the ready, holding their weapons tightly as their eyes dart all around, with beads of sweat forming on their hideous faces.

They never even see what hits them as Angel shoots

out from behind the stage and lights them up with sanitizer bombs. The projectiles from this first volley hit four germs each, easily clearing the ring of rainbow soldiers. Colorful slime flies everywhere. Her bombs even irradiate the stink of these guys as they melt onto the stage.

She cartwheels toward center stage to address the gang who is standing over Gary coughing in his face. "Nobody messes with Gary!" she shouts. Then, without further ado, she wipes them out with four quick sanitizer blasts, two from each hand.

The antiseptic splashing on his face starts to wake Gary up. Angel tries to scoot him toward the backstage door. Realizing her wheeled base would come in handy, Ivy zips over to help Angel move Gary. When she reaches center stage, Angel seems surprised to see an IV pole there, but she doesn't have too much time to think it over. She loads the oversized green lizard onto the makeshift dolly in a hurry and pushes him toward the backstage door. By this time, The Chemo Kid has run over to the door and opened it for her.

"Thanks," whispers Gary the Green Dragon from Ivy's base.

"No problem," replies Angel as she yanks Ivy backwards launching the dragon out the door.

She grabs the door out of The Chemo Kid's hands and slams it shut. The Kid isn't sure if she saw him but he looks to the floor shyly in any case, avoiding eye contact. If she can see him or not, he still wishes he had the words prepared to address his dream girl properly. By the time he looks up, Angel has shoved a plastic branch diagonally through the handle to safely lock Gary out

233

and has strode back on-stage, ready to re-engage in the battle.

The Kid and Ivy are surprised to see the germ-gang is nowhere in sight. Even the frantic screaming children are gone. All they see is Angel stepping softly over puddles of bubbling bacteria goo. She silently prowls through the spray from the sprinklers overhead, searching for signs of danger. Angel moves like a cat through the cluttered theater, eventually creeping up on a doorway that is partly open.

"He's in there!" Ivy alerts The Chemo Kid.

"How do you know?" he asks.

"I can see him. I can see past the corner by manipulating an image off of anything reflective in the area: a wristwatch, broken glass, or anything that is reflective or extra shiny. I can just see Neuro's shadow. He's in the right rear corner, behind some boxes. She's got him cornered."

"Or does he have her right where he wants her?" asks The Kid.

He cranes his neck to see if he too can catch the reflection. He gives up quickly though, realizing he doesn't have the benefit of highly sensitive digital sensors like Ivy. Instead, he mounts his robot partner and races quietly to Angel's side.

Angel spins around as they approach and freezes. This time it is obvious that she can see The Chemo Kid. He doesn't know whether to be happy or sad about this, because, at first, she seems annoyed. However, once he and Ivy get to her side, Angel softens and gives The Kid a wink.

He is excited by the intensity and acceptance he sees in Angel's face. Neither say anything to each other. Angel just smiles and looks upward, closing her eyes and then opening them again. Her eyes glow so blue that Duke nearly falls back on Ivy. She smiles again then turns to the doorway. The Kid and Ivy follow step for step behind her. As she approaches the door she turns and blows a kiss and opens the door. A bright light shines all around her, and she walks inside. The door closes behind her and the light goes out.

8

"I think he's waking up," Maggie announces to the half-dozen or so who have overfilled the room and the hallway outside. G.G. and Poppy have been waiting here the whole time because they couldn't stand to sit through the scan. Aunt Ne-Ne is here because she couldn't stand to sit through work. She took the day off to support the Dillan family. Mom-Mom Jo and a few more supportive faces appear in the glass, steaming it. Everyone is hoping to get a view of their favorite kid as he wakes from sedation.

Duke begins to stir but feels like he's been beaten up. His head is spinning with thoughts of Angel and what the dream could mean. When he takes a peek through half closed eyelids, the faces he sees in the window are contorted and unfamiliar. Even the faces of his parents are unrecognizable to him at first. He shifts to his right side, and sees Ivy standing beside him. She looms larger than usual from this vantage point, and he almost doesn't recognize her either until a warm feeling slowly filters through his veins, reminding him of their friendship.

235

Duke waits a second, for this comfort to clear his mind, then turns over with a smile for his mom and dad.

"I want min-yum. I want moke," he says, sounding like one who is not yet awake, or maybe drunk. Poppy looks at Maggie and says, "What did he say?"

"He wants a banana and milk," she replies with a grin. She and her husband have learned the subtle nuances of their son's newly forming language. Duke giggles to himself, mostly because he is still feeling the effects of the sedation, but also because he is proud of his ability to mimic the subtle nuances of a child's newly forming language.

"You can give him a banana and milk… but not too much," Nurse Mike says. "We don't want him to throw up. I gave him something that would help his stomach, but you never know after they wake up from sedation."

Duke pays no attention to the nurse's advice. He grabs the banana and shoves half of it in his mouth.

"Slowly!" Mike insists.

Duke knows he'll be fine. He hasn't been this hungry for a long time.

Chapter Fourteen

From Dreams to Reality

1

Ivy stands silent in the corner of the room, inanimate, more like a fancy hat rack than a decorated hero. It's been twenty-five years since she was actively involved in high stakes action like this. The physical part of it is just as dangerous and fun as she remembers, but the emotional attachment she's developed with Duke scares her. She doesn't know if she'll be able to handle the pain if something were to happen to him.

She knows this scenario all too well from her many adventures chasing bad guys on the sixth floor. When one of these guys gets you into their sights, they go for the jugular, and if they can't get you, they'll get someone close to you. It's a brutal game. Ivy has more than her share of scars, and not the kind you see on the outside either. They can polish her shiny metal frame to a brilliant sheen, but who can wipe away the pain of friends lost?

Duke can read the distress in Ivy's monitors even though she is trying to hide it from him. All this down time from his sedation and testing has brought back difficult memories that she had been able to put away after a quarter century alone in a broom closet.

Duke doesn't know what to say to Ivy so he doesn't try. He stands up on his mattress and walks across his bed to the side closest to Ivy. He puts his hand through the bars and touches her pole. With eyes closed, Duke and Ivy share a silent prayer that only the two of them can hear, the two of them and God.

It doesn't happen immediately, but Duke notices, after a few minutes, that Ivy's pumps are starting to churn with a positive rhythm. He opens his eyes and sees the sparkle return to her monitors. Duke's wordless gesture rejuvenated Ivy's confidence. Even though her friends are no longer fighting beside her, Ivy knows that with The Chemo Kid and God's help, she will make them proud. Duke is happy he was able to lift his friend up by using the advice he's heard his missionary Uncle Simon say... "When you don't know what to do, pray."

2

"We need a plan," Duke says to Ivy as he's pacing back and forth in his bed. "We can't wait for Neuro to come attack us. We need to set up a trap for him."

Duke's got his Gary bath robe on and his dad's discarded bandana from the day before. Nurse Mike ordered him to stay in his room, with the pulse/ox band-aid around his finger, so he can be monitored for the next couple of hours until the effects of sedation wear off completely. He's making the most of his quarantine, though, harkening back to his 'Duke of Dragons' days. The same groove is being worn down in his mattress that would be in his bed back home, but this time it's not just make-believe.

"What do we know about Neuro?" he asks Ivy.

She responds with a couple beeps. A skull and cross-bones appears on her main screen.

"You got that right! He's a huge blob of liquid evil that strikes without warning and has a full cavalcade of germ warriors who can't wait to put their butts on the line for him. Oh yeah... and only kids who have had cancer can see the real him."

The young hero stands tall on his children's hospital bed with a determined, yet blank, look on his face. The truth is that neither Duke nor Ivy knows much of anything about Neuro at all. Where did he come from? Where is he headed? What are his strengths? What are his weaknesses? Does he have a goal, or is his mission simply indiscriminate evil? And the most common question asked about him... Why?

Suddenly, a light bulb appears on Ivy's main screen with a ding! Duke perks up with his head turned to the side and his brow furrowed.

3

By eight o' clock that evening, Duke has fully recovered from sedation and his parents have returned to the room. Jesse and Maggie are passing out on the aero-bed and Duke is trying his best to fake sleep so they don't wake up. In another fifteen minutes, the couple is out cold. This last week has been rough on them.

As Duke sits up slowly, he looks down at his parents. They've both given up their jobs to stay here with him. He heard them saying earlier, "'I don't know how we're going to pay the bills, but suddenly money just doesn't seem that important anymore..." At twenty-one months he could never really understand the importance of it anyway, but it sure does seem to make people crazy.

As Ivy slowly creeps around the bed, Duke begins to

climb over the rail. One false move now and the folks will be waking up for sure. Luckily, the TV is on full blast, as usual, so no one notices when he falls over the top rail to the ground with a thud directly onto Ivy's base. Duke rises to his feet extra slowly in order to gather himself. This vault over his bars wasn't as graceful as his previous. Maybe his day of testing was more strenuous on his body than he thought.

Ivy slides him over to the closet, and Duke steps inside. Whoever controls the mechanical arms inside the closet certainly seems to think that this battle is going to be tough. His super-onesie is literally sagging beneath the weight of his many cancer-fighting weapons. "What am I going to do with all this stuff?" The Chemo Kid muses once they are in the hall. Ivy emits a few authoritative sounding beeps and the assorted weaponry shifts around on his suit like a pack of mini-robot cockroaches.

"Yee-Ah!" The Chemo Kid yipes and dances back off of Ivy. Before The Kid sets off the mini-bombs on his chest by swatting at them like bugs, they quickly settle down and into their new places. The sanitizer grenades stack up in perfect little rows from his left shoulder to his right hip, then up his back to connect with the shoulder strap. If he pulls them off, one by one, another will feed up to the top until they're all gone. His Chemo Cannon is nowhere to be found, but when he reaches into the back of his waistband he easily pulls the massive needle-firing gun from wherever it was hiding. Ivy and The Kid look at each other and chuckle at the thought of where it was stashed. Even after he slips it comfortably back in his waistband, The Kid *still* can't tell where it is disappearing to.

The two purposefully take the long way in order to pass

Angel's room. It's dark and empty. He knows it was just a dream, but around here it doesn't seem to matter. He'd do anything to see her face again.

They continue past the Nourishment Room which causes Duke to shudder with the recollection of his mortar attack dream from the other night and the strange way that James the Janitor found him in the darkness. He shakes off the feeling. Down the halls they go to the very same corner where they staged their ambush attack on the germ warriors on his first trip to the place he and Ivy now know as 'Chemo Cove.'

This time, as they approach the playroom, there are no henchmen of the big Nasty there guarding the door. However, as The Kid tries to propel Ivy closer, she holds her ground.

"What is it? It's all clear, right?" The Chemo Kid asks. He's so ready to get going that he's jumping out of his skin. He would have made a costly rookie mistake and ran right out there if it weren't for Ivy.

"It seems clear... but look closer," Ivy says as she spins and tilts so he can see a nasty glob on the upper part of the doorway across the hall. It looks like the wall has a huge greasy pimple.

"What is it?" The Kid asks.

"It's a camera, I'm almost certain. It's been likely placed here to guard the door since Neuro can't trust his band of stink-monsters to guard it anymore... at least not with you around!" Ivy chimes and makes a funny face that looks like the Mr. Yuck stickers that are plastered all over the cleaning products under the sink at home. This makes Duke chuckle under his breath. "Can you hit it with one of your sanitizer grenades from here?" asks Ivy.

"I don't know. My old man always said I have a good arm... but it's pretty far," he says as he studies his target.

"Well... be sure, because if you miss, I'm sure they'll know we're here," she says.

"Great! No pressure!" The Kid replies.

He tears one of the grenades away from their Velcro strap and focuses his eyes to better gauge the distance. The Kid mutters a silent prayer then winds and fires. The miniature cylinder hurtles across the corridor until it lands directly on the spot and splatters, sending nasty multi-colored goo dripping down the wall. When the sagging mess finally reaches the ground a tiny metal chip frees itself from the mess. It trickles away from the glob on a drop of condensation as it sparks and steams until finally coming to a halt in the middle of the hallway. The Chemo Kid starts to move toward it, but Ivy stops him again.

"Let's go back to the Nourishment Room and grab a napkin or something. We still don't know if that thing is working or not. This way we can throw it over-top of the camera before we pick it up."

Ivy's always got the best ideas. They quickly backtrack to the Nourishment Room and find a dark cloth napkin that will just do the trick. Instead of chills, this time The Kid is thankful for the room's close proximity. He remembers the cold milk that James and his father found for him in the refrigerator and decides to grab a quick sip for energy before returning to the hallway.

When they return to the playroom entrance, the tiny

camera is still fizzing in the puddle of goo. They throw the cloth over it and head to the door. They are inside without incident. The code is entered into the Baby's First Laptop, and they slip into Chemo Cove, as if they have done it a thousand times before.

"Now, let's go see Starr and the others and fill them in on the plan," The Chemo Kid says.

4

As they roll through the nerve center of Chemo Cove, the reaction by the other kids is much different than the first time they came through. Everyone is high-fiving The Chemo Kid and murmuring about 3S19. Apparently, word spreads around here quickly. The Kid is somewhat of a popular one with the ladies these days as well. Girls are blushing and giggling as they pass, and a couple even blow him kisses. The Kid's got a big smile across his face and Ivy is absorbing every adulation. At least for the moment, all is well in Chemo Cove.

"Kid!" Trooper shouts from across the hall. "What's up, Dude? How did your scans go?"

"OK, I guess." The Chemo Kid says as he gets to where Trooper is standing. "I had the craziest dream while I was under, though. It actually gave me a pretty good idea about how we can set a trap for Neuro. Where's Starr? I want to get this all set up so we can start soon."

"Here, follow me. She's in the training room," says Trooper. "I swear it's no wonder she's so skinny. She works out all the time."

They walk over to the training room door. When they open it, they see Starr doing some type of martial arts

243

training. She does a 360-flip in mid air. When she lands, she knocks the feet out from under a fake germ warrior with a sweep kick.

"Whoa!" The Kid shouts. "That was awesome! You can really kick some butt!"

"Aww, that's sweet… but you haven't seen nothin' yet!" Starr exclaims.

She runs back across to the other side of the training room. From there she goes into a series of twisting and flipping moves that Bruce Lee would be proud of, knocking down practice dummies along the way with a "Yah!" or a "Hey!" She picks up a long stick and begins to twirl it in the air around her head and then her feet, bounding over it at all of the right times. Finally, she completes a pole-vault over the last dummy and lands just inches short of giving Duke a fresh black eye with her stick. The Kid falls to the floor in fear.

"Oops!" Starr giggles. "I'm sorry. Sometimes I just get a little carried away with myself."

Trooper rolls his eyes. He's seen all of this before.

"Now what brings you gentlemen here today?" Starr asks as one of her tiny assistants hands her a towel. She uses it to wipe the sweat from her face, then throws it to the floor. The same assistant quickly sweeps it up and shuffles off.

"Duke's got an idea he wants to run past you," Trooper replies. "And from the way he ran in here, it must be a doozie!"

The sassy acrobat cheers with glee, "Ohh goodie! I love strategizing! Let's call a meeting with the others, shall we?"

Before they know it, The Chemo Kid, Ivy and Trooper are sent away to gather key members of the team. Starr jogs to her office, along the way shouting out orders to Trooper and her two little assistants to go find the rest.

"Chop, chop people! We've got work to do!" she cheerfully directs with a smile.

5

The Chemo Kid and Ivy arrive at Starr's office with Mario Genioso and Tom the Medic. By the time they enter the doorway, there are already five other kids there: Trooper, the two Little Sluggers, and two older kids that The Kid has never seen before.

"Who are they?" The Kid asks a little nervously.

"Ohh, don't worry about them, they're the Hodgkins Kids, Dave and Kate," explains Trooper as they find a seat in Starr's office. "We call them in for the big jobs, you know, for the heavy lifting. You see, kids who get Hodgkins are usually a lot older, but they're every bit as important as us little guys. The only difference is that it's a lot harder for them to get around without being spotted. We had to sneak them in dressed as Environmental Services!" He points out a pile of blue scrubs on the floor. Everyone chuckles a little at the thought of Dave and Kate skulking around in janitor's clothes.

The Chemo Kid isn't in on the joke. Instead of laughing he says, "Actually, I think they could pass for custodians pretty well, if we just make their poles look like mops and buckets!"

"Brilliant idea, Mr. Dillan!" Mario interjects. "I'll begin

245

the schematics immediately!" Mario crashes through the group on his way to Starr's desk without taking his nose out of his laptop. Once he reaches the front of the room, he sits on a secondary office chair set perfectly for his dimensions. It looks diminutive and cheap next to Starr's throne, but he doesn't seem to mind. He is focused and excited, typing and peering over the monitor occasionally to eyeball the dimensions of the Hodgkins kids and their poles.

"People, people, people!" Starr blares like an actress bursting on stage for a grand entrance. "Welcome!" she proclaims, ignoring the fact that she is the one arriving. All of the side-conversations stop when she walks in, and the two little assistants quickly grab her fuzzy pink coat and scurry behind the desk to toss it up over the back of her chair. The coat makes her plush throne look even more comfortable.

"I trust you all have taken the liberty of introducing yourselves. You all already know who I am. I have been informed that Mr. Dillan has a plan to share with us," Starr announces. "Mr. Dillan, you have the floor. Hopefully you aren't wasting our time."

Everyone turns in unison to look at The Chemo Kid. He is startled by Starr's purposely caustic introduction. He wasn't prepared to be put on the spot so suddenly. However, with a bit of silent affirmation from Ivy and a pat on the shoulder from Trooper, The Kid stands up.

He can feel perspiration forming on his forehead as he takes a deep breath. All eyes are on him. The room is dead silent when he speaks.

"Hi… My name is Duke. I'm The Chemo Kid."

246

6

"I had a dream yesterday when I was under sedation. Ivy and I were in the audience at the Gary the Green Dragon show, and his special guest was a peculiar character I hadn't seen before. Under the cheap dinosaur costume I could see the stink waves rising up, like the guy was in a sauna or something."

"The experience was completely different than any dream I've had before. It was weird... like we were watching someone else's dream, actually. I think it may have been Angels dream!" explains The Chemo Kid. With that last statement, he turns to look at Starr. She is fully engrossed in his story.

"No one could see us, so we just watched. Angel snuck off-stage and got herself set-up to attack the creepy monster, but the germ warriors pulled the fire alarm. It was a trap, but she smoked them all before following Neuro into a dark room. We tried to follow, but the door closed in front of us. That's when I woke up."

As The Kid was telling his story to an enraptured audience, Starr slowly rose to her feet behind her desk and walked to the window. She stands with her back to the rest of the team with a far off look on her face. "She told me about that dream," Starr says. "Just before she passed... I kept telling her to wait for help, but she believed that she was meant to do it on her own." Then she turns to look The Chemo Kid directly in the eyes. "You see Mr. Dillan, around here, dreams and reality are one in the same."

7

"So what's the plan?" they ask as they all huddle closer.

"We're going to lure him out into the open, by setting up the same trap that he set for Angel." The Kid replies. "But this time, we'll have backup."

Chapter Fifteen

'No More Mr. Nice Guy'

1

Duke couldn't sleep all night. He just laid there thinking about everything. First of all, he just couldn't get Angel's face out of his mind. She's so beautiful. Secondly, he's got revenge on his mind. He won't be satisfied until Neuro pays for taking Angel and all the other terrible things he's been doing to kids around here.

Duke has lost track, but he goes over the plan in his mind again for what must be the sixteenth time. He hardly realizes when his mom opens the blinds letting the light in for the first time all morning.

"C'mon Dukey... We're going to go downstairs to the atrium. They're having a carnival for all the kids on the Oncology floor," she says. "They're going to have face-painting and a costume contest! Do you want to wear your Dukey Dude outfit?"

The regular crowd is gathering around his crib. GG and Poppy are there, as well as Mom-Mom Jo and Aunt Ne-Ne. They are awaiting Duke's answer with bated breath

"Nooooo..." whines Duke in his best little kid way. "I want to wear the dragon one GG buy me!" His smile makes the women in the room get all excited as usual.

"Ohh... well, OK," she says with a very well, how-do-you-do tone and a smile. Duke chuckles a little and says,

"Ohh Mommy!"

"I wanted you to save that for Halloween," she responds, "but you can open it now."

"Dukey Dude!" his dad exclaims as he strides in the door with his morning coffee. "How's my little buddy today?"

"A-good!" Duke responds, which sends a smile to his dad's lips. His old man has always liked it when Duke says it like that. Duke doesn't have the heart to let him know that he really doesn't talk like that anymore. He likes to make his folks happy however he can.

"Good! Are we ready to go? I think I saw some of the All-Stars players down there!" Duke's dad has his jersey, hat and the glimmer in his eye of a twelve-year-old boy who might get to meet some of his favorite guys from the team. Duke imagines his dad as a kid, but with his grown-up sized jersey and hat. He giggles a bit at the image, then smiles up at his dad, which makes both of his parents smile.

Jesse picks up his son and brings him down to the couch where he helps him into his costume. Maggie starts to tear up when she sees her son in his little dragon costume. She wasn't supposed to look yet, so she's got her hands over her face, peering between her fingers.

"Mommy... ready!" shouts Duke.

She removes her hands from in front of her face and says, "Whoa! You look so cool! Here, let me get Andrea to disconnect you from your tubies so you can be free to play..."

"Noooo, my Poe," he says as he steps on Ivy's base and

holds on tightly to her pole. Andrea strides through the door just in time to hear the exchange.

"Yeah, they actually want him to stay hooked up, for hydration, I mean. If it's a big deal I could page the resident to see if it's OK to unhook him…" she says.

"No, it's Ok, I guess," replies Maggie. "He seems to be getting really attached to that thing."

2

On the way out of the room, Duke points to Angel's room as has become his custom. He just wants to get one more glimpse of his friend. She's all he's been able to think about lately. He knows that she isn't really here in the flesh, but he's sure that she is as real as anyone else in The Children's Hospital. The door is closed and it's dark inside as usual.

"C'mon bud," his dad says. "I don't think there's anyone in there.

"Noooo!" Duke whines as he grasps at the air over his dad's shoulder. Jesse is right though. She's not in there. He carries Duke around the corner where Andrea and the mini-entourage wait.

3

Duke's family approaches the atrium en masse, and they smell the popcorn and cotton candy on the air in unison. It makes each of them think about home for just a second. The people here are great about putting on these little functions to try and retain some sort of normalcy for the families who are stuck here for weeks and months on end. Mostly people are very appreciative, but some families avoid the events at all cost. They'd rather not remember what they're missing at home. Some of the other kids are so sick, that they're not even allowed out of their rooms. Duke is counting his blessings that he's not that sick… not yet anyway.

He pauses for a minute as he thinks about the kids less fortunate than him at this moment. He even says a little prayer before he finally snaps back to it. The sounds and smells of the Oncology carnival bring him back. Despite the fun and frolicking, it is business time for Duke and his partners in the battle with The Nasty Neuro. Hopefully everyone is where they are supposed to be.

He looks around and immediately spots Trooper across the huge lobby on the staircase, just next to the scale-model of the hospital. He's decked out in his custom Stanley Steam-Engine get-up. He gives Duke a nod, and a 'choo-choo' motion with his fist. He motions with his eyes to the area that leads to the cafeteria.

"Look, there's The Big Guy!" Duke's dad says as he swings Duke around to see the All-Stars big slugger. Instead of looking for his father's favorite professional baseball player, Duke eyes the crowd that has gathered for autographs and photos. Brandon and Tommy are standing at the front of the pack in their baseball outfits. It's the perfect spot to cover the right flank, plus, while they are waiting, they've practically been able to meet the whole All-Stars team.

Tommy says something to Brandon and points his bat to where Duke is standing. Brandon looks in Duke's direction. He tips his cap and then blows a huge bubble. It explodes all over his face, sending his mother in with the paper towel that she wet by licking. Duke chuckles as he watches the kid try to wiggle away from one of the worst tortures known to kids.

Just then, and right on time, Starr Powers comes strolling down the staircase opposite of where Trooper is standing. The perfect distraction, she struts in complete with a camera crew from Channel 2. They're snapping photos and shooting footage for the upcoming prime-time telethon. Their goal is to pull on America's heartstrings with these shots of the famous, sick, Starr Powers. With the excuse of the cameras and her entourage, Starr is able to hang back to cover the left flank.

"Daddy, Daddy... I show MY costume!" Duke says, pointing to the stage where a pop-up tent is standing with a line of kids waiting to be entered into the costume contest. Mario, watching over the whole scene from his room overlooking the atrium, takes the cue, glances to all the lookouts to be sure they are set, then signals Trooper to make his way over to the sign-up tent.

Big Tom the Medic got himself set-up to work the sign-up booth outside the tent, since he's too old for all of this kid stuff. Once Duke and Trooper are checked into the contest, he gives a wink in Mario's direction. He can't see the pint-sized genius, but he's definitely up there in his room behind the Jurassic Park T-Rex that is painted on the window.

Mario jets over to the phone in his room and dials up Chemo Cove. "Pizza and Milk," he says into the headset. With that, the mousetrap is set into motion.

4

On stage, under the tent, the kids in the costume contest line up from tallest to shortest. The Hodgkins Kids, Dave and Kate, are there to assist them.

"We need a few bigger kids, if you catch my drift," Dave says into the microphone. "Are there any adults out there who would like to join our costume contest? You sir… that's a very funny costume!" he shouts to a parent in the front who is wearing his favorite jammies. The crowd laughs as the overweight man climbs up onto the stage in his pajamas. "Ok, we need one more. Who's it going to be?"

This is the moment of truth. The Kids all nervously watch to see if Big Nasty will take the bait. Silence prevails for a long minute as everyone in the crowd looks around to see who will be the last volunteer to have a little fun poked at him onstage.

"Here! I'll do it!" comes a voice from the crowd. At first no one can see who spoke. The sea of people eventually parts, allowing a hunched figure in a dingy T-Rex costume to make his way through. A thunderous applause from the crowd prompts the man to raise a paw in the air to acknowledge their cheers.

"OK, we have our contestants. Now you can all place your votes over here at the ballot box. In fifteen minutes we'll announce the finalists," Dave announces to the crowd.

Amid the commotion, Duke locks eyes with a beautiful little girl standing all by herself in the middle of the crowd. It's almost like she's glowing.

"It's her! It's Angel!" he says to Trooper, who has made his way behind him in line. Duke practically jumps out of line to go see her. Trooper has to grab him by the shoulder to snap him out of his trance.

"Dude, it's not her!" Trooper snips.

Duke looks again and sees that it's actually another little girl who only looks a little bit like Angel. The girl sees Duke looking and blushes as she turns away.

"Stay focused, buddy," says Trooper. "We got him right where we want him." Trooper waves his open hand in front of Duke's eyes. "C'mon, man… They're taking us back to the room."

5

When they get to the Clean Room, they take everyone over to the sani-station to sanitize their hands. The big guy declines because he's got a full body suit on that covers his hands too. The team is all huddled up pointing out the big T-Rex.

"That's our guy, right Duke?" Dave asks.

"It's got to be him," Kate says.

"I can't tell," replies Duke. "In my dream I could see the stink lines coming off of him and his suit was open in the back." Duke doesn't seem so confident. "It's got to be him though. Go ahead with the visual capture, Kate."

"Ahhhh, I'm going to beat all of you little pipsqueaks in this contest!" the T-Rex shouts to a group of other kids as they all try to climb on top of him.

T-Rex is grappling with the annoying kids. Kate takes advantage of his distraction to pull out her camera and a take of picture of the dingy dinosaur. In the camera flash, Duke sees the creep's eyes under the mask turn briefly red.

"That's got to be him!" Duke pipes excitedly. "I've seen those evil red eyes before in my dream. Let's move!"

Big Dave moves first. He heads to the front of the room and prepares to have each contestant file by him as they re-enter the stage for the finals. Duke blocks the doorway to the bathroom. He looks around to be sure Kate and Trooper have their doors covered, and then gives Dave the signal to call for the contestants' attention.

"Alright, I need everyone to line up in a single file line in this order: Kopelsky, Truman, Smith, Kraft..." Dave lists off the official child entrants first, leaving the T-Rex last. "Alright... once our meat-eating carnivore, T-Rex, lines up at the end, we'll head onstage," he says. "Alright group one, here we go, follow me."

When Dave makes the announcement, Duke inhales a deep cool breath of air and runs his hand across the purple spikes on the top of his fuzzy green head. He has to remind himself to wait for Dave to get back before he makes his move. As he looks around the room, it seems like the rest of the crew is in the same boat. They look like a pack of dogs held back by invisible leashes. It is hard to hold themselves back, but they'll need to work in unison in order to have any hope of restraining their nemesis until the rest of the troops get here.

6

The kids in the contest are slowly filing out the doorway. Duke can see the T-Rex, last in line, start to tap his paws impatiently. Finally, without waiting to verify that it is him, Duke, Trooper and Kate spring into action once they see Dave's shadow in the doorway foreshadow his return.

The four converge on the figure in the ratty dinosaur costume, full speed, from all directions. They leap in the air simultaneously, feet and fists in attack mode. The apex of their flights turns to slow motion. Each team member

256

is focused on bringing down the Nasty One, and their individual poses are fierce.

With a surprisingly awkward CRASH!, they resume normal time and collide with the dinosaur. His surprise is so absolute, he hasn't even had time to react. The group tumbles to a pile on the floor. Dave grabs a right arm. Trooper takes hold of the tail. Kate hugs both legs together. Duke grabs the prehistoric costume tightly and tries to rip it off.

"Hey! What are you all doing to me?" the man in the T-Rex suit shouts. "Get off of me!"

"Get 'em," shouts Dave.

"It's him… It's the Nasty Neuro!" adds Kate.

"Duke! Get the mask!" Trooper shouts.

Duke gets to his feet and quickly grabs the mask off of the guy's head. He yells, "Ah-ha!" as he yanks it off.

"Wait, what?" Duke sees the man's face. "It's not him!"

7

"What do you mean, it's not him?" Trooper shouts from underneath the man's costume. He releases the stranglehold he has on the dinosaur tail and rolls over to take a better look.

"It's… Dr. Maloney?!" Trooper half asks-half exclaims. He is confused and embarrassed that he just had a wrestling match with the tail of his Opthomologist. "Uhh, sorry Dr. Nick," he says and stares at his steam-engine wheels.

"That's OK, Trooper," the tall man replies as he gets to

his feet. "What were you kids doing?" he asks.

Before anyone can answer, they hear strange sounds coming from the atrium.

BOOM! CRASH! HISSSSSSsssss!

Dave quickly swings the door open to reveal a melee unfolding on the other side. All around, splatters of germ warfare sizzle down the walls. A few of the doctors and nurses are standing in the center trying to keep everyone from panicking… but it's no use as the masses of people stream for the stairs and try to get back to their respective rooms.

It is surreal to see the Crayola-colored monsters attacking the innocent and vulnerable carnival attendees. Every kid who is hit by a germ starts coughing and doubling over with sickness. The parents and nurses don't react as violently, but they are afraid and desperate to get their immune deficient wards away from this mess. Kids and parents are running in every direction as laughter and violence reigns down from the squadron of evil bacteria-warriors.

Dave slams the door shut just as a stink bomb blasts the doorway. It's reeking glob of goo drips down to the floor and starts to seep through the crack underneath. Dr. Nick, freed from his T-Rex costume by the attacking team members just a moment ago, shoves his mask and cloak in the opening before the red, shimmering, germ-filled sludge can do any damage to the kids inside. He then turns and looks at all of them with wide eyes. He keeps one hand on the door handle, which starts to shake as he takes a deep breath to gather his senses.

Duke, still guilt ridden from their mistaken attack, starts

stammering, "Dr. Nick… I'm so sorry… we just thought you were… it must have just been red-eye from the flash… I can explain…"

"It's OK Duke, I'm not mad at you," Dr. Maloney replies. "From the looks of the scene outside, I'm starting to understand that you and your friends were just trying to protect yourselves from whatever that is."

He reaches one of his huge hands over and wraps it around Duke's bald head. "It's going to be alright, buddy." Dr. Nick then wipes a tear away from Duke's eye. "You make sure that no one leaves this room until I come back and give you the all clear. I'm going to go out and see what I can do."

With that, the adult steps out into the battle. Dave pulls the door shut and turns around to find all of the others in their super hero costumes. Their pedestrian outfits for the costume carnival are strewn on the floor. Trooper in his Stanley the Steam Engine outfit is replaced by Firebird. Kate's street clothes are upgraded to her Hodgkins Kids blue and whites. No one will mistake Duke Dillan for Gary the Green Dragon anymore. Now he is The Chemo Kid.

Dave tries to calm the team down. "Fine… I get it. I know we wore our super-clothes underneath our costumes, but Dr. Maloney said not to let you guys go!"

Suddenly something huge slams into the door, nearly ripping it out of its frame. Trooper races to the translucent window beside the door just in time to see Dr. Maloney fall to the floor. "Dr. Nick!" he shouts and lunges for the door handle. Dave stops him from heading carelessly into the danger without support. "Wait!" he yells and quickly strips to match his sister's blue and white Hodgkins Kids attire. He looks straight in Troopers eyes and whispers, "We got your back."

Trooper doesn't hesitate to snap down the handle to the door race into the atrium. Dave and Kate follow closely behind. The Chemo Kid takes a deep breath, mounts Ivy, and follows his team into the fray.

8

When they get outside, it's as if the whole world is empty except for them. They roll through the wreckage, past overturned chairs and party streamers littered on the floor. The stench is unbearable. The Chemo Kid clips his super air-filtration mask, and Trooper follows suit.

"It's like a ghost town," The Kid says. "Where did everyone go? It was just a full blown war scene in here!"

Ivy quickly spins them around when they hear footsteps scurrying behind them. They don't see anything until Dave and Kate peek from behind a pillar under the stairway. The sound must have been them rushing to find a safe base.

Ivy spins them around to face to the open space where the battle had been waging just moments ago. Again, there is no movement, just the aftermath of Technicolor destruction. The air, however, now has that hazy quality to it. The Chemo Kid knows just what that means.

"Be on the lookout for germ warriors," The Chemo Kid whispers.

"Way ahead of ya'," says Trooper, pointing to his wristwatch. "I've got our eyes in the sky right here."

The Kid looks up to see a flicker from the window of

Mario's room.

"Mario, what do we got?" Trooper whispers into his watch.

"You guys are surrounded," comes the reply. "I can see two Blue by the information desk, two Red by the ladies restroom, two Green behind the stairs, and a Purple on the second level."

"What about Starr? Is she OK?" asks Trooper.

"I lost her in the commotion. She was with Tom and the news crew when everything went crazy. If you guys head over to the main entrance, you can probably get a shot at the Blues and the Green... but hurry, Purple is ready to ambush you guys. Get to that security desk STAT, and you'll be covered," Mario says.

Upon hearing the report, The Chemo Kid pulls four rounds of sanitizer bombs off of his belt and hands two to Trooper. "Ivy," he commands, "Trooper is going to hop on your base with me. I want you to take us to that security desk by the main entrance as quickly as you can. The Hodgkins Kids should be fine on their own. Spin us around once we get there. Trooper, you get the Greens behind the stairs and I'll clear the Blues near Information. Ivy will watch out for the ambush from the second level. Ready?" He doesn't wait for an answer.

"GO!"

Ivy speeds toward the desk. Duke lobs a couple grenades over their heads and the battle begins. Stink bombs start to fly from every direction, and Ivy makes evasive maneuvers to dodge the first wave. The Chemo Kid and Trooper lean out and toss their grenades toward their targets. The Kids's makes contact and blue slime explodes all over the information desk. Trooper misses with the first, but dives to the ground and tosses one mid-roll that injures both of the green warriors.

Ivy notices a barrage from Purple on the second level and spins around, lying back on one wheel, so The Kid can see the projectiles against the skylight. The Kid holds on tight, takes Ivy's cue, and fires his own missile that catches a stink bomb in mid-air. The resulting shrapnel extinguishes the remaining projectiles before they splatter on Trooper. This frees Firebird to finish off the two green ones with a second dive-and-roll attack and a pair of grenades. He quickly admires his work then runs toward the security desk.

Trooper's temporary lapse of focus costs him. On his way to their objective, he is tripped up by a tangle of streamers and falls to the floor. Meanwhile, The Chemo Kid and Ivy have just completed their 180 behind the desk. The Kid sees Trooper sprawled on the floor. He tries to hop off his IV pole and race out to help his friend, but Ivy yanks him back using their tubes, just in time to avoid another purple bomb.

Trooper tries to get the streamers untangled from around his feet by himself. Purple and red bombs are exploding all around him and the germy ammunition splashes all around the vulnerable Firebird. The Chemo Kid wants to help his friend, but Ivy won't let him go from behind the desk. He is horrified to see two red warriors run out to finish off Trooper. The Kid can't believe they forgot to account for them from by the ladies room! As they get to the center of the room, certain to pulverize Trooper, they both explode like giant ketchup bottles in a microwave. Red goo splatters the room in all directions.

At the sight, The Chemo Kid fully gives into Ivy's pull and falls back onto her behind the desk. From their covered location they can't see who blasted them. Ivy creeps them around the corner of the desk, where they see Starr Powers twirling through the air. She lands in the middle of the atrium, scoops up Trooper, spins, and launches a bazooka blast of sanitizer towards the second level. Purple goo splatters the windows of the second floor. Starr's sanitizer gun has defeated the last of the germ warriors.

The Kid turns to see if Trooper is OK, but he and Starr are both gone. The Chemo Kid and Ivy are the only ones left in the atrium.

9

The last embers of sizzling germ warriors bubble away to mere Kool-Aid stains on the floors and walls. Silence prevails as The Chemo Kid sits on Ivy behind the security desk, motionless. With his legs crossed and his hands folded in his lap, The Kid prays for Trooper and Starr's safety. He also prays for all of his other friends. He tells God that he doesn't care what happens to him, but he just wants all of his friends to be OK. If robots could cry, Ivy would have let it all out at that moment. She can feel his sincerity and humbleness. Instead, she sends a warm sensation through their connected tubes. This makes The Chemo Kid smile. He squeezes her a little tighter so she knows he appreciates her.

After a moment, he looks up at Ivy and says, "C'mon, let's end this."

The Kid gets to his feet on Ivy's base. She turns them around to see the carnage that has made this atrium look like a junior-high cafeteria after an epic food-fight. They slowly roll through the muck to the middle of the atrium where Starr rescued Trooper from the last of the germ-monsters.

The Kid looks up to Mario's window, but doesn't see the flicker that he saw before. He then looks anxiously at the various places where the bad bacteria had hidden before being splattered all over the walls and floors. He's nervous that another wave of stinking ammo will come flying towards his head. None comes. No one or nothing is moving in eyesight. The silence is enough to drive The Chemo Kid insane. Trooper and Starr are gone. Dave and Kate are gone. There are no signs of Mario, Tom the Medic, Brandon or Tommy. The Chemo Kid and Ivy are truly alone.

Just then, the giant fluorescents overhead start to explode, one by one, showering sparks and shattered glass down on the floor below. Ivy scoops up The Kid and spins them to safety, but the surging electricity throws an overpowering wave of energy through the atrium. Lighting crashes down to the floor and The Kid holds onto Ivy for dear life as they are blown back against the wall and tossed to the floor by the invisible force. The new darkness is only broken by stray sparks that touch down around them. As they wobble back to their feet to regroup, the emergency lights start up with a crack and a buzz of their own setting the whole room aglow like a psychedelic canvas of modern art as the red exit signs glow ominously at each corner of the room. Exit seems like no option as the choking cloud of smoke builds in all around.

BOOM! The ground shakes, and the concrete floor beneath The Kid and Ivy cracks.They crash back against the wall once more as the quaking earth jumps and shifts beneath them. Bellowing laughter echoes up from deep beneath the crumbling floor.

"HA- HA! HA-HA-HA-HA!-HA!" resounds and repeats through the acoustic atrium as the terrible voice swirls around them.

The huge glass encased kinetic sculpture,which is an ever-moving ringing and chiming mouse-trap in this gallery-style atrium, lets out a "Dong!" like some clock tower ringing in the zero hour. The whole thing then explodes glass and twisted metal into the hour, sending various sized marbles shooting all around like bullets as they spin around a corner to safety and dive to the floor.

Ivy has to react quickly to get the two of them upright, jumping and dodging acrobatically to stay on the larger sections of the floor as it disintegrates beneath them. The broken marble crumbles into a steaming sea of bubbling goo. Ivy leaps off the last floating chunk of floor to the foundation that is still connected to the main hospital. The stinking lava jumps up and tries to singe Ivy's base. She's backed herself and The Kid up to the wall to keep as safe and clean as possible.

"Nicely done!" booms a gravelly voice from the deep. More maniacal laughter follows, shaking the walls of the atrium. "You've done well against my half-witted henchmen. But you are no match for me!"

The thunderous tones echo to the ten-story high glass ceiling, causing it to shatter. Another shower of broken glass rains down on Ivy and The Chemo Kid. Ivy quickly spins them away again, keeping close to the wall in order to avoid the bigger pieces that crash to the remaining floor. She also wants to keep a safe distance from the cauldron of sludge. There is not much room to maneuver.

The Kid looks up from his death grip on Ivy to see his worst nightmare rising from the depths. The earth shakes as a mighty Tyrannosaurus Rex steps up from the murky deep.

10

"RAAAAAHHHHH!" the monster roars, sending nasty green spit droplets onto The Chemo Kid and Ivy. The beast leans in and breathes his hot breath into The Kid's face. Willfully controlling his fear, the Kid shoves a sanitizer grenade directly into the terrible lizard's mouth. The monster barely flinches. He just steps back and spits the goo into the steamy sea.

"HA! Ha-ha-ha-ha! That won't work on me!" he boasts.

Ivy tugs on The Chemo Kid's line. She's trying to show him the spot by the elevator, just a few feet away, that she could possibly jump onto. The Kid is paying absolutely no attention. His hand is reaching back into the waistband of his super-onesie. He feels the handle of his Chemo Cannon and takes hold of it. With a smirk on his lips, he pulls it out and points it in the face of his growling opponent.

"This is my Chemo Cannon! Don't move, or I'll blast you!" he shouts up at the gigantic beast.

Ivy, flashing and beeping away, is trying to signal him. It's to no avail. The Kid has got his finger on the trigger and he's ready to fire.

"HA! HA! HA! HA!" the monster howls, once again shaking the very ground they stand on. "I wouldn't do that if I were you! You don't know who you're messing with!"

The Kid closes his eyes and says a split-second, silent prayer. When he opens them, he pulls the trigger. Nothing happens. The massive beast grabs the gun out of his hand with his massive jaws like a toothpick and tosses it over his shoulder. The Kid watches his weapon fly out of reach and with it, most of his confidence. He closes his eyes and slowly turns back to face the Tyrannosaurus.

"You fool," the monster roars, "that weapon is useless to you. You haven't even had one dose of chemo yet!"

Ivy twists toward The Kid, but the monster deftly spins 360 degrees in less than a second, knocking her to the floor with its tail and severing their connection. The Chemo Kid is having a hard time containing his emotions at this point. His fear of dinosaurs, his inexperience with fighting, and his lost connection with Ivy are almost too much for him to bear. He stands frozen, and alone, in front of The Nasty Neuro. With hope for a miracle and a tear in his eye, The Chemo Kid looks to his right at his robotic friend who lays motionless on the floor.

"Aww, is the baby going to cry?" Neuro asks with a dastardly smile.

The beast spins back the other direction so fast that The Chemo Kid doesn't know what hit him. He finds himself clinging to the few remaining marble tiles above the sea of red goo far from his lifeline and gasping for breath. He feels himself fading in and out of consciousness, but is pulled back when he hears the voices of his friends.

"Duke!"

"Hang on! We're coming, Kid!"

The Chemo Kid can barely see. His bad eye is nearly

swollen shut, but he forces it open to see Starr and Trooper come out of nowhere to save him. Starr is attacking with a laser-beam that has the monster reeling. The charge seems to be coming out of the palms of her hands. She twirls and throws a crushing blow at Neuro as she lands next to The Kid. The laser blasts the Nasty One temporarily back into the gooey ocean.

Trooper flies in from the second floor landing. He looks like he's on fire as he crashes into the belly of the beast as it rises up from the lava after Starr's attack. Firebird bounces off the dinosaur gracefully and rolls across a floating island of marble to retrieve The Chemo Kid's Chemo Cannon. He grabs it and leaps back to stand by Starr and The Chemo Kid, who is still lying, breathless, on the hospital foundation.

Neuro is hit… and injured badly. He's writhing and twisting awkwardly. The monster takes a step backwards into the bubbling deep and then makes one last lunge toward the team.

Spooooooosh! Spooooooooooooooooshhhhhhhhhh!

They were preparing for a thunderous attack, but instead, Starr, Trooper and The Kid see James the Janitor and Dr. Houston burst through the doors with fire extinguishers. The room quickly fills with white foam. The snowy cloud obscures everyone's view. No one sees Neuro slip back down into the abyss.

"Duke…. Duke!" Trooper screams. "Somebody help! Help!"

Duke slips fully out of consciousness.

11

*"Duke… Duke… Duke…" rings like an echo in his ear.
He tries to lift his head in the darkness but can't see who
is calling his name. The cries of his friends grow weaker
and more distant until he is alone in a black weightless
dream. The voices coming from the atrium and the battle
in which he just partook have drifted away to a foggy
place in his mind where memories hibernate.*

*He tries to prop himself up but can't feel the floor
beneath him. He grabs at the air, expecting Ivy to
be there, but there is nothing. As his eyes become
accustomed to the lack of light, he finds himself floating
above the forest in the starry twilight from his recurring
dream. The realization shoots waves of dread through his
veins. His muscles tighten and lock, freezing him stiff. At
first he thinks he is falling to his death, but then a warm
breeze lifts his head and sits him upright. The stars tingle
his flesh as they nestle in all around him, carrying him
across the sky like a golden chariot through the heavens.*

*He is approaching a beautiful light, warm and bright.
More stars gather around him as he gets closer. Duke
closes his eyes and enjoys their radiant glow as they
softly kiss his face. When he opens his eyes again, he
sees beauty personified in a little girl gracefully floating
just ahead. She is dressed in a white dress, so wonderful
that it makes him want to smile and cry at the same time.
She reaches her hand toward his and Duke returns the
gesture by touching her fingertips. Feeling like he did
when he was in his mother's arms as a baby, he holds her
hand and smiles.*

*"Angel? Is that you?" asks Duke, trying to wipe the
tears from his eyes.*

"Yes, Duke, it is me." she answers softly.

"W-Where am I?" he asks, looking around, this time seeing no signs of the forest or path below. All he comprehends are stars that have gathered in close. "What is this place?" he asks again. "Is this heaven?"

"Almost... but not quite," she says in a soft harmonic voice that sends a tingle through his spine.

"Are you an angel?" he asks, not wanting to know the answer.

"I am," she says.

Duke begins to cry. Angel reaches out to wipe the tears from his cheek.

"Don't cry, Duke. There is nothing to be sad about. I am happy."

"But, I don't understand... What is this place?" he asks.

"This is the place where we gather our light to help illuminate the paths of those who still fight. We have all earned our wings, and now we live together. There is no more pain or sadness. I have been assigned to you, Duke... assigned to watch over you. You have a very important job to do, and I will help you in any way that I can." Her voice is clear and resolute.

"It's so beautiful here..." Duke replies, trailing off as he looks around again. This time he notices faces in the stars, the faces of children. Their smiles brighten the skyline as he pans the horizon.

"Are all of you..."

"We have been given the honor, as heroes, to help those

who are still in the fight. We live in the light of love, and that love gives us a power greater than any that can be summoned on earth. I will do my best to pass this power onto you."

"But will I ever see you again?" he asks.

"It is not for me to say. I can tell you that I will be with you always... in here," she replies and places her hand on his heart. "You must go back and fight for the others. I will be watching you, and I will help you."

The multitude of stars gather even closer and reach out to touch Duke. Their light shines into him, until he is so full of light that he shines like a beacon. Lying down again on a bed of pure light, he drifts back out into the twilight.

Chapter Sixteen

'It's So Hard to Say Goodbye'

1

When Duke opens his eyes, he's even less sure of how long he was out than when he woke up in his bed on 3 South the first time. Has it been hours? Days? Weeks? He wouldn't find it hard to believe that he was knocked out for a month with the way Neuro had laid him out. His folks are asleep on the air-bed on the floor which is the only thing that tells him that it's morning at all. The sky-lit E.R. waiting room projects rare warmth that, so far, he has only felt in the mornings. Duke closes his eyes to let the refracted sunlight shine on his face. He can almost convince himself that he's sitting on a warm, sunny Florida beach.

That's when he starts to recall, like when a dream is pieced back together, his meeting with Angel. Duke's mind can't yet complete the picture; it's confusing. Where… who… what is returning to his consciousness? The warm sun from the E.R. room reminds him first of gently floating stars. They were aglow with a light brighter than anything he'd ever seen or felt before. Someone was glowing too… Angel! Her luminance was powerful, yet easy on the eyes. Duke dares not open his eyes again until he can fully recapture the memory of their meeting. His progress stalls, however, when a big, fluffy cloud floats above the hospital, stealing the warmth of the sun from the skylights.

Instead of re-capturing the image of the girl he can't wait to see again, the loss of sunlight shoves back into his mind the image his clock getting cleaned by an oversized lizard in the atrium. It's not a memory Duke cares to relive. Before his regretful performance during his showdown with The Nasty Neuro, Duke had convinced himself that he wasn't scared… that he was really some kind of tough guy… that he was The Chemo Kid, a hero everyone looked up to. But now, he can't help but shudder at the thought of coming face to face with the monster again.

It doesn't matter if his failure was the result of a lack of self-control, preparation, or simply being overmatched in the most important confrontation of his life. In any case, the beautiful image of Angel floating in the heavens has now been irreversibly replaced by one of Neuro and his stink soldiers, embarrassing him, and escaping to continue on with their horrific infections. This is at least enough to make Duke mad again, which has him feeling a little tougher, at least for now.

2

Duke turns over in his bed to look for Ivy. He assumes that by the time he completes his roll, she'll be lit-up and focused on him, having read his mind. He couldn't be more wrong. She's nowhere in sight. What's worse is that she's been replaced by another pole. This one is nice enough… for an inanimate object… but thoughts of the worst possible outcome surge into his mind as he remembers how Neuro tossed her aside, leaving her motionless on the floor.

Duke starts to cry. He is so worried that Ivy might be gone forever. Sure, she's got a reputation in the underground community, but he's afraid no one in the surface system of The Children's Hospital really knows how incredibly special she is. He imagines a custodian or maid, slogging through their daily rounds, not hesitating to toss her aside in a pile of other broken poles. Worse yet, given her date of manufacture, they might send her off to the scrap heap all together.

Duke is utterly frantic at the thought of losing his best friend. On top of his tears, he starts to shake and moan into the bars of his children's hospital bed, uncontrollably. By now, his mom and dad have woken up and are at his bedside, trying to console him. They assume it is a standard night terror. Duke is screaming and kicking at his IV tube. Jesse tries to lift him up but doesn't get a good grip so he has to set him down again in the bed.

Duke takes a breath at this moment and cries, "My Po!" He stretches his hand in the direction of his new, non-Helper-unit.

"Buddy, calm down… please!" pleads Jesse. "They hooked you up to this new pole when you came back up. The other one got knocked over. They had to set you up with all new IV tubes." Jesse is actually a bit mad, having been woken with screams and convulsions… all over a silly pole. "This one's just as good!" he shouts.

"No! My Po!" Duke cries.

Maggie's maternal instincts require her to console Duke, so she steps in front of her husband to pick her son up in her arms. As she does, she gives Jesse a look as if to say relax… that's not helping!

Jesse continues his explanation to his son, but his eyes

are focused on his wife as she rocks Duke in her arms in order to communicate, non-verbally, that he understands her feelings. "That other pole has a broken wheel. It's not so bad, but it wobbles. That's why they gave you a new one."

This causes Duke to increase the volume of his wails. Even if his father says "it's not so bad," Ivy's been hurt, and he can't do anything to help her. He feels weak and useless without his Helper IV pole. He doesn't think he can continue with The Chemo Kid routine without her. The Nasty Neuro really has gained the upper hand. More than simply injuring Duke's confidence by showing him up in the atrium, he has completely crushed it into driveway paver dust by potentially separating him from Ivy forever.

"Is everything OK?" a voice asks from the doorway. Nurse Andrea looks into the room. She and the other nurse in the hall look worried, having overheard Duke's fit. "I just got in and heard Duke crying."

"We're OK," Jesse replies. "He's upset about his pole. They gave him a different one when we came back up from downstairs. The other one has a broken wheel."

"No! *My* Po!" Duke interrupts. He shoots a sad look in Andrea's direction.

"Watcha' mean? This here po?" shouts a voice from behind the nurses.

"Hey James!" exclaims Andrea.

James the Janitor slips past the two nurses in the doorway, pushing Ivy into the room.

"Ohh, yeah... old James ain't gonna leave his buddy

hangin' all weekend with some old junker!"

James walks the pole over to the side of Duke's bed, where he extends a hand to Maggie, then to Jesse. He forgoes the introduction, assuming that they heard Andrea's exclamation as well as his 3rd-person reference on his way into the room.

"Yeah…. I saw this last night, and I know she's special. I seen the way they been ridin' around together." James points at Duke and sweeps his finger back to the IV pole in his hand to accentuate their connection.

Duke is no longer crying. He stopped the second James walked in. He had gotten himself all worked up thinking that, without Ivy, he didn't have any other friends who could help him in this place. James deserves a big smile, so Duke makes a production of giving him one, eliciting the typical oooh's and awwww's from the ladies in the room that follow his trademark cuteness.

"Wasn't no thing little buddy… Just had a busted wheel, that's all. I got a whole drawer of new ones. Just put one on there and figured I bring it to ya, before I left."

"I can change all the tubes over when I come back. I just have to get the report from the night nurse and I'll be back in," Andrea chimes with a smile, happy that Duke is no longer upset.

James already has Ivy plugged in as he turns and says, "Alright lil' man… Old James be back again Monday. Don't be getting yourself in too much trouble over the weekend." He shakes the hands of Duke's parents again. They thank him repeatedly for making Duke smile after a long, horrible week.

"Bye!" Duke yells as James makes exits the room. James turns and gives him a wink, then disappears into the hall.

"What a nice guy!" Maggie exclaims.

Duke agrees with a smile, and a hug for his mom.

3

After Maggie unsuccessfully tries to get Duke to eat breakfast, another knock comes to their door. A woman pulling a wagon full of bags and toys introduces herself, and Duke's mom opens the door, inviting her in. She enters, followed by a bald little two-year-old of her own. Duke turns to see Trooper Phoenix holding onto his own mommy's pant-leg. As the mothers talk, Trooper walks over to the plastic sofa where Duke's mom put him down after his crying fit.

"Hey, dude! Everyone was really worried about you," he says. "I heard about Ivy. I'm glad to see she's OK. I made my mom stop in here so I could say goodbye to you before we go."

"Go? What do you mean... go?" Duke asks.

"I'm going home. My treatments are done and my counts are back up. I'm sorry. I wish I could have told you sooner, but I didn't even know until this morning. And as soon as my parents heard we could leave, they packed up the room and... now we're leaving." Trooper keeps eye contact with Duke after describing his status even though there is a little tear in his eye, ready to drip down his cheek.

"When will I get to see you again?" asks Duke. "What about Neuro?" He doesn't fully understanding how Trooper could have not known he was leaving until today. However, he is also not surprised to find out that life around here will be getting even harder pretty soon without Trooper.

"I have to come in every Friday to see my doctor in clinic. I'll tell my mom to bring me down to see you then. Believe me, I don't like this any more than you. I, too, have unfinished business with Mr. Neuro. But they say it's time to go… so I have to go."

This time Trooper turns away from Duke because he can't stop the tears running down his cheeks. Duke and Trooper's mom finish talking and walk over to their sons. Trooper's mom grabs his hand and leads him out of the room. On the way out, Trooper turns his head towards Duke, but fails to make eye contact out of embarrassment. "Bye, Duke," he says.

"Wait!" Duke says. Their moms hear the statement more like a baby crying Waaaa! Duke takes the moment of attention to hop down from the plastic sofa, sprint over to his bed and grab the Stanley Steam Engine medallion that Trooper had given him a few nights ago in his room.

"You," he says. Duke is trying to act his age in front of the adults but still articulate to Trooper how much his friendship means to him. He slaps the medal into Trooper's hand. Trooper finally looks up. Duke can see the tears in his eyes.

"No, you," Trooper says. He squeezes the medallion back into Duke's hand, then he walks out into the hall with is mother. He's gone.

All the rest of that day, as hoards of friends and family come for a visit, Duke holds the medallion, running his fingers over the raised letters. He was mad when Trooper told him he was leaving, but he knows that no one can stay here forever. Duke is just at the beginning of his journey with cancer, but Trooper's treatments are over now. It's time for him to go home.

Duke's parents relive the story of the last week over and over again to the people who visit throughout the day and night. Duke listens to each storytelling, but each time, as it should be, his parents leave out the parts about scary monsters, horrific dreams and confrontations with timeless evils. Not to discount the struggles his parents have gone through, but Duke smirks each time, because his adventures have included quite a bit more than what Jesse and Maggie are sharing.

Duke is realizing that he won't have much help from the regular people if he hopes to defeat the Nasty Neuro. Thankfully, he'll at least have help from Ivy, Angel and the rest of the Fighters. These are the kids who have been touched by something that can't be seen… something that has to be believed in without seeing in order for it to make any difference. Children have this ability to believe, much more commonly than adults.

As the last of the visitors leave, Duke Dillan, still clutching the medallion, looks up past the plastic liner on top of his baby hospital bed and prays, "Though I walk through the valley of the shadow of death, I will fear no evil, for you are with me."

He reaches his hand to Ivy who slides into position. He hangs the medallion on the hook next to her pumps.

Trooper and Starr, and all the other kids from Chemo Cove, his parents and family, the little girl who was in the room next door until just a few days ago, as well as a power beyond even his advanced comprehension fill Duke's thoughts.

"I will fear no evil..."

To Be Continued...